D1047450

The
Surface
Breaks

The Surface Breaks

 LOUISE O'NEILL

SCHOLASTIC PRESS

New York

Library of Congress Cataloging-in-Publication Data available

ISBN 978-1-338-33260-5

10 9 8 7 6 5 4 3 2 1   19 20 21 22 23

Printed in the U.S.A. at Berryville Graphics in Berryville, Virginia   37

First US edition, August 2019

Book design by Abby Dening

For Aine Loughnan,
my first best friend,
and
for my beloved godson,
George Gillan.

Chapter

1

YOU ARE NOT *ready, my child. Be patient. Your time will come.*

I have been listening to my grandmother say these things to me for as long as I can remember. "But when will I be ready?" I kept asking her. "When, Grandmother? When, *when*?"

And she told me to be quiet. "It's for your own good," she said. "You know how your father feels about the human world. Do not let him catch you speaking in such a fashion."

I have never been allowed to talk much. My father doesn't care for curious girls, so I bit my tongue and I waited. The days of my childhood kept turning over, dissolving like sea-foam on the crest of the waves. I have been counting them, the days and the nights, the weeks, the months, the years. I have been waiting for this day.

And now, at last, it has arrived. I am fifteen and I shall be allowed to break the surface, catch my first glimpse of the world above us. Maybe there, I will find some answers. I have so many questions, you see. I have spent my years swallowing them down, burning bitter at the back of my throat.

"Happy birthday, my beloved Muirgen," Grandmother Thalassa says, placing a wreath of lilies on my head. I am sitting on a throne carved from coral, staring at my reflection in the cracked mirror in front of me. It is a relic from a ship that was wrecked two years ago. The Rusalkas rose to the surface to sing the sailors to a watery grave, stuffing death into their bloated lungs. They sing so sweetly, the Salkas do. They sing for revenge for all that has been inflicted upon them.

My room in the palace is full of such finds: remnants of humans that descend from their world into ours, and that I hoard for my collection, piece by piece. A broken comb that I use to tame my long, red hair; a jeweled ring that my sisters covet and beg to borrow, but I shall not share. A statue of alabaster white, of a young man's face and torso. I wonder who he is, he whose face has been whittled out of marble. I wonder if he ever looks at the sea and considers its depths, ponders what could be found in its belly if he looked hard enough. I wonder if he knows that we even exist.

"It is difficult to believe that it is your fifteenth birthday," Grandmother says. "I remember the day you were born so clearly."

Everyone in the kingdom remembers my birthday, but not because of me. She knits a pearl into my fishtail, piercing the flesh with a razor shell. I watch as the blood drips away, trembling on the water before it melts. The pearls are large, heavy, and I must wear six of them for fear the other mer-people will somehow forget that I am royalty and therefore their superior in all ways. "It was clear you were special," my grandmother says. "Even then." But not special enough. Not special enough to make my mother stay.

Grandmother scrapes the scales away, ignoring my gasp of pain. Thalassa of the Green Sea does not care to hear such complaints. *One cannot have beauty for nothing*, she would tell me. *There is always a price to pay*, and she would gesture at her own tail with its twelve pearls. My grandmother is not royalty-born, so she is expected to be grateful for this decoration bestowed upon her by her son-in-law, the Sea King, and even more grateful that the privilege wasn't revoked when her daughter . . .

misbehaved as she did. Grandmother's family was of high birth, and well respected, but my mother was their ticket to the throne. Perhaps my grandmother did not realize the price her daughter would have to pay. Perhaps she did not care.

When my grandmother calls me "special," she means "beautiful." That is the only way a woman can be special in the kingdom. And I am beautiful. All of the Sea King's daughters are, each princess more lovely than the next, but I am the fairest of them all. I am the diamond in my father's crown and he is determined to wear me as such. He will hold my prettiness out for display, and he will take any ensuing admiration as his due.

"My name is Gaia," I say. "That is what my mother called me."

"Let us not speak of your mother," Grandmother says. "Muireann had many ideas that would have been better ignored."

My breath catches a little. *Muireann.* We hear my mother's name so rarely. "But—"

"Shhh," she says, looking over her shoulder. "I should never have told you the name she chose for you."

But she did. My fifth birthday, and I begged her to tell me something, *anything* about my mother. *She called you Gaia*, I was told, and when I heard it, I felt as if I was coming home to myself.

"Gaia is not a name of the sea, my child," my grandmother says now.

"But it was what my mother wanted, wasn't it?"

"Yes," she sighs.

"And my father, he agreed, didn't he? Even though Gaia was a name of the earth, and not of our kind."

"The Sea King was very fond of Muireann in those days. He wished to see her happy."

They thought my mother's love of the human world was innocent in the beginning. That was before she started to act strangely. Before she disappeared for hours at a time, giving increasingly elaborate excuses to explain her absence upon return. Before she was taken.

"And then my mother—"

"Your mother is dead, Muirgen," my grandmother says. "Let us not speak of her anymore."

But I don't know if she is dead, despite what they tell me. All I know is this: When someone disappears on your first birthday, your entire life becomes a question, a puzzle that needs solving. And so, I look up. I have spent my life looking up, thinking about her.

"She could still be alive," I say.

"She's not."

"But how can you be so sure, Grandmother? All we know is that she was taken. Maybe—"

"Muirgen." Her voice is serious. I meet her eyes, blue, like mine. Everything is blue down here. "It does not do a woman good to ask too many questions."

"But I just want—"

"It doesn't do a woman good to want too much either. Try and remember that."

Muireann of the Green Sea wanted too much. *You're so like your mother*, the old folk tell me (though only when my father is out of earshot—my father will not have talk of my mother at court), *the resemblance is . . .* (Freakish? Odd? What?) But they never finish their sentences. *Such a pity what happened to her*, they say instead. They have all accepted she's dead, even if we never had a body to bury in the deep sands. They think it's a shame, but what else could a woman like my mother expect? She had her own needs, her own desires. She wanted to escape, so she looked up too. And she was punished for it.

My grandmother picks up the final pearl now, her tongue sticking out in concentration. My tail must look perfect for the ball this evening. My father is always in a rather exacting mood on this date.

I wait until she is rapt in her work, and I look up again. I look at the dark sea, the crashing waves, straining to see the faint light beyond. That was where my mother went, up there. And that is where I must go to find the answers I need.

Grandmother tugs at my tail but I keep my head tilted back, staring at the surface. For I am fifteen now, and I can do as I please.

Chapter

2

I PAUSE OUTSIDE my sisters' bedroom, listening to them argue. Raised voices, squeals of annoyance. *Shrill*, my father would say if we ever behaved in such a fashion in front of him. Not that we would dare. We are the daughters of the Sea King, and daughters must be good at all times.

"That's my comb."

"It's not, Talia, your comb is black."

"I have a black comb *and* a coral comb, and you're using my coral comb. Give it to me right now."

"Talia," Cosima says as I push the door open. She and Talia are floating in the middle of the room, my other three sisters ignoring them from the safety of their beds. "Not everything belongs to you. It's *my* comb."

It is a huge space; vaulted ceilings lined with seaweed in greens and browns, the floor paved with pearlescent marble. There are two single beds on either side and one double at the head of the room by the window of stained sea-glass, where Talia has slept since we left the nursery eight years ago. "I am the eldest," she said when she claimed it for her own, ignoring Cosima's protestations. "I shall have this bed until I leave the palace for the house of my husband," she said then, with a grand wave of her hand. Talia doesn't make comments like that anymore. We all know that Talia shall be a long time waiting to leave this palace.

I used to have a bed in the dormitory too, falling asleep with my hand stretched out to hold Cosima's. I had nightmares then, visions of the acute pain the humans might have inflicted upon my mother when they captured her, and Cosima would shake me awake, reassure me that everything was fine. *Don't worry, Gaia*, she would say. Cosima was the only one who called me Gaia, because she understood how much it meant to me. But then I celebrated my twelfth birthday, and everything changed.

Cosima, quietly crying herself to sleep at night, each rasping sob a rebuke. *It's not my fault*, I wanted to tell her. *I didn't ask him to pick me. I didn't ask for any of this.* In the end, I requested to be moved to the tower at the top of the palace, pretending not to care that none of my sisters objected. "But there's no ceiling in the tower." My father had frowned. "Only the sea above you." I told him I didn't mind, and I smiled at him the way he liked, like a good little girl. He relented, saying, "Anything for my Muirgen," and he granted me permission to move my belongings to the high turrets, dragging my bed and my mirror and my comb and my jewels with me. And the statue, of course, although I had to do that when my father wasn't looking.

The Sea King hates the humans. The only time he is happy to hear of them is when their corpses sink into the kingdom, eyes still open as if searching for something. A loved one? A rescue that will never come? I can't be sure. Not that it matters to the Sea King. *A dead human,* my father would say, smiling grimly as a body floated past the dining room window, *is the best human.* (*But can you blame him?* my grandmother said. *Can you blame him after they took your mother?*)

"Give it back," Talia says now, wrestling the comb out of Cosima's hands with a triumphant *"ha!"*

"Good day, sisters," I say, and they both turn to look at me.

"You're late," Talia says, running the comb through her black hair. She is the only one whose hair refuses to curl, no matter how carefully she wraps it around conch shells. We tease her that she must be half-Rusalka; with hair that straight, she cannot have pure seawater running through her veins.

"Have you gone up yet?" Cosima asks.

"Not yet," I reply. "I will go at first light tomorrow morning."

"Goodness," Cosima says. "I assumed you would have been racing up there at the earliest opportunity. Perhaps you are not so like that 'mother' of ours after all. It would have been a terrible shame if you had inherited that woman's sickness."

"Don't talk about our mother like that," I say, anger flaring.

"Why not? She abandoned us, didn't she?"

"She didn't abandon us."

"Muirgen," Cosima sighs. "She knew the dangers and yet she kept going to the surface, day after day. She was reckless. She might not have meant to be captured, but she still brought it upon herself. She abandoned us."

What can I reply to that? *Perhaps we were easy to abandon.*

"Come now, Cosima," Sophia, my third-eldest sister says. "Leave Muirgen alone. Have you forgotten that it's her birthday?"

"Forgotten? How could any of us forget what day today is?"

"Okay, Cosima," I snap. "I get it. Today is a cursed day and I am a cursed mermaid. Are you happy now?"

"Hush, sister," Sophia says. "This is your birthday and we are happy to celebrate it. *All* of us." She swims towards me, her waist-length brown hair floating behind her. She hugs me, smelling of salt and tin, of weeds draped around her neck and wrists. She smells the same as all of us do. (Up there, the women wear the fragrance of flowers on their skin; they smell of rose and lily and jasmine. Up there, flowers carry scent, seeping perfume from their buds.)

"I know it's your day, Muirgen," Talia says, biting her nails. She is always tense on my birthday. She was seven the year I turned one and thus she remembers the infamous party. Talia remembers everything. "But that doesn't excuse you being late. We'll all get in trouble too, you know."

"I'm not late, Talia."

"You're late," Talia insists. "Isn't she late, Nia?"

Nia is by the window, fingers pressed against the clear green glass, staring at the fish drifting past. "What?" she says. "Yes. Yes, you're right, Talia. You're always right." She attempts to smile at me. "But happy birthday all the same, Muirgen."

"How many pearls did you get?" Cosima asks. "It looks like Grandmother gave you seven pearls. Did she give you *seven* pearls? Why would you get seven pearls when the rest of us only have six?"

"I only got six pearls too, Cosima," I say as Sophia takes my hand, holding back the gossamer curtain wrapped around her bed so I can swim through. "The same as the rest of you did. Grandmother wouldn't have it any other way."

"Oh, I'm sure you did. Precious Muirgen," she mutters under her breath, returning to the mirror that is mounted at the head of her bed, decorated with cockles and red algae. "Typical."

"To be perfectly honest, the concept of wearing pearls is archaic," Arianna pipes up. She is lying on her stomach, her mint-green tail folding over to skim her back as if scratching an itch. "If any of you bothered to come with me and Sophia and Grandmother when we visit the Outerlands, you would understand what a *horrendous* waste of resources it is. We should be spending palace money on improving conditions for those folk rather than this frivolous vanity."

"Yes, Arianna, you've mentioned that before," I say. *About a hundred times.* Grandmother visits the Outerlands every week, to where my father has sent the "undesirables," the mer-folk that he cannot stomach to see within the palace walls. She brings them food and unctions the healer has prepared, and while the Sea King does not approve of our grandmother's demonstrations of good will, he does not forbid them either. I think he might be wary of what could happen if the folk in the Outerlands got too hungry.

"But it's not like it's our decision to wear the pearls, now, is it?" I ask Arianna. Nothing is ever our decision.

"And that's why I don't wear decoration in my everyday life, out of *principle*," Arianna continues, ignoring me. "But, then, I'm not as obsessed with this nonsense over pearls and mirrors and which comb belongs to whom and whose hair is the curliest. I mean, really, if you just came with Grandmother and me the next time we go on a charity mission, then you would see how terrible the conditions are, those poor folk are—"

"The mer-folk in the Outerlands are *fine*," Cosima interrupts. "Better than fine. They're lucky that we allow them to remain here at all. *Unnatural creatures.*"

"Unnatural?" Nia asks, her voice sharp. I glance at her in surprise; Nia never gets involved in arguments. "They can't help being the way they are."

"Please." Cosima rolls her eyes. "They could change if they really wanted to. And anyway," she turns her attention back to Arianna, "you're wearing your pearls today, Ari, for all your talk of *principles.*"

"Today doesn't count. You know that I can't . . ." Arianna doesn't finish her sentence. But I know what she would say.

I can't because there is a ball at court today.

I can't because Father will be there, and he will expect us to be properly attired.

I can't because the Sea King will be angry if we do not do as he wishes. He will not stand for female insubordination, today of all days.

And we know what happens when our father is angry.

"Let's not talk about this anymore," Sophia says, quick to make peace. "You look beautiful, birthday girl. Zale won't be able to take his eyes off you."

"I think Zale has more important things on his mind," Cosima says, her jaw tightening. Yet another thing she can be angry with me about. I wish Zale would take his eyes off me and put them back on Cosima. At least she enjoyed it.

"Oh," I say. "Cosima is entirely correct. I'm sure Zale won't even notice me." *I hope he won't.* "Too busy trying to figure out a way to kill every Rusalka under the sea, no doubt."

"And why shouldn't he?" Cosima asks. "Zale is just trying to protect us. The Salkas are dangerous. They're not like us. They were not born of the sea, as we were."

She says this as if it is new information, as if we have not been told this story since we were children. Or versions of it, anyway. Grandmother's version was more compassionate: *The Salkas are wretched,* she would say. *They have been hurt, and therefore they lash out. Be kind.* The Rusalkas have been in these seas as long as the mer-folk have, but they are not of salt. They were human women once, but they sinned. They had to be punished, as fallen women must be, and they died crying, sobs caught in their throats, tearing the life out of their chests. *The drowning girls,* my grandmother calls them. The dead who somehow found a way to breathe underwater, even before the Sea Witch decided to become their champion. Grandmother was the only one who thought the Salkas deserved pity, despite the fact that they had taken the life of her only son during the war. *Why are you not angry with the Rusalkas after what happened with Uncle Manannán?* I once asked her, but she said that I was too young to understand.

The other version is what everyone else told us. Stories about the Salkas' behavior when we were at war, the damage they had wreaked and how they had smiled for the duration, hungry for more blood to be shed.

"The Salkas must be controlled," Cosima says, twirling a blonde curl around her finger, still gazing into her mirror.

"Lucky we have Zale, then," I say. "He enjoys nothing more than controlling women." My other sisters laugh, then stop instantly. We are not allowed laugh at the mer-men, no matter how high our birth.

"Enough of this," Talia says. "We're *late.* The light is shifting in the water." She herds Nia and Arianna from their beds, pulling Cosima away from her reflection. "We're going to get in trouble." She turns at the door to stare at Sophia and me. "Well? Are you coming?"

"Just a minute," I say. I need to gather my strength before this spectacle begins.

"Muirgen, I forbid you from delaying any longer."

"I'm fifteen now, Talia. You can't 'forbid' me from doing anything. You're not my mother."

"I am very much aware of that," she says quietly, and I wish I hadn't said that. Not to Talia. "Very well, then. I forbid nothing, but I'm *advising* you that being late would be a grave mistake."

"I won't be late."

"This is your birthday, Muirgen. You can't be late for your own party." I almost laugh. Whatever tonight is, it has very little to do with my birthday. "I'm serious," she continues. "Father will—"

"Father will be fine," I say. "I will join you at court in five minutes."

With an exaggerated exhale, she leaves, the others close behind, waves of thick hair swishing in their wake.

"Seven pearls," I can hear Cosima complaining. "And a ball thrown to celebrate her bir . . ." Her voice fades away and the room becomes peaceful, for once.

"I'm so glad I don't have to sleep in the dormitory anymore," I had told my grandmother when I was moving to the tower. "I need to be alone, sometimes, to think my thoughts."

She touched her hand to my cheek. "You are so like your mother," she said. *Why?* I wanted to ask her. *And in what way?* Tell me about her, Grandmother. Tell me about the day she was born and what she was like as a child and what her favorite games were and her favorite foods, what songs she liked to sing. Tell me, tell me, *tell me*. I have so many questions and I know none of them will ever be answered. Not down here, at least.

"Cosima needs to stop this, I don't get any preferential treatment. Not from Grandmother, anyway," I say, when I am sure they are out of earshot.

"You know why she behaves in such a way," Sophia says quietly. "Try and understand."

"That doesn't excuse her from being rude," I argue. "Or Talia for being so bossy. *Hurry up, Muirgen. You'll be late, Muirgen.* She'll never get a mer-man if she keeps acting like that. And Nia is worse, always agreeing with everything Talia says. She should develop a backbone."

"Be kind," Sophia says. She wraps her hair up into a bun, holding it in place with a piece of broken conch. "Talia is twenty-one and not yet betrothed. She knows she is the talk of the court; it is all she can think about."

"Maybe she's better off," I say, and we fall silent. There is nothing that can be done to save me now, and we both know it.

"And as for Nia . . ." she continues. "Well. Nia has her own problems."

"What do you mean?" I ask. "Nia is betrothed to Marlin. Her future is secure."

"And do you believe that Nia *wants* to be bonded with Marlin?"

"I—" (The palace kitchens. Last year. Nia sobbing, her skin blotchy—Father would not have been happy if he had seen her like that. *Please, Grandmother*, Nia had begged. *Please don't make me. I can't. I'm not like that, do you understand me? I'm not—* Grandmother silent. Then she saw me. *Muirgen*, she snapped. *What are you doing? Stop eavesdropping.*)

"Sophia," I say now. "What do you mean?"

"It doesn't matter," she says. Her eyes meet mine, blue on blue on blue again. I wish mine were another color. Up there, the stories go, the women have eyes of brown and green and violet and hazel. Their skin is brown and black and pink and white. Up there, the women are allowed to be different.

"What do you think Mama would say if she was here today?" I ask, and Sophia glances behind her nervously. We all do this, I've noticed; as if we are afraid our father will be there, waiting for us to make a mistake.

"I think she would kiss you and wish you a happy birthday," she says. "And then she would tell you she loves you."

But she didn't love me enough to stay.

Sometimes I wonder if I should be angry with my mother for that, like Cosima is. But I'm not. I miss her. And I want to know the truth about what happened to her.

The court room is shimmering; gemstones embedded in the coral walls. Blood-red streamers hanging from the ceiling, woven from every sea-flower within the vicinity of the palace, swaying in the fluttering water. Enormous cockle-shells have been prized open and dug into a circle on the sand, mer-people nestled in their hearts, wishing me a happy birthday as I pass.

Midway up the back wall, a balcony has been carved out of the palest sandstone and studded with oversized pearls. The Sea King is there, my father, hands bearing down on the balustrade, my sisters in a single-file line behind him. His hair is cropped close, as is customary for mer-men, a thin gold crown circling his head. The trident is resting against the balcony wall; he has no need of a weapon at an event like this, yet he keeps it close to him anyway. His jaw is working back and forward, a furious click of bone, *snap, snap*. My father hates this ball, and yet he continues to insist that it be thrown, the festivities more elaborate with each passing year. He shall prove to the mer-folk, once and for all, how little he cares about my mother's desertion, and we will believe him, if we know what's good for us.

"Muirgen. Sophia." My grandmother loops around us, a crown of battered metal plaited through her long, graying hair. "Where have you been? You know the Sea King does not like to be kept waiting." She pushes us before her, swimming until we reach the Sea King. Sophia joins my sisters at the back of the balcony, Grandmother settling at her side. I approach my father—I must present myself to him before remaining at his side for this part of the festivities.

"Is there any particular reason that you are late?" my father asks as I hover before him. His left eye is twitching, never a good sign. "I do not appreciate this tardiness, Muirgen."

"I'm sorry, Father," I say. "I wanted to ensure that I looked my best before leaving my bedroom."

"Well, let me see if the delay was worthwhile, then." His gaze licks up from my tail to my crown. I keep my face very still. He does not like it when we flinch.

"You are pleasing to me, Muirgen," he says finally. "Most pleasing indeed." He tosses a compliment back at my grandmother. "You have done well this evening, Thalassa."

"Thank you, Sea King," my grandmother replies, relaxing. "But the praise should surely rest with you. For it is you who has created her. It is you who gave her life, is it not?"

"This is true," he says. "Hopefully she will take after me in other respects too, for her own sake."

He takes me by the shoulders then, turning me around to face the crowd. I blink in the bright light, wondering at the vast numbers of people, most of whom are unknown to me. And yet they all know my name, of course.

"Greetings, mer-men, mermaids, all of my loyal subjects. It is a pleasure to receive you at court today, on this, the celebration of my youngest daughter's birthday."

The mer-folk swim out of the cockle-shells, gazing up at us with envy and fascination. We, the chosen ones. "Today is a wonderful day. Not only do we celebrate the *cleansing* of our kingdom, the *decontamination* of the palace . . ." He gives the same speech every year, and yet his indignation never seems to dissipate. "But to add to our joy, Princess Muirgen turns fifteen today. An important age, as you all know. An age that brings extra privileges, yes, but also extra responsibilities. I have no doubt that Muirgen is up to the task of both. She is my most beloved child."

Out of the corner of my eye, I see Cosima scowling before she remembers her manners, her face smoothing into a blankness that I recognize too well. I shall pay for my father's comments later. "And the most attractive," the Sea King adds. "She resembles me, does she not?"

The mer-folk cheer, even though everyone knows that I look like my mother. I watch them clapping for my beauty, as if it was something I had earned.

"Sing," they shout. "Sing, Princess!" The words bubbling up to meet us, demanding to be heard.

"The people have spoken," my father says. "You shall sing, Muirgen."

"I am tired, Father," I say. My voice is one of the few things that is mine, and mine alone. I do not want to share it with this baying crowd. "I was hoping I could rest this evening."

"I said, *sing*, Muirgen," he repeats, his tone shark-threat. "I too want to hear your voice. You will not deny me, your father, will you?"

The Sea King cannot be denied. I learned that lesson a long time ago.

"Of course not, Father," I say. "Whatever you want."

I breathe in, and I can feel the notes trembling at the base of my throat, forming without any real effort. I open my mouth and the melody spills out, slithering through the water, turning everything it touches translucent.

The mer-folk look up at me, spellbound, the melody lacing us together as one. It has wound its way into their bodies, shivering through them. This is my gift, but unlike the much-admired symmetry of my face, this gift actually brings me joy. For the last few years, I have noticed that it is only when I am singing that I ever feel complete, as if my body and my soul have finally found one another. *There you are*, they whisper, curling up in each other's arms. *I've missed you.*

"What a treat for you all, what an honor," my father cuts in before the end, the song scurrying out of my reach, as if frightened away. "Such clarity. Such *purity*. I'm sure we can all agree that my daughter's purity of voice has no parallel."

"Thank you, Father." I repeat the lines that I have been taught to say since birth. "Thank you for bestowing this gift upon me. I am fortunate to have been born as your salt-kin."

"You are most welcome," he says, kissing my forehead. "A father's love for his daughter knows no bounds. And that is all any child needs, wouldn't you agree?"

"Yes, Father."

"Yes, Father . . . what?"

"All a child needs is the love of her father."

"Very good. But let us not waste any more time chit-chatting," he says. His eyes move from one sister to the other and each of us tense when we realize what is coming next. It never gets easier, somehow, no matter how often it happens. "Talia, you go at the end," he says, grimacing as if he can barely stand to look at her. "Then Arianna, then Sophia." Arianna looks momentarily perturbed, despite her claims to be above such "vanity." "Nia," my father says, "you are looking quite pretty today. Marlin is a lucky man." My sister stares at the balcony floor. "And now," he says, when it is only Cosima and me remaining. "Which of my daughters deserves prime position today? Who shall win the honor of standing closest to me, your beloved father?" His gaze lingers on Cosima for a second, just long enough to give her hope. I wish he wouldn't do this. "Cosima, you can go in second place," he says. "And Muirgen, that face, that *face*! You are the winner, as it should be. Stand next to me, my love."

I take my position behind him, lining up with my sisters. "Sorry," I whisper when I accidentally brush against Cosima, but she doesn't acknowledge me, just tosses her hair back as if she doesn't have a care in the world. The opaque amber doors to the court are pushed open, and the chorus mermaids swim through, their voices blending together to create a wall of sound. The other mer-folk cheer at their arrival, taking to the water to dance, twirling with exquisite fragility.

"Oh, how lovely they all look," Cosima says. "The maids in particular. See, Father? See how their pearls shine as they dance?" He affords her a rare smile and she lights up. "I feel sorry for the men," she says to him. "How sad that they must live without such decoration."

My father laughs at the thought. The men do not need to be beautiful. I watch them as they dance. They are not weighed down by pearls; their movements are a fraction faster than the mermaids, their limbs loose. *Free.*

The party continues and my family remains on the balcony, maintaining a dignified distance as we watch the revelers below. "It is late, Sea King," my grandmother says when the light disappears, the water slicking black. "With your permission, I might put your daughters to rest. They are looking weary."

"Yes, Thalassa," my father says. "Some of the girls may go. It is essential they get adequate beauty sleep— particularly you, Talia." My sister just nods. "But Nia and Muirgen, you will stay behind. I am sure your betrotheds would like to speak with you."

"As you wish, Sea King," my grandmother says, beckoning my sisters to follow her. Cosima turns back, and I know whose face she hopes to catch a glimpse of. *Oh, Cosima.*

My father picks up his trident, banging it once on the balcony floor for Zale and a second time for Marlin. The two mer-men are huddled in a cockle-shell with their friends, but at my father's command, their bodies rise out of the shell as if an invisible lasso is fastened around their waists, dragging them against their will. Zale struggles initially, but then he acts like he doesn't care, that he desired an audience with the Sea King anyway. I watch as he gets closer to me, this man who will be my husband, and my stomach clenches, threatening to spit its contents out through my teeth.

"Sea King," Zale says as he is pulled onto the balcony. Every time I see him I am struck once more by how old he is; his hair is thinning, with patches of gray fuzz, and he has deep-cut lines on his forehead. He is nothing like the handsome prince foretold in my grandmother's nymph-tales of true love. My sisters and I, so small, nestled in our beds, waiting for her to finish the story with *and they all lived happily ever after.* I used to wonder then why my mother didn't get a happy end-ing. Maybe they were reserved for girls who did as they were told.

Zale bows his head in deference to my father and Marlin does the same just a beat later.

"Many thanks for a wonderful evening, Sea King; your generosity is unparalleled." Zale's voice is so obse-quious, I would think he was being insincere if I didn't know better.

"Today must be celebrated," my father replies. "For fourteen years, I have ruled this kingdom by myself."

"Indeed, and you have done such a difficult job with great wisdom and strength," Zale says. "Good riddance to bad rubbish, sir." I bristle at my mother being referred to like this, but I contain myself. *Anger is not alluring in maids*, my father says. "If I may be so bold as to ask," Zale continues, "to what do we owe the honor of an audience with the royal family?"

"It is late," my father says. "And my daughters are tired. I thought you would want to bid them farewell."

Marlin blushes. "Good night, Nia," he says, reaching out a hand to touch hers, shuddering as if he has been electrified when he makes contact. My sister is motion-less, her tail barely beating, eyes downcast. I do not understand such a muted reaction. Marlin is a little insipid, yes, but he is kind. Gentle. He will be good to her. I envy her that.

"You may go, Marlin," Father dismisses him, and Nia gives an imperceptible sigh of relief. Marlin bows his head to the Sea King again, and swims away, his skeletal torso a sliver of flesh slicing through the water. My father releases Nia with a wave of his hand, and I silently beg her to stay, to protect me. But she goes, because my father has told her to do so, and I am left alone with them.

"Sea King," Zale says, digging his spear into the ground. Zale is never without that spear, although there is no need for it. The kingdom is at peace, and has been for many years now. Much to Zale's dismay.

The war between the Salkas and the mer-folk had dragged on for ten years, the old folk say, and there didn't seem to be a respite in sight. And then my mother—not queen then, just an ordinary mermaid at court—went to my father and begged him to call a cease-fire. In exchange, she promised to marry him on her sixteenth birthday. That was something the Sea King had long yearned for, apparently, but any maid under the age of twenty needs to have their father's permission if they are to be betrothed. Or their father's decision, as in my case. You're so lucky, they tell me when they hear I am to be bonded with Zale. *I am so very lucky.*

As if on cue, Zale begins to talk, and it is his favorite subject. *War.* "We need to talk about the Sea Witch and the Salkas," he spits, as if the word *Salkas* is burning a hole through his tongue. "They are becoming—"

"Zale," my father says softly, and my spine straightens. I know that tone, and what it means, too well. "Have you forgotten that we have company?"

There is a pause as Zale's eyes go to my face. "Of course not," he says, smiling as if he wants to eat me whole, and then chew on my bones for comfort. *We will be bonded in a year*, I remind myself, *me and this old man*, and my throat closes up. "How could I possibly forget, when such loveliness stands before me?" he says.

"Well, then," my father says. "I'll ask you not to discuss such things in front of my daughter, or any maid for that matter. This is none of their business."

Zale runs a hand over his shaved head, his eyes narrowing. They are blue, like the rest of the mer-folk, and yet they seem darker as he imagines battles, sword striking sword, heads cleaved off torsos. Zale will not be happy until his spear is smeared with blood. Preferably a Salka's, but I don't think he's overly particular. "I apologize, Sea King," he says. "And a very happy birthday, Muirgen. Fifteen at last, you must be excited."

My name is Gaia. That is the name my mother gave me. Perhaps if Zale was a different kind of man, I could ask him to call me by the name that I prefer. But I don't think he would care for such niceties. All he is concerned with is that I am the most beautiful daughter of the Sea King. I am a prize to be won, and Zale likes the taste of victory.

"Did my daughter not sing sweetly tonight?" Father asks, exhibiting me for Zale's approval. I breathe through my nose, trying to remain calm. It will be over soon.

"Such talent," Zale says, although I suspect he has no love for music.

"And doesn't she look radiant? One of the great beauties of the kingdom. A great, great beauty."

"That is the truth," Zale says. "I still remember the night of that ball, when it was apparent she would become the fairest of your daughters. I knew then that she should be mine."

I remember that night too. I had just turned twelve. That was the night that Cosima began to cry.

"You were smart," my father says, pressing his fingertips into my shoulder blades. "You got in early. If Muirgen were not my daughter, perhaps I would have chosen her for myself."

He and Zale laugh, and I try and smile too. *Just merman talk*, I think. No need to be so sensitive.

"But really, sir," Zale says, somber again. "We cannot wait much longer. There has been movement . . ."

"Aye, I suppose we should," my father says. "Shall we discuss this now?"

Zale nods. The two men stand side by side, uncannily similar with their gray buzz cuts and broad shoulders. They could be brothers. The Sea King unlocks an ornately carved door at the side of the balcony, opening it into the war room. I see a flash of silver, racks of spiked weapons, waiting patiently to be used.

My mother sacrificed herself to ensure that this door would remain locked forever. But my mother is gone.

"Muirgen," Father says. "You may leave." Neither he nor Zale checks to see if I obey his command. There is no need.

For I am the daughter of the Sea King and I will do as I am told.

I knock on the open door of my sisters' room, waiting until they grant me permission to enter. Each of my sisters is lying alone, bodies made shadow by the white gauze wrapped around their beds. They are awake, and yet none of them speak to me, not even Sophia. They always end up resenting me on my birthday.

"Muirgen," Grandmother says. "Come in."

I did not see her there, tucked into the corner of the room behind Cosima's bed, sitting in front of a mirror bordered with crystals cut into the shape of stars. It is the largest mirror in the kingdom, falling during the Great Storm that cracked the sky open and tore the sea apart. I had wanted it for the tower but Cosima had refused. "No," she had said, folding her arms. "I found it first. It's mine. You can't have *everything* you want." We both knew she wasn't talking about the mirror.

"Sit with me, child," Grandmother says. She is sitting on a cockle-shell seat, and I align my body with hers, my dark green scales a stark contrast to her silver tail. She runs her fingers through my hair, unpicking the braid. *It should be my mother who is doing this.* My mother would be thirty-seven now, still relatively young. Would she have allowed the betrothal to Zale to occur, if she had known how revolted I was by him? Would she have been the only one who could have stood up to the Sea King, or would have cared enough to do so? I stare at my grandmother and myself in the mirror, our faces fine-boned and sharp of angles. I can see the foreshadow of what is to come as the years pass and my beauty fades, my skin folding in on itself, my hair shedding its vibrant color. Is this what my mother would have looked like one day, when she reached her hundredth year?

"You're bleeding, Grandmother," I say, looking down at her tail. The pearls are twisting, the weight pulling down, plucking tendrils of flesh away. There is a gap between the gemstones and her tail, open wounds filling with bubbles of blood. "Are you in pain?" I ask. "Shall I call the healer?"

"No," she says, reaching to unscrew another pearl, wheezing as it comes away in her hands. "Ah, but I am too old for such finery. No one cares for the pitiable attempts of an old woman to retain her youth."

"Then why do you wear them?"

"Your father desires that all women be properly adorned at court. And I am the mermaid of the highest birth since . . ." *Since your mother left.*

"But—"

"The Sea King has willed it, Muirgen," she says. "And that is that."

I let it go, nestling against her as she strokes my hair. "There, there, my salt-heart," she says. And for a second, I pretend that she is someone else, another woman who dreamed too much. Another woman who looked up.

"Grandmother," I say. "Tell me the story of the first time you went up."

She groans, but she cannot refuse me today.

"It was my fifteenth birthday," she begins, and I mouth the words along with her. I have heard this story so many times before. It was the lullaby that rocked me asleep when I was a baby, the soothing croon that calmed me after a fight with one of my sisters.

My grandmother was fifteen and she looked up, following the sun to the surface. "And I felt heat for the very first time," she says now, as she always does. "A heat so intense that I had to dive back under; it seemed as if my skin might be peeled from my bones." She broke the water's skin again, seeing fish that flew in the air (*Birds, my child, they call them birds up there.*) and ships (*What are they like, you ask? Well, they are like giant whales made of wooden planks, I suppose.*) floating past in the distance. Grandmother Thalassa stayed there until the sun fell beneath the waves and she dropped deep into the sea's chest to search for it, to hold that scalding gold between her fingers; but it had disappeared.

"It was beautiful," she says now. "But not as beautiful as the Sea Kingdom."

My sisters whisper their agreement, their voices closer than expected. I blink to find them in a semicircle at our tails, gazing at our grandmother, rapt in her story. When she is done, they tell their own. The dawn of their fifteenth birthdays, a whole new world to be found. A dazzle of stars strewn across a midnight sky or wild swans dashing through crimson clouds with a loud battle cry. Icebergs glittering in a glacial sea, impaled by a sudden spike of lightning and sheared in two. Human children (*They looked so innocent*, Sophia said. *They had not yet turned bad*, Cosima replied. *Give them time.*) splashing in shallow water, a barking animal at their side (*a dog*, my grandmother explained). The children were somehow able to swim though they had no tails; it was most peculiar, they said. The clatter of people living in coastal towns, from whom my sisters kept a safe distance. The roar of engines, the soaring church spires reaching for heaven's graze.

"Beautiful," each of my sisters says now. "But not as beautiful as the Sea Kingdom."

For the last five years, I have watched my sisters rise out of the water, one by one, wishing I could go with them. And for the last five years, I have watched as my father has awaited their return. "Well?" he asked each of them, his teeth clenched. "It was fine, Father," they all replied. "But I have no desire to go back." It is strange. The Sea King could simply ban these expeditions, forbid us from traveling to the realm that claimed our mother and took her life. But he does not. Perhaps he wants to gauge the depths of our loyalty. Perhaps it is a test to see if we are showing signs of turning, like our mother did before us.

"And tomorrow," Grandmother says, "it will be your time, Muirgen. And I hope you too will see that the world up there is charming, but it has not been designed for the likes of us. It is not safe for our kind."

Then why show it to us? Why risk our mother's fate? But I stay silent, for fear that such questions will result in my being unable to travel to the surface, and I must see it for myself. I *must.*

"Of course it is not safe for us," Cosima says. "Not after what they did to our mother."

"Your mother," Grandmother says slowly, "was so young. Only fifteen when she promised her hand in marriage, sixteen when your father took her as his bride."

I am only fifteen too, I feel like reminding her, and I am to be wed next year; but it will be of no use. "And at the time of their bonding ceremony, your parents seemed . . ."

"Happy?" Talia asks hopefully.

"They seemed settled," Grandmother says. "They had you girls so quickly, one after the other." So many girls, and all my father wanted was a son. Another way in which Muireann of the Green Sea failed him. "And your mother was fine. I thought she was fine."

"She was fine until you were born, Muirgen," Cosima mutters.

"Stop that," Grandmother says. "Your mother always loved the human world; she visited there often after her fifteenth birthday. She would regale your grandfather and me with the sights she had seen, the things she had witnessed. Your grandfather, the sea gods bless his memory, he warned her to be careful. He warned her that the humans were not to be trusted. But she didn't listen. She was so tempestuous, that girl. There was no controlling her."

"Our mother started to visit the surface more often." Talia picks up the story for Grandmother Thalassa. We know it well. "She stopped eating. She complained that she was tired all the time."

"And the Sea King thought she had fallen sick," Arianna joins in. "And he got the healer to brew potions for her, but nothing worked."

"And then on the day of my first birthday party . . ." I start, but I cannot continue. My grandmother squeezes my hand.

"We were all gathered for the celebration," she says, so I don't have to. "But we were waiting on your mother

and the Sea King to arrive. There was no sign of either."
She takes a deep breath. "And then the Sea King burst
through the palace doors, looking as if he had been
struck by lightning. And he told us."

He told the mer-folk how he had followed my mother
to the surface that afternoon and had seen her become
ensnared in the human nets. Her body thrashing, the
men on the boat jeering, touching her tail without permission, screaming with laughter at my mother's cries for
mercy. He could have stopped them, the Sea King told
those congregated at my crib; he was the most powerful
man in the kingdom after all. But if he did, then the
humans would know there were more creatures like my
mother to be found. They might come looking for us,
hunting us. And while the Sea King could have protected
himself easily, he didn't want to risk the lives of every
other mer-man or maid under the sea in order to save
just one of our kind. So he watched as they took our
mother away. And then he told us that she was dead.
Which she was, probably; she would not have survived
outside of the water for that long. She is dead. Of course
she is; it is the only logical conclusion to the story. And
yet . . . We never closed lids over frozen eyes, nor rested
tiny pearls upon her lips. We never sang hymns by her
lifeless body, nor prayed to the gods to dissolve her soul

to sea-foam and scatter it on the waves. We were just told that our mother was selfish, that she had abandoned her six daughters to see the wonders that the world above the surface had to offer. And then we were told that she was dead, and we were expected to believe it.

"We are blessed to be where we are, living in this kingdom," my grandmother says now, and she kisses my head, murmuring love into my skull. "It is time for bed now, little mermaid."

I wish my family good night as I leave, swimming the long corridor from their room until I reach the spiral staircase to my tower. The steps are cut out of packed sand, the walls a mosaic of sea-glass and broken shells, like the bones of fallen sailors that the Salkas steal to make their homes in the Shadowlands, that realm far away from here that the Sea Witch has made her own.

Two maids pass me on the winding path, pushing their backs into the wall. "Apologies, Princess Muirgen. We did not mean to disturb you." I recognize the prettier girl immediately: Lorelai, whose husband abandoned her and the children. She had been banished to the Outerlands for a time, but she was allowed to return to the palace as a member of the chorus when the Sea King decided he missed her perfect falsetto. No one ever calls her husband "unnatural" for abandoning his children; no, instead they whisper that Lorelai must have failed to satisfy him. Her former husband is re-bonded now, but no merman will take on Lorelai. No matter how pretty she is, the weight of a tainted maid with a reputation is beyond endurance.

"Don't worry," I say, allowing them to pass without further objection.

I close my bedroom door, leaning against the heavy coral with a sigh. *Gaia*, I whisper, as if summoning her from deep within, telling her that it's safe to come out now. I have left Muirgen on the stairs outside; I could not bear her for much longer. I am alone, so I can be true again.

I look up.

The tower opens to the roiling black sea, waves stirring as shoals of fish twist past, a glimmer of metal in the darkness. Moving to the seabed for safety, it seems. *Storm*, the water whispers to me, its voice as familiar as my own. The gods must be angry. A shape passes over the palace; a whale, perhaps, or one of the ships from the human world that my grandmother warns my sisters to be wary of when they go swimming. Not that she need worry; my sisters have broken the surface only once since their respective birthdays. They say it is safer that way; they are reducing the risk of being spotted and imprisoned—*we don't want to end up like our mother*, are the words that are left unsaid. I wonder what it must be like to be one of them, to have their curiosity so easily sated. I reach my hands up towards the surface, as if to touch the ship or the whale, but it is too far away. We are buried alive down here.

"Mother," I say aloud, the word unfamiliar on my tongue. I am not supposed to say her name. I am not even supposed to think of her. "She didn't think of any of you, did she?" my father told us time and time again. "She didn't care enough to stay."

Mother.

Chapter

3

I T IS STILL dark when I wake, a tiny pinprick of light burrowing its way into the palace, promising the coming day. *It is time*, the water whispers to me.

I am strangely calm as I prepare for my journey, the journey I have been waiting to take for so long now, but I cannot help but picture my mother's fifteenth birthday. I imagine her, wild hope caught between her teeth, her bone-knowing that she was meant for more than a life of combing her hair and singing for survival. Betrothed to a man much older than her, a man who saw her as a toy, a shiny thing that he couldn't wait to get his hands on, and yet she married him anyway, putting aside her own needs to make others happy, because that's what maids are supposed to do. *Zale makes my skin crawl*, I would tell my mother if she was still here. *He looks at me like he wants to destroy me.* Sometimes I wish I could hate my mother, that I could resent her for leaving us behind. But all I can do is long for her.

The darkness is collapsing into a murky gray, chasing me upwards. I swim out of the open tower, looking down at the palace beneath me. Thousands of fish surround the walls, a circle of phosphorescent skins, cowering for shelter. They can smell the storm too, can sense shattered sand. Their fear today is greater than their usual trepidation about the nets the humans cast to trap them. It is difficult for me to fathom, but it is said that up there they eat fish the way the Rusalkas eat men, teeth tearing flesh, sucking juice from bones.

We mermaids are not so easily caught. We are rare, and that makes us precious. The humans who believe we exist want to capture us and exhibit our bodies, for that is the only way they can make us real for their skeptical brethren. Most humans cannot believe anything that they cannot see with their own eyes, touch with their own hands. But we are more clever than mere fish; we know how to avoid such snares.

I follow the dawning light, fighting through tangled lumps of seaweed, avoiding the fields of jagged coral that would tear my tail apart, keeping the tattered scales as ornaments. Dodging sucking currents that ache to consume bodies, throwing them back and forth, as if it is a game of catch, like the mer-children play. And then a shark grazes past me, eyes sly and mouth closed to hide its sharp teeth. I stay very still, hoping that it will pass me without incident, holding my breath until it has gone. I keep going, ignoring the niggling twinges in my arms, tired from swimming such a great distance. The light becomes easier, dappling the water in a way that I have never seen before, and I know now I must be close. Panting as I break the surface, my gills fit to burst with the extra oxygen pumping through them. Pushing snarled hair down my back so I can see this new world without impediment, I open my eyes, wincing as the unfamiliar gleam scours my eyeballs. It is too bright, the sun in the pale sky razing heat across my skin. I have never experienced such warmth. My grandmother tried to explain what this would feel like—but how could I understand this sensation? I was born in the water and I was born of the water. The cold is all I have ever known.

It's too much—the dazzling glow of the sun, its warmth licking my skin, the screaming *caw-caw* of winged fish (*birds, they are birds, Gaia*) swooping in the heavens. There is a rock jutting out of the sea's skin and

I swim to it, shooing the seals bathing on its surface away so I can hide behind it. I duck under the water for comfort, soothing my sun-seared face. Panic is twisting my gut, thick-thick, but I cannot give up now. For what would my sisters think if I returned so early? I have been the most eager to see the human world, the one who wanted this adventure the most. *Typical Muirgen*, Cosima would say. *I wasn't afraid when I broke the surface, I was brave. Zale will not allow you to act like such a baby once you are bonded.* As if courage is something that Zale would ever want in his bride.

I grit my teeth, wrapping my arms around the rock to hold steady. I shall stay here until the sun sets and then I will return to the kingdom, spinning pretty stories the likes of which my sisters have never heard. I shall not be shamed.

"There. Over there." A male voice, calling out. I cannot tell where it is coming from, the sun blinding me. The voice is harsh, the air refusing to lull its tone as the water does. "I definitely saw something, I'm telling you."

I clamp a hand over my mouth in horror. Those are human voices, and they sound close to me. *Too close, Gaia, they are dangerous. Be careful.* I should duck beneath the sea, return immediately to my father's kingdom, but I do not. Perhaps I am too curious. These are the creatures my mother loved, that she risked so much to be near. And so, despite myself, I stay quiet behind my rock, my breath coming fast and shallow. *The humans will see you*, I try to convince myself. *They will cut your tail off and stuff you, display your body above their fireplaces. They will slit your throat without a thought, just to see what color your blood is.* I should swim away as quickly as I can. But I find myself unable to move. I want to see them, I realize. They might know what happened to my mother.

"Oh, Oli," comes another voice. A girl's this time. "It was probably just a seal."

"I could have sworn . . ." The first voice stops. There is bewilderment in his tone. Where are they? The voices are close but they cannot be swimming, not this far out to sea.

"Sworn what?" A different boy, laughing. "Did you see a monster? A mermaid?"

"What's the difference?" the girl asks. I take a deep breath and, so cautiously, peek around the rock.

I find a large boat there, painted white, with three balconies at the back and a flat open surface to the front. Thick sticks are growing out of the paneled wood, a cream canvas on top, like a kind of flatfish. There are about a dozen humans on the boat, of different shapes and sizes, their bodies a variety of shades from the palest white to the darkest black. Most of them are lying on beds made of the same cream material as the canvas, dozing with an indolence that seems strange, given how ferocious they are reputed to be.

"Time for another drink, mate," the second boy says, and there is a smashing noise, glass against wood, the sun setting the shards on fire, dazzle-white.

"Geoffrey Gupta, why are you such a dolt?"

"Shut up, Viola."

"You shut up, or I'll tell Mum that you were drinking too much *again*. And call Mabel to clean up this mess. Someone will cut their feet to absolute shreds."

Feet. Feet are what the humans call the stumps they walk upon. The humans will cut their feet on the broken glass and it will hurt them, as the coral slices our tails in the kingdom if we are not careful. These creatures are not impervious to injury, it seems.

"Shall we drop anchor here?" Viola says. "Seems as good a spot as any, doesn't it, Oli? Oliver? Are you listening to me?"

A boy walks to the side of the boat and stares at the rock that I'm hiding behind. And I see him.

Oh.

A sharp intake of breath that seems so loud, almost a gasp really, and I realize that it is coming from my own mouth. I stare at him, this boy. He is tall, his hair and skin dark, and he is more beautiful than I have ever dreamed a boy could be. *Who is he?* I want to know. I need to know. I would happily spend the rest of my life finding out everything about him.

"A girl," he says, a hand cupped over his eyes. A strange heat flashes through me, a heat that has nothing to do with the sun. "I thought I saw a girl."

Chapter

4

I REMAIN BEHIND that rock for the rest of the day. I no longer want to flee; all I want to do is watch the humans. Watch *him*.

We have been told often how evil they are, how depraved. These are the people who are responsible for my childhood, for nights spent searching in the darkness for a comforting hand that would never come.

But they seem so innocent now that they are before me. I count them, seven girls and eight boys, on the precipice of adulthood with their awkward limbs, the material they swathe around their hips and chests so they are not naked. "I love your swimsuit, Lizzie," one girl said, sticking a finger down her throat when the human called Lizzie turned away. They seem oddly ashamed of their bodies, particularly the girls. They tug at stomachs and rub thighs, pulling down the edges of their suits to conceal more flesh, refusing offers of food because "I've eaten so much today, I'm *disgusting*." It appears as if the humans, boys and girls, have come to sea to celebrate a birthday. His birthday.

"To Oliver on his twenty-first," they shout, demanding that Mabel bring more champagne, whatever that might be. Oliver keeps walking to the side of the boat, staring out to sea. He is searching for me.

"Oli." Viola's arms around his waist, resting her head against his back. Her hair is cut to her chin and she has very long, brown legs. "You're missing all the fun." Oliver kisses her, and my throat feels as if it is made of teeth while I watch them. Are they betrothed, Oliver and this Viola? *Keep looking for me*, I urge him silently.

The sun becomes weary as afternoon stretches into evening, wilting in the lilac sky. Voices curve and become indistinct, dripping at the edges as if doused in liquid. The sticks—*umbrellas*, they called them—have been removed so the humans can dance. One has brought an instrument and he is making music with it, the others yelling out songs that they wish for him to play next. Oliver and Viola in the center of the boat, bodies close, swaying to the tune. I should leave, I tell myself, counting the ways that the humans are bad, how often my father has warned that they promise destruction and ruin. *They killed your mother, Gaia.* I should leave, but I know also that I would sooner die than do so. As odd as that sounds, I would rather dissolve with this sight burning in my eyes, Viola's half-smile as Oliver murmurs in her ear.

"Are you ready for the finale?" the boy called Geoffrey yells, pointing to the heavens. All of them stare at the sky, and I follow suit. For a moment it is as if we are all one. Even here, the humans look up, searching for something more.

A screech of a whistle, a bang, and an explosion of gold dust. The stars plunge, raining light onto the boat, and my heart drives its way into my chest with fright. My skin will surely burn, I think; these bursting stars will tear our faces apart—but nothing happens. The lights re-emerge, flaring into the air, sprinkling red and silver and gold on the world, in spinning circles and shooting rockets. The humans grin, the glitter reflected in their eyes. They are dazzled by the display, hypnotized. Only Oliver is looking around him still, frowning. A murder of crows are spinning through the air, flying in chaotic circles, crashing into one another with a screaming cry. The sky is bruising purple, as if battered by the birds.

"Wait," Oliver says, and everyone turns to him immediately, as they do in the kingdom when my father speaks. It is a kind of influence that I cannot imagine. "Did you feel that?"

"Feel what?" Viola asks, running her hand up his arm. "Are you enjoying the fireworks? It took me an age to organize."

"Of course I am, my darling," Oliver says, but he's staring out at the sea and I don't think he's looking for me anymore. "I just . . . something isn't right."

I dip under the surface, tasting the water as it wakes up around me, stretching its arms out, ready to play. *Hello,* it says, and it begins caressing the left side of the boat, then the right, just enough to inform the humans that it is here. The water does not pay much heed to the boats ripping through its skin, but occasionally the humans must be reminded of the water's generosity in allowing them to do so.

I rise up again to watch the humans. A glass walks off the table, exploding as it hits the floor. No one calls for Mabel this time.

"Rupert did say the weather looked dicey," Viola murmurs.

"Never mind Rupert. You said you checked the forecast this morning, didn't you, Gupta?" Oliver says.

"I did," Geoffrey replies, grabbing a railing at the boat's edge to steady himself. "It didn't say anything about a storm."

A sudden fork of lightning, a serpent's tongue licking the sky apart. A girl's scream.

"Okay, we all need to stay calm," Oliver says as the sea begins to grumble. *Hungry*, it tells me. "Everyone put their life jackets on. It's going to be fine." He turns to Geoffrey. "Where's Teddy? He's the only person who knows how to sail a yacht this size."

"Teddy is asleep."

"Then wake him up, for fuck's sake. We need to get back to port right now."

"Oli, Teddy has been drinking since noon. I doubt he can even stand, let alone steer this boat."

Oliver curses. The sky is broken again, flashing brilliant, and another human screams, more desperate this time. They scramble for these life jackets that Oliver spoke of, ashen faces against the luminous yellow. The wind lifts its heavy head, sniffing deeply, inhaling the sea's anger. It wants to join in. It wants to put the humans in their place too.

"Oli," Viola says. She is not crying, like some of the other girls are, but her face is tight. "Oli, what are we going to do?"

Something slithers past me, a substance like seaweed sliming my skin. A head bobs out of the water, then another, and another. Right on time, as they always are. They will have been anticipating this moment all day, as soon as they smelled the storm, no doubt. Pale green hair slicked down their backs, the whites of their eyes flashing in the dark. They circle the boat, holding hands, their song gathering at the backs of their throats. *Oh, come, human men. Come to us. We will teach you a lesson you shall never forget.*

"What was that?" Viola says, staring into the water as a Salka moves forward. "Did you see that?"

They never believe in us until it is too late. The sea begins to climb, stacking wave upon wave—it is a giant with a gaping mouth, looking for something to feast upon. The humans offer their useless prayers to their gods, as if anything can save them now. Pressure builds behind my eyes, like I might cry. Cry for these creatures who would see me as a freak if they knew I existed? Cry for those who took my mother from me? *What is wrong with you, Gaia?* But if they die, *if he dies*, then will I ever feel this way again? Never feel heat pooling in my stomach, that urge to take his hand in mine and never let go? I cannot bear the thought of it. A whip of a vicious wave, a snapping sound, wood crumpling between the water's death-grip fingers. The boat lurches desperately to the side, the water gushing in while the humans scream. They scream and they scream. And all I can do is watch.

The Rusalkas begin to sing, the tune vibrating sharply in my teeth like gritted sand.

Come to us. (Their song is so beautiful.) And the humans cease struggling.

Accept your fate. (Their song is so terrible.) And the humans close their eyes. They beg for mercy.

And the Salkas move.

Limbs and planks are torn apart by the wind and the sea, tossed from one wave to the next, and for some reason that I cannot name just yet, I find myself swimming, heading into the wreck, narrowly avoiding being crushed by a thrashing beam. I ignore the salt sizzling hot in my veins, warning me of certain death if I continue. I refuse to be frightened, not now. The water twisting and devouring the boat. Arms and legs and screaming mouths and eyes wide open, beaten into submission. The bodies that descended to the kingdom looked so peaceful; I did not realize that their demise would have been so violent. The girls are left to swallow death as the Salkas claim the men for their own.

Left, right, peering into the lashing water, searching for one person only. *Where is he?*

I see him. A Salka has her hand against his chest, hunting for his heart.

"No," I say. And then, "Not him."

Her head spins completely on her shoulders, in one clean movement.

"And why not?" she asks, her tongue waggling past her teeth. "Why should I spare this man?"

"I—"

"Don't be foolish, little mermaid," she murmurs. "Human men will bring you nothing but pain."

"No. You can't have him," I say, that heat tingling through me once more. I don't know what this is but I want to hold on to this feeling forever. "You can take her instead." I point at Viola, struggling in the water, fingers clawing wood as she reaches for a beam to hold on to, her features twisted in what looks more like fury than fear. A warrior, that one. She would have made a good Salka if she had died in a more tragic fashion.

"You would trade a girl's life so easily, would you, little one? For some man you don't even know? And besides, what use would I have with a *girl*?" the Salka says. "It is not women that must atone for their sins."

"You can't have him," I say again. "I am telling you now, Salka. I am Princess Muirgen, sixth daughter of the Sea King. I am betrothed to Zale, leader of our kingdom's troops. And I command you to let this human go."

I wrestle Oliver's body away from the Salka, ignoring her promising war and destruction after me.

"Ceto!" she screams. "Ceto will hear of your actions. You will regret this."

I ignore her. In this moment, I do not care for my own safety or what retribution the Rusalkas will seek for this flagrant transgression of our laws. I don't care if my decision upends the uneasy truce we have brokered between our kingdom and the Sea Witch's Shadowlands. All I care about is this man, the blessed weight of him in my arms as I drag him to safety. *Oliver.*

He must live.

Chapter

5

"MUIRGEN." HUMAN MEN *will bring you nothing but pain.*

"Muirgen." *Human men will bring you nothing but pain.*

"Muirgen! I shall not tolerate such insolence from you, girl."

An elbow to my ribs. *"What?"* I hiss at Arianna, rubbing my side. She tilts her head towards our father. He is sitting at the top of the mother-of-pearl dining table, glaring at me.

"What is it, Father?" My voice is strangled, even to my ears.

"I asked you a question, Muirgen," he says. "And when I ask a question, I expect you to answer me immediately."

"I'm sorry, Father," I say. He looks at me strangely, and my skin prickles with dread. *Does he know what happened? Does he know what I have done?* "I was distracted." I have been distracted these past two weeks, waiting for the Salkas' response to me saving the human boy. Each day brings a silence that is increasingly unnerving. The peace between my father and the Sea Witch is brittle, fragile; hard fought for and easily dismantled. I have put us all in danger.

"And you haven't touched your dinner," he continues. "Did you not enjoy it?"

"It's perfectly fine, Father. I'm just not hungry."

"Muirgen is never hungry at the moment, Father," Cosima says eagerly. "She has barely eaten anything in weeks. That's not right, is it? Not when you do so much to provide for us."

"Perhaps a loss of appetite might not be a bad thing," my father says, looking pointedly at her empty plate. "We don't want any suitors put off—or preferring another sister again, do we?"

"No, Father," she says, pressing her lips together. She won't cry, no matter how upset she is. Not in front of him.

"Well, I think it's disgraceful," Arianna says, taking another spoonful of greens. "Such a waste of food; it is most ungrateful of you, Muirgen. And think of all the mer-folk in the Outerlands, practically starving to death. As if it's not bad enough that they live in constant fear of an attack from the Salkas." She shudders at the thought. "You have no idea how much they would appreciate this dinner."

"Sister." Sophia is uncharacteristically cold. "Do not talk nonsense. The Salkas will never invade the Outerlands without the Sea Witch's blessing—they fear her powers too much—and the Sea Witch is just as invested in the armistice as we are, if not more." I shiver. Little do any of them know how I might have already ruined that armistice beyond repair.

Grandmother places a hand over Sophia's, reminding my sister of her place. None of us speak after that; the room is so silent that all we can hear is the lapping of water against the sea-glass window.

"No, no," Father says. "Let the girls speak. Such lively debate is . . . interesting." He taps his fingers slowly against the table, one at a time. I repress a shudder. "You speak of the 'starving' mer-folk in the Outerlands, Arianna. I hope you are not insinuating that there are people within my kingdom who are not adequately provided for."

"Of course not, Father," she says cautiously. "Those in the Outerlands are most grateful for your support."

The Sea King seems to be waiting for her to say something else, all of us holding our breath.

"A-a-as they should be," Sophia rushes into the silence.

"And as for you, Sophia . . ." He smiles, and it's sinister, that smile; he's relishing this. Would he smile at me like that if he found out that I saved a human life, risking the kingdom's peace in order to do so? Risking all of our lives? Or would it be worse? Would he cut my tail off and hang my torso on the palace walls, call me a traitor to the crown? Banish me to the Outerlands, damn me to a life of famine and misery with the other undesirables? I don't know. The only person who ever disobeyed the Sea King was my mother, and he didn't need to punish her. The humans did that for him.

Human men will bring you nothing but pain.

"I'm sorry, Father," Sophia says. The rest of us stare at our plates as if to pretend that none of this is happening. We are never brave in times like this; we are all too afraid that Father will direct his attention onto us instead.

"You're sorry?"

"Yes, Father."

"And what exactly are you sorry *for*, daughter number three?"

Sophia's eyes dart to Grandmother, as if hoping she will intervene on her behalf, but our grandmother sits still, eyes down.

"I'm sorry for . . ." she says, and I can barely hear her. "I'm sorry for mentioning the Sea Witch at dinner."

"Oh, I think you did more than just *mention* the Sea Witch, didn't you?"

"Yes, Father."

"I think you might have implied that she had . . . what was the word you used?" Sophia doesn't reply. "Sophia," he says, her name thickening between his lips. "What was the word you used?"

"Powers." The word jumps out of her.

"Ah, yes. *Powers*. Surely you weren't suggesting that the old hag has abilities akin to my own?"

"No, Father." Her voice is faltering, like a shadow moon. "I'm sorry, Father."

"No one in the kingdom has powers like the Sea King," Cosima says, with indecent haste.

"Precisely," my father says, passing his trident from one hand to the other. My eyes follow it back and forth, the metal glittering with the promise of destruction. "Everything I have done is to keep you girls safe. I hope you're not becoming ungrateful, Sophia. I'm sure you remember what fate has befallen ungrateful women in this family."

"Yes, Father," Sophia says, gulping. "I'm sorry, Father."

"Under my reign, the mer-people are the most prosperous they have ever been," he says. "The *rightful* mer-people, that is; those allowed the privilege of life within the palace grounds. No one can deny that I have made the kingdom powerful again, can they?"

"We are blessed to be living in the time of your sovereignty, Sea King," Grandmother Thalassa says. She picks up her knife and fork, cutting some weeds into smaller chunks. We are the only ones who use such human items, collected from the ruins of shipwrecks. My mother insisted on it, apparently, and even then, no one thought to question how she knew to use them, how she came to be familiar with their names. My mother said the utensils were glamorous and refined, and my father, always keen to make his family more "special," agreed. He did not suspect any threat in his wife's interest in the humans then. The tradition of formal dining has never been broken, despite the Sea King's hatred of the world above the surface. "Now eat your food, Muirgen," Grandmother says. "You need sustenance."

I stare at the bowl of weeds in front of me. The humans on the boat had sipped frothing bubbles from gleaming crystal, and unwrapped little powdery cakes from colored paper. They wouldn't eat this. They would laugh, call us animals. Maybe they would be right. My hand slips under the table and I tear at my fishtail with my nails. Maybe we are half-beast, after all.

"You most certainly will need to keep your energy up, young Muirgen." Father winks at me. "What with Zale calling to visit you after dinner." A lump of nausea throbs in my throat at the mention of Zale's name, clotting deep. He turns to Nia. "Don't worry, daughter. Marlin will accompany him. You shall not be left out." He shovels another forkful of green into his mouth. "At least *some* of my daughters are betrothed, isn't that right, Talia?"

"We are fortunate," Nia murmurs as Talia stares at her lap. I don't want to be like Talia, twenty-one and unloved, and yet I don't want to marry Zale either. But what other option do I have?

"Thank you, Father," Nia says. She returns to the window. If I have spent my life looking up, then Nia has spent hers looking out, staring into the depths of the sea. Past the Outerlands, past the Sea Witch's realm of the Shadowlands. It is as if she thinks there might be somewhere safe for her beyond that. *What are you searching for, Nia?*

Of course Zale is coming tonight; it is Saturday. He has visited every Saturday evening since my twelfth birthday. I was still half-child then, half-maid, just becoming interested in mer-boys my age. Hoping to hold someone's hand, have their lips brush chastely against mine. I thought nothing of my father and his old friend huddled in the corner, brows furrowed. I didn't know that my body was being sold to the highest bidder.

I want to get to know you better, Zale said that birthday night, his hands on my shoulders as he leaned in to kiss my cheek. His lips lingering too long, my stomach turning over with something between shame and fear. *Beautiful,* he said, and I would rather have torn off my own face than have him look upon me with such pleasure again. But I smiled, and said, *Thank you.* I have always been a very polite girl.

"Muirgen? Did you hear me? Zale is coming to see you."

"Wonderful," I reply, attempting to smile, but it is a struggle, every muscle in my body taut with anxiety. What if I have brought war back to the kingdom? Grandmother Thalassa has told us of what the last one was like, of starving children, their bones twisting out of flesh as their tails withered away. She told us of fathers and husbands and sons and brothers sent to fend off the Sea Witch and the Salkas, women who were frantic to claim the kingdom as their own. She told us too few of our mer-men returned and those that did were utterly changed; they were silent, quick to take fright, their sleep broken by sweating dreams and pleading sobs. Then my mother's brother was taken by the Salkas, his bones sucked dry and sent back to the court as proof of purchase, and that was when my mother went to my father. Offered herself to him so that there might be no more bloodshed.

She sacrificed herself for an uneasy peace.

A peace that, two weeks ago, I put in jeopardy. My chest tightens. And for what? For a human boy who thought I was a girl because he only saw me from the waist up, a swirl of pale flesh and tangled hair?

(Human men will bring you nothing but pain.)

I wasn't thinking of the kingdom that day, as the storm raged on. I hauled Oliver's body to the nearest beach. It was deserted, only one small building nearby. The inlet was enclosed by a semicircle of trees with fruits of yellow and orange upon them, flavoring the air with a sharp tang. No mermaid had ever ventured onto human land before and returned alive.

And yet, I did not feel afraid. All I cared about was that I save Oliver. I laid him down on the beach, smoothing back dripping hair from his face, willing him to wake up. I sat there, watching him, waiting for him to open his eyes. Until finally, he did.

"Viola," he groaned, trying to sit up. "Viola."

He reached his hand out to touch my face, the face he thought was Viola's, but I crawled away from him, dragging my tail across the coarse sand until the water took me back. Of course he would call for her, Viola, the girl with the charming laugh and dark eyes. He was in love with her. She was not a monster or a mermaid. She was just a girl.

"Muirgen," my father says again sharply, and I jump, banging my wrist on the table. He laughs, the rest of my family joining in while I rub the stinging skin. Every time he says my name, I think that he knows, *he knows*, and what will he do to me?

"Eat your food," he says. "You have been acting peculiar these days, Muirgen. Anything you want to share with the rest of us?"

"No," I say, and my heart is pounding so loudly that I fear he must be able to hear it. "I have nothing to say, Father."

Chapter

6

*E*AT, THEY TELL me. *You look so thin, Muirgen. You look so pale. What's wrong, Muirgen? Tell us what's wrong.*

I smile and say that I am fine. I sit at the dining table and I pretend to eat my food. (And all I can think about is him, his tight curls and those dark eyes. How he made me feel, my insides turning soft. I need to feel like that again.) But then I remember my father, and the Salkas, and the Sea Witch's attack, which must be imminent. *What are they planning?* Fear grips me so tightly that I can barely breathe.

It is difficult, feeling as I do, when you are a part of my father's court, meeting his demand that his daughters be charming at all times. *Entertain me,* he says. (*Earn your keep,* he means. *Prove to me that you are not like your mother.*) We must tell stories or jokes, we must dance in swirling loops, we must raise our voices to the gods and hope that we have pleased him.

I do all those things. And underneath it all, I pray. I pray that the Salkas will not attack.

"Very good, Cosima," my father says, after she sings a song that she has composed herself.

"I am pleased you enjoyed it, Father," she replies, her cheeks pink.

"But your youngest sister's voice is still the sweetest," Father says. "Do try and listen the next time Muirgen sings. You might learn something."

He insists that I sing then, and I do as instructed, of course. But I have lost all joy in it. Singing was the one thing that made me feel content, and even that has been tainted—as if fear has scratched its nails across my vocal cords, leaving them bleeding and raw.

Zale and Marlin continue to visit, Marlin sitting by Nia silently, while Zale regales us with stories of his youth. "Such a long time ago," he says to me after a particularly dramatic account of a battle with the Salkas during the war. "Years before you were even born, little one." His lips against my cheek, too close to my mouth. It is as if he wants to peel my skin away from my body and taste it on his tongue. *Patience, Gaia*, I tell myself.

The nausea might subside once we are bonded. I might learn to like him, in time.

"It's getting late," the Sea King said one night, when he arrived to tell the men it was time for them to go home. Zale stopped mid-story, instinctively knowing that such boasting would not be appreciated by my father. Our betrotheds left, and my father gave Nia and me a long look. *Does he know? Does he know what I have done?* "You're very quiet tonight," was all he said.

Nia and I are always quiet when the men leave. "I hope you both know how fortunate you are," my father said. "Particularly you, Muirgen. Zale could have had whichever of my daughters he wanted."

"Thank you, Father," I replied, wishing that Zale had chosen someone else, *anyone else*. Why did it have to be me? "Thank you for bestowing this gift upon me."

I cannot stop thinking about Oliver. When I wake up, the first thing I see in my mind's eye is his face. I wonder if he is safe. I remember the Salka, her claws spiked and her mouth screeching, and I imagine the horrors the Sea Witch is dreaming up to exact her revenge upon us. I cannot sleep for worry, circling my room, around and around.

Human men will bring you nothing but pain, the Salka told me. Does she know what they did to my mother? My mother, who was taken when I was so very young. My mother, who is dead.

My mother is dead.

Isn't she?

Another long night of half-dreams and worry. I press my hands into my eyes, blinking back tears. Water is our life force; it runs through our veins, turning our insides to blessed salt. It should not be wasted by crying.

"In bed already?"

I start, but it is only Grandmother speaking.

"You're very jumpy at the moment, Muirgen," she says, floating by my bed. Her gray hair is tied in a knot at the base of her neck, a necklace of seashells hanging between her breasts. *How long has she been there?*

"I'm fine, Grandmother."

"Your sisters are going swimming tomorrow. Just as far as the pools, I believe, so it shouldn't be too taxing," she says. "I thought you might like to join them."

"No."

"Are you sure?"

"I said no, didn't I?"

"That's a shame. You used to love going swimming before."

Our swimming expeditions were the only times I ever felt free. My sisters and I, mer-children then, our hands gripped on to a dolphin's fin, screaming at the speed at which we were towed through the water. The joy of it, the exhilaration. Back then, Cosima and I were best friends. A team. Just us against the world. Cosima had been promised to Zale since birth, and she talked often of the wedding, what she would wear in her hair, how adorable their mer-babies would be. That was before I turned beautiful, before I became something that Zale wanted to possess. That was before I lost her too. It seems that I am forever destined to lose the people I love.

"I'm too tired, Grandmother."

"You're always tired these days," she says as she strokes my hair. I close my eyes and pretend that it is Oliver's hand on my hair, his voice whispering to me. I pretend that I am just a girl, not a mermaid or a monster. "Can't you sleep, Muirgen?"

I sleep a little but I do not rest. How can I? I am holding my breath until I hear the Salkas' battle cry, the clash of metal as blades are sharpened in anticipation of tender throats to be slit. My dreams fracture into splinters every night, breaking me apart from the inside out.

I dream of brown eyes and skin, of long legs, and a perfume made of a flower that I cannot name.

I dream of my mother, chains looping her tail, binding her wrists together. *Roll up, roll up, see the mermaid! See the freak! Genuine article, or your money back guaranteed!* In some dreams, all I see is my mother's heart, torn from her chest and placed under a magnifying glass for inspection, still beating. In others, she is contained in a large tank, trapped, begging for someone to rescue her. *I'm coming, Mother*, I say, but I make no sound. *Wait for me.*

And I dream of walking on two legs, walking towards Oliver, my steps sure. *You are beautiful*, he says, and he is not looking at my face, but at the legs that have grown from my body. *You are so beautiful.* I awake gasping, fumbling down my body to see if it's true, if I am free, but no. All I feel beneath my fingertips are scales of oil, not human flesh. Then I remember what I have done in order to save the boy. I lie in bed for hours, awaiting my destiny.

"Shall I call the healer?" Grandmother asks now. "She will brew a tonic for you."

"I'm fine." The healer is said to have mind-reading abilities, and I am afraid of what she might see in me, in the murky depths of my subconscious. We are not allowed to describe her skills as "powers," not when the Sea King is in hearing distance. He despises the healer, but he must tolerate her. His need for her services is too great to banish her to the Outerlands with the rest of the misfits.

"I don't think you *are* fine, actually," Grandmother says. "Please talk to me."

What can I say? I cannot tell her about Oliver, about what I have done. I turn over on the bed, a wasteland of loneliness spreading infinite in my chest, hoping my grandmother will get the hint and go. *A girl*, he said. *I thought I saw a girl*. And even though we are in the depths of the kingdom, the same heat ripples through me, starting at the base of my stomach and radiating out through my arms and tail. I have never felt anything like this before. I don't understand what it is.

I look out of the tower when Grandmother has left my room. The water is still tonight, so clear that a counterfeit moon is hovering near the surface. When I was a child, I would have thought it remarkable. I would have assumed that this weak reflection was all the world had to offer. But I know the truth now. I have seen how much more there is to experience than what I have been told to be satisfied with.

I cannot resist climbing out of the tower again tonight, aiming for the true moon. *I should not be doing this.* I rise and I rise until I reach the same place that I go every day. An inlet. Yellow flesh-flowers on the trees, cutting sharp. A white building, a steeple, a bell calling time. But no Oliver. I try to come at different times of the day and occasionally at night, hoping to catch a glimpse of him. I see other humans but never him; it is never him. I keep my distance as I watch them, attempting to learn them by heart. The girls that pour out of that building once the bell rings, they argue and laugh and sulk; they whisper secrets to one another, promising to never tell, *cross my heart and hope to die.* They sigh over how pretty one another is, proclaiming themselves ugly in comparison. I am struck by the similarities between them and my sisters, the same games that we play, despite everything we have been told about the humans and how barbaric they are. It is cold up here tonight, the air tight with frost. *Winter is near,* the water whispers to me, the stars forming constellations of ice on the horizon. I hear no voices and see no one, but I wait until the last light has been turned off in the white building (Is he inside there still? Those full lips and laughing eyes, a man more perfect-looking than I ever thought possible? Is he calling out her name in his sleep? *Viola, Viola.*) before I force myself to dive back to the kingdom.

Every time I return, I am struck by how small our world is. How insignificant it seems, and by extension, how insignificant we are. I bite my lip at what my father would do if he heard such traitorous thoughts. I bite so hard that I taste tin-blood.

In my bedroom, I run my hand across the statue, pretending that it's Oliver and that he has reached my tower, that he has somehow found a way to breathe in water, his ears morphing into gills. I imagine the two of us, and a life on-the-swim, always trying to stay out of tails-length of my father, but happy because we have each other, and that's all we need. I sit in front of my mirror, folding my hair under until it resembles her neat bob, imagining my skin as brown as hers. *Viola.*

"It doesn't suit you like that."

I start, allowing my hair to fall around my shoulders. And then I see him, in the shadows by my door, his eyes hungry. He always seems to be watching me, ever since I was a small child.

"How long have you been there?" I ask.

"I've been waiting for you. Where have you been?"

"Zale, you shouldn't be in my bedroom," I say, my mouth dry. "The Sea King would be furious if he knew you were here."

"The Sea King approves of me, little one. We have been the closest of friends for decades now," Zale says, moving behind me and resting his hands on my shoulders, forcing me towards the mirror again. I look so young next to him, as if posing for a portrait with my grandfather. "And we are betrothed, are we not?"

"We are betrothed, Zale, but we are not yet bonded." I do not want him touching me. Ever since he decided that it was the sixth daughter of the Sea King he wanted rather than the fifth, I have felt his fingers on my skin. Just a light touch to the waist or the cheek, trailing across the small of my back. Nothing that he could be reprimanded for. Just enough to remind me who I belong to.

"We shall be bonded on your sixteenth birthday," he says, and I look away. I do not want him to see my fear. "So soon, little one." It is tradition in the kingdom that maids are not to be bonded before their twentieth birthday, but it seems that rules can always be broken by powerful men. They created the laws, after all, and they uphold them, therefore they can shape them to their own desires.

"Regardless of that fact," I say, "it is an invasion of my privacy to come into my room like this. And at such an hour."

"Oh, I do apologize, young Muirgen."

"Zale, I'm serious. My father—"

"Your father? I'm sure your father would be interested to hear about how often his youngest daughter has been traveling to the surface."

How does he know that? "I am fifteen now," I say, trying to ignore my uneasiness. "I will have you remember that."

"Yes," Zale says, and his eyes drift down my body. My heart beats too quickly, like a song made up of broken chords. "You most certainly are."

Watch the fish, my grandmother had told me when I came of age and I began to ask questions of an intimate nature. *Watch the fish and you will understand.* And so I did. The male fish chasing the female fish around and around, biting her fins, nipping at her tail, waiting for her to fall down in exhaustion so he could claim her as his own. I could not tell if they were fighting or making love. Perhaps it is all the same, in the end.

"Fifteen," he says. "And I have been so patient these past three years. I feel like I deserve a small reward, don't you agree?"

I swim away from Zale, floating up towards the surface. My breath feels leaden, as if it wants to break my ribs. I wish Oliver were here to rescue me, take me away. I wish my mother were still alive. I wish someone would ask me what *I* want, just once. I wish for so many things, and I know that none of them are possible for girls like me.

"Always looking up," Zale says, floating easily beside me. "Tell me, what is it about up there that fascinates you so much, Muirgen? Is there anything you would like to tell me?"

"What do you mean by that?" *(Does he know? How could he know?)*

"Nothing," he says. "I was just wondering."

Zale has never even been to the surface; it is a point of pride for him. *Why would I?* he says. *Why would I even want to be near those disgusting creatures?*

"And all of this nonsense," he says now, pointing to the statue and the precious things on my table. "This human rubbish. I don't know why your father indulges this obsession of yours."

"It's not an obsession." *And my father does not know anything about me.* "I just think they're pretty."

"Typical girl," Zale says. "Distracted by shiny trinkets, regardless of their provenance. Things will change when we are bonded. These visits to the surface will come to a stop, for one. It's too dangerous, your risk of capture increases with each return. Perhaps you should heed what happened to your mother. There's a lesson in that, isn't there? A lesson I'm sure you would do well to remember, especially when you belong to me."

What he says is true; I will be his. I belong to my father, and my father has chosen Zale for me. I shall be passed from one man to the next, ownership transferred with the ease of a handshake, and I will be expected to smile as the deal is done.

"Do you mind being betrothed to Marlin?" I asked Nia a few months before my last birthday. The others had gone on a rare trip to the surface to watch a lightning storm (*Don't tell Father*, Talia warned me. *You know how he would get if he heard we were going up there*.) and I had to watch jealously as they swam away from the palace. Bored of sitting in the tower, waiting for them to return, I found Nia in the dormitory, staring out the window.

"Do you mind?" I asked her again when she didn't answer me. I couldn't stop thinking about that conversation between her and Grandmother that I had stumbled upon: Nia's despair, her pleas that our grandmother do something to help her. Both of us remained still then, listening to each other's breathing. We were waiting for the other to be the first one to tell the truth. "Do you love Marlin?"

Nia was quiet for a long time. "Muirgen," she said eventually, "you can't always get what you want. We should know that better than anyone else."

"Zale?" I ask now. "Do you . . ." I am unsure of how to phrase this. He moves through the water until he is floating in front of me, reaching out to caress my hair. Something heavy pulses in my throat.

"Delicious," he murmurs, examining each bare inch of flesh and scale. Next he will ask me to show him my teeth so he can check for cavities. "What were you asking? Do I what?"

"Do you love me?" I need to ask him this. If Zale feels the same way about me that I do about Oliver, if he dreams about me, if he can spend hours thinking about holding my hand, maybe it will all be okay. He will treat me with kindness when we are bonded. I could learn to be content if I was treated kindly.

"*Love* you?" he says. "What has 'love' got to do with anything? This isn't one of those nymph-tales your grandmother has filled your head with, Muirgen."

"I don't think it's the most absurd question in the kingdom," I say, anger rising in me. "Considering we are to be bonded on my next birthday."

"Don't be such a child," he says. "You are the Sea King's favorite daughter. Your beauty is unrivaled and therefore you are the correct choice for a man like me. He has no sons, so once we are bonded, the Sea King will have to honor me as rightful heir to the throne. I shall make certain *improvements* that need to be enforced around here."

He has never spoken so freely about his ambitions for the future before. There has always been a chaperone present, an elder there to safeguard my purity. But in a few short months, there will be no one there to protect me from this man. I will be alone with him, forever.

"But I am the youngest," I say, ignoring the pain in my chest, my lungs feeling as if they are too big for this body to contain. "If this is what you want, surely Talia would be a better match. She is the first-born. Or Cosima, the way it was supposed to be. Zale, she still adores you, she would—"

"You're being ridiculous," he says, his mouth tightening at the mention of Cosima's name. "You are just girls. Your looks are the only thing that distinguish you from one another, and I want the best." He touches my face, as if testing my beauty to ensure it is worthy of acquisition. "You remind me of your mother," he says. "I wanted Muireann myself, you know—every mer-man did at that time—but the Sea King had first priority." He smiles at me. "But you're the next best thing, little Muirgen. With you by my side and the Sea King's trident in my hand," he closes his eyes, as if imagining the power flooding through him, "the kingdom will be mine. *All* of it. I will make sure of that."

"You don't mean—"

"Yes, I do," he says, opening his eyes again. "It is time to be rid of the Salkas for good. We were so close to victory the last time—if your father had remained resolute instead of allowing a mermaid to persuade him to concede. We had nearly destroyed them when he agreed to this joke of an armistice."

The armistice that my mother was so anxious to achieve. A crown of white lilies in her hair, my father's hand on hers. Peace, that was what Muireann of the Green Sea wanted, the stories go. She wanted peace so badly that she gave her body to a man old enough to be her father. I would not see that legacy so carelessly dismantled.

"That 'joke of an armistice,' as you put it, has worked for so long," I say. "No one wants a return to the times of war, Zale. The mer-folk nearly died of starvation before. Why would you want such a thing to happen again?"

"It won't happen like that this time. This time, we shall be the victors."

There are no victors in war. "But why would you want to take such a risk? When things are peaceful now . . ." We have heard the stories of the Sea Witch, and the atrocities that she is capable of. If provoked she will eat our young; she will send her Salkas to scalp our women, shave our hair, and wear it as their own. And they will kill every last mer-man they find in the kingdom. There is no guarantee of our victory, no matter what Zale might think. He is so blinded by prejudice that he cannot see his own foolishness.

"It is not a risk," he says. "The Salkas are an abomination and must be destroyed."

"But—"

"Enough back talk, girl. I am a man, not a fish," he says. "And men go to war."

"Why do you hate them so much?" I ask him. "What did they ever do to you?"

"Muirgen. They came from the world above, from the *human* world." I am silent; that is all he needs to hate, I think. A human touch is enough to make him venomous.

"Besides," he says, and there is an amused smile on his face, "a war should make you happy. Are you not afraid that they will come for you? They must have been most displeased at your little . . . *intervention.*"

"What?" I say, and the water is ice suddenly, frost chipping into my bones. "What are you talking about?"

He tilts his head to one side, a smirk playing on his lips. "You know exactly what I'm talking about, don't you? I saw you. I saw you the night of the storm."

"But, but you never go to the—"

"—dragging that *human* away from the Salka."

My hands are trembling so I clasp them together to make them stop, as if in prayer. "That isn't true. I don't know what you think you saw, Zale, but—"

"Don't lie to me," he barks, and I shut up. "I wanted to keep an eye on you, little one. Your mother's blood is in you. I wanted to make sure that, along with her red hair and her"—he stares at my breasts and I resist the urge to shudder—"*form*, you had not also inherited other, more displeasing traits. It was such a disappointment to discover the truth, but don't worry," he says, and he rubs his tongue against his top teeth as if he's sharpening it.

"I can purify you. I can purify you in ways that you have never imagined. It would be my pleasure."

"Zale," I say. I begin to drop down into my room, too weak to stay afloat, and he follows closely. "Zale, I beg you. Please don't tell my father. There hasn't been any word from the Sea Witch, no hint of a reprisal. No one need know. This could be forgotten—"

"Oh, I don't think I'll be forgetting this in a hurry."

"What do you want from me?" I say, sinking onto the bed, fear spinning me dizzy.

"Well," he says, tapping his fingers against his jawline in an exaggerated pose of thoughtfulness, "there is *one* thing you could do."

"What?" I'll do anything he wants. Anything. So long as my father does not find out.

"You think I don't see how you flinch when I look at you? How you pull away when I touch you?"

"I don't—"

"Yes, you do," he says matter-of-factly. "I don't mind a bit of reluctance. That can be fun, actually. But in public? It won't do, not anymore. I won't be made into a laughingstock." He places his hands on my waist, leaning in to whisper in my ear. "You will be mine soon, little one; you had better get used to it."

"Are you going to tell my father?"

"I haven't decided yet. But what fun I am going to have with you in the meantime." He tightens his grip and claims my lips with his, his cold tongue invading my mouth like a greasy sea slug. "Good night."

As the door closes behind him, I can feel my stomach clenching, propelling something up through my chest and my throat, spewing out of my lips. A dark yellow cloud, a shadow on the waves, floating away from me. And I watch it dance.

That was my first kiss.

Chapter

7

TIME PASSES, AS it always does in the kingdom. The winter festival comes and goes. The court room is adorned with silver and gold in its honor, and goblets are held in the air to toast the Sea King. "Thank you for your graciousness," the mer-folk say. "Thank you, Sea King, oh, blessed Sea King." The chorus maids sing songs celebrating the ice, thanking the winter gods for another year of peace.

Peace. Yet I do not feel relief. I don't feel very much at all. I have become resigned to my fate: I will never know true love. This is as good as it gets for maids like me, maids who should be content with beauty, wealth, status. Perhaps it is greedy for me to want to be happy too. But I am hungry, so hungry, for something more. My desire is carving a hole in my stomach, leaving me hollow.

"Sing," my father says to me as the festival celebrations become wilder, his eyes blurring from the drink. "Sing, my darling." (That's what Oliver called Viola, *my darling*.) Thinking of that night, I sing a song of my heart, something strange, full of longing. I sing a song for *him*. When I am finished, the crowd is quiet, some wiping tears from their eyes. "That was fine," my father says. "Though a tad melancholic for my tastes. Remember, Muirgen, the winter festival is supposed to be a celebration."

I am still my father's favorite; Zale kept his promise and has not told him of my misdeed. And I uphold my side of our bargain as well. He continues to visit, late at night when everyone else sleeps. I envy them that. They still possess an innocence that I will never know again. He does not take my purity—he knows that would be a step too far without my father's blessing. But he is rough with me. He pulls my hair, his fingers forceful on my skin, leaving discolored marks that I struggle to explain to my grandmother and sisters in the days following. "You're hurting me," I tell him, and he only laughs. "Better get used to it, little one," he replies.

Spring breaks slowly that year, spilling light through the water. The eggs hatch, the next generation of mer-babies unfurling themselves in a new world. There are more girls born this year than ever before. I want to tell them to be careful. I want to tell them to swim away at first light. I want to hold a pillow over their mewling faces and bury their last breath inside their mouths. They would be safe then, safe from men who watch them all the time. Men who come to your bedroom every night, demanding you pay the toll for their silence.

When Zale leaves, I curl up in a ball, nursing my disgust like I am feeding an infant at my breast. *Summer will be here soon*, I think. Summer means my sixteenth birthday. It means a bonding ceremony with Zale. This summer will also bring the anniversary of the shipwreck, of the boy in my arms on that beach. Watching as he was reborn and the humans took him, helping him to his feet, helping him walk away from me. He didn't look back. I've stopped going to the surface to try and find him. I spend my days lying in bed, weary, staring at the water-softened sky, jolting at every unfamiliar sound for fear that it is Zale.

He continues to visit in an official capacity, smiling when I float into the reception as if he hasn't seen me every night. Cosima rushes to his side as soon as he arrives at the palace with a: "How are you, Zale?" and: "You look so well. Doesn't he look well, sisters?" and: "Are you comfortable, Zale? I can get you another cushion if you so desire." She fusses incessantly, until Father sends her to her room, complaining of an earache.

"Why can't you be more like your sister?" he asks Cosima. "Muirgen is always quiet. It's much more attractive for a maid to be quiet."

I am quiet because I have nothing to say. Every Saturday, Nia and I sit in the palace's reception room with Zale and Marlin while Grandmother hovers in the corner, keeping a close eye on us to ensure we don't behave inappropriately. *Where are you at night-time? I want to ask her. Why don't you protect me then?*

"You do seem rather quiet," Zale says to me, after he told me a joke and his punch line landed into silence. "I'm sorry," I say automatically. I can't afford to anger Zale, not now. "I found it hard to understand. Can you explain it to me? You're so intelligent, Zale." I see Grandmother's head jerk up as if in surprise at my response, but then she nods. *It is easier for girls to be agreeable,* she has always said. *Don't you want an easy life, my child?*

"Muirgen."

I am counting the fish as they swim past my tower. *One fish, two fish, three fish more.*

"Mama used to say that counting fish helps you fall asleep," Talia told me when I was little. "Look out the window and tell me how many you can see, Muirgen."

I would fall asleep soon after, dreaming of fish and a woman with hair as red as mine. Talia was seven when our mother left, and she can remember. Those memories might be patched together with half-forgotten bedtime stories and kisses on foreheads and whispered *I love you*s, but they are more than the rest of us have. And we resent Talia for that.

"Muirgen," my grandmother says again.

Gaia. My mother called me Gaia.

"Muirgen, I know that you are awake." Grandmother swims closer to the bed, sitting by my side. "Muirgen, look at me," she says, and there is an urgency in her voice that makes me roll over and face her. "My child, you must not worry. You must not worry about the Salkas."

"What . . ." I need to find words. Safe words. Words that will not get me in trouble. "But why would I be worried about the Salkas, Grandmother Thalassa?"

She is unadorned at this time of night; the hair hanging freely around her face is the same silver-gray as her tail. There are tiny gaping wounds in her tail from the pearls, the flesh taking longer to heal these days.

"I know what you did, my Muirgen. And I need to tell you that there will be no retribution from the Salkas for your actions. I have spoken with Ceto and all is well."

I push myself to sitting on the bed. "What? You spoke with the Sea Witch?" She nods and I carry on, bewildered. "After what her Salkas did to Uncle Manannán?"

"Don't." My grandmother raises her hand, as if she wants to push the words back down my throat. "Do not say his name." Her voice cracks. "Do not speak of things you do not comprehend, Muirgen."

"I'm sorry, Grandmother," I say. "But how did you find out what I did? What did the Sea Witch tell you?"

"So many questions," my grandmother sighs. "All that matters is that you are safe."

"She will not attack us? She hates the Sea King so . . ."

"Oh, your father and Ceto have fought since they were children," she says, suppressing a small smile. "They are two sides of the one coin. They need each other, as much as they are both loath to admit that."

"Need each other? Father and the Sea Witch are mortal enemies."

"There are many things that you do not understand about the ways of the kingdom, my child. About its history," she says. *Then tell me, Grandmother. Tell me that which I do not understand. Let me learn.* "All you need to know is that your father will never hear of this," she continues. "Surely that is the most important thing?"

Hope flares in me briefly—*I am safe*—and then dies down just as swiftly. This does not change much. Zale will still visit, and I am still not allowed to say no. I hate him, and I hate myself more. And my bones still ache and I will never see Oliver again, and what does it matter? For he woke with her name on his lips. *Viola.*

"This is good news," I say. "I am grateful, Grandmother Thalassa."

"There is more, is there not?" she asks. "Muirgen? I know there is more that you want to tell me."

I pause, unsure if I can trust her, but I need to talk to someone, *anyone* and then—

"I love him," I say, the words shredding my throat in their desperation to be heard. My grandmother is silent for a moment, but her expression is not unkind.

"Love him? This human man?" she asks. I nod. "After everything they have taken from us?" She runs her hands through her hair, silver strands like rings on her thin fingers. "You cannot tell a soul of this, Muirgen. Whatever you think you 'feel.' Do you understand?" I catch the edge of panic in her voice. "Your father will . . . I can't lose you too. I just *can't.*"

"But maybe my mother isn't lost." I watch my grandmother close her eyes as if in pain, but I press on, regardless. "We never had a body to bury. Maybe if I go to the surface, I can find out what happened, finally discover the truth of it all. What if she's still up there, waiting for us to find her?"

"Stop it, Muirgen." Grandmother's voice is ragged. "Your mother swam too close to the shore. She was impetuous and headstrong. She was taken by the humans and she died in captivity. That is the end of it."

"But it doesn't make sense. Father said that she chose to go, that she left us of her own free will—but he also said that she was captured. Which is it? And you always said that mermaids are too wily for the humans' nets, so how did they take my mother if—"

"Muirgen. I said *enough*. The Sea King told us what happened. His word is law."

I cannot deny the truth of that. None of us can. "Was he upset when she was taken?" I ask instead.

"What?"

"The Sea King. Was he upset when my mother was taken?"

She hesitates, but only for a second. "Of course he was upset. He was outraged. As he should have been; he had lost his wife, the mother of his children. He was . . ." She breaks off, swallowing hard. "I don't want to talk about this anymore. It was a difficult time for us all. I still don't know why your mother did what she did. I thought I had raised her better than that."

"I don't think she loved my father," I say. "It must be very hard to be bonded to someone who you don't love."

"Oh, Muirgen." She softens. "I'm sorry. Zale isn't a bad man, I'm sure of it."

You are wrong there, Grandmother.

"He's so old," I say. "The bonding age is twenty. Can't I have a few more years, at least?"

"Your father was sixty-three when he was bonded to your mother, and she was only sixteen. Exceptions are made, from time to time."

And I will be sixteen too. Soon. So very soon. "But I want—"

"I've told you before, *wanting* has never brought anyone in this family any luck," she says. "A woman wanting more than what she can have only results in pain and loss and small children crying for someone who will never return. Wanting has brought—" She stops herself. "Muirgen," she says, more calmly. "All you need to know is that the humans are different from us. They don't even believe that we exist, not really. They tell stories about mermaids, stories they believe to be myths, legends. They are fascinated by us, and terrified by us as well. Do not underestimate that fear, and what they might do with it. Some men are very afraid of women, my child. And those men long for us the most, and are the most dangerous when they do not get what they want."

"But why would they be afraid of us? We have no powers."

"Of course we don't," she says, looking away from me. "But the humans do not understand that. They fear that their men will be overcome with madness and dive into the depths of the water to make a bride of one of us, finding only death instead. And then they blame us, as men have always blamed women, for prompting their lust, for fuelling their insatiable greed for something they cannot have."

"But . . ." I know that I am about to say the unsayable. "Why *can't* they have us? If that is something a mermaid wants in return. What is to prevent it then?"

My grandmother skims her fingers across my tail. "Have you forgotten something?" she says. "The humans find our tails disgusting." I stare at the dark green scales flecked with silver, catching the moonlight and making it seem as if I am aglow.

I can believe that. I can believe it easily.

A mermaid or a monster? What is the difference?

"Yes," she continues, mistaking my silence for shock. "They prefer their own legs, those clumsy stumps that allow them to walk upright. It is most puzzling."

"But could they . . ."

"Could they what, child?"

"Could a human learn to love someone with a fish's tail, do you think?" I hold my breath.

"No," she says, not ungently, and I feel something split inside my chest. "A man would need a woman with legs. For all our beauty, to the humans we are freaks, curios." She rubs her eyes and I can see how weary she has become.

"If only . . ." I whisper. "If only I could find a way to . . ."

"Find a way to what?"

"A way . . ." Grandmother leans in to hear me properly. "Find a way to grow human legs. Father has powers—perhaps he could . . ."

She rears back. "Have you gone mad, child? The Sea King despises the humans, especially after what happened to your mother. He would rather see you dead than what you're suggesting."

She is right. My father would rather bury me in the shifting sands than see me happy with a human above the surface, and a part of me always knew that. I must obey his rules, be a good girl and live the life that he has chosen for me. I will wait here in the kingdom until the end comes and my soul is scattered on the waves for the fish to feed on.

"You are of the sea, child," my grandmother says. "This is where you belong."

But I do not want to belong here.

"I will leave you now," she says. "Muirgen, you are young, beautiful. You have the purest voice that has ever been heard in this kingdom, a gift that could make hardened sea-warriors shed precious tears. You have your sisters. You are betrothed to the most respected man in the kingdom after the Sea King. You are blessed, child."

"I can't, Grandmother." I am gasping now, the words breaking apart. I can't seem to control them. "I can't be bonded to Zale. I would rather die."

"There's no need to be so dramatic."

"I'm not being dramatic," I say, stung by the accusation. "It's not true love with Zale."

"True love? My dear, those were nymph-tales. That's not real life."

But it could be. Oliver has proven that to me. He represents the possibility of love, of something more than a life under the sea has to offer me. "Grandmother," I say,

"Zale frightens me. And sometimes," I gather my courage, "sometimes, he comes to my room at night and—"

"Stop it," my grandmother says. "That is not true. Zale is a well-respected member of the kingdom; I do not believe that of him."

And I know then. I know it is over. My grandmother was my last hope.

There is a clanging noise outside, metal hitting the pearl steps, and both of us shrink back.

"What was that?" I say as Grandmother swims to my bedroom door to check. "Is someone there?"

"There's no one there," she says, peering into the dark. "It must have been a fish."

"That sound was too heavy to be a fish."

"There's no one there," she says again. "We are tired, and it is the darkest hour of night. It was nothing." Our eyes meet, uncertain.

"Good night, Grandmother," I say.

"Good night, Muirgen," she replies, and she doesn't return to my bedside to kiss me on the forehead or tuck me in, to tell me she loves me and to pray to the sea gods to protect me while I sleep, like she normally does.

I lie there, imagining the phantom legs that I know must be trapped inside of me. I picture them, stretching, pushing, ripping my tail apart. Craving the earth beneath them, solid.

There have been rumors before, of mermaids who decided that two hundred years was too long a time to spend in the kingdom. Maids who have wrapped sea-weed tightly around throats and scraped sharpened sea-shells across wrists, praying to the sea gods to melt their bones to foam when their pain became too much for them to carry. *Defective*, the whispers in the nursery went. *Broken*. More like Rusalka than maid, and it was always mermaids who chose this fate. No man would ever feel so utterly without hope.

I am desperate now, more desperate than I ever thought possible. But I still have hope. There must be a way to escape this. *There must be.*

Chapter

8

*T*T IS DARK that night when I leave the palace, the kind of dark that suggests that, above the surface, the moon has been smothered by clouds. I waited until the palace had fallen silent, only leaving my bedroom when I could be sure that everyone was asleep. Tracing my fingertips over my comb and mirror, murmuring good-bye to my marble statue. I won't need them where I'm going.

Down the stairs of my tower, past my sisters' dormitory. Pausing outside the door, wishing I could say good-bye. But they would make me stay. Stay here and marry Zale. They would have me spend my life dreaming of Oliver. Dreaming of my mother. Dreaming until I dream no more. I can't do it, but still, I wish I could tell them that I love them. That, like my mother before me, I must leave them.

Creeping through the foyer, the floor smooth in diamond shapes of gold and pearl. Holding my breath in case I wake the servants, wretched fear paralyzing my thoughts, stuttering them into words rather than sentences.

What if... Father... Zale... Oliver...

My mother. My mother. My mother.

Winding through the narrow streets of sand, daisies of red and purple lining the paths, seashell houses crammed together. They are all closed at this time of night, the lips of the cockles pushed up to meet one another. I imagine the mer-folk nestled inside, and I wonder what their dreams are made up of. Have they ever dreamed of the escape of an open sky the way that I do?

As I swim away from the kingdom and into the Outerlands, the darkness thickens, and although the path ahead is clear, it feels like I am wading through tangled seaweeds. The water is drier here, a desert wasting on my tongue, the sea grass and flowers withering, as if diseased. The shantytowns, made from shattered gray shells and a prayer, seem to sway with the pull of the tide. I have never been here before. I refused to accompany Sophia on her charitable visits, certain I would say the wrong thing or be caught staring at the Outerlands mer-folk.

They are different, those who live here. Not different like the humans or the Salkas; they are still mer-folk, but the Sea King does not wish them to live within the palace grounds. The ones who pray to the forbidden gods, those whose bodies were hatched misshapen, maids who did not adhere to the standards of beauty my father prefers, those who were sterile or barren. "I'm not going to *exterminate* them," my father said when I asked why the Outerlands even existed if he found the people living within so objectionable. "It's just better that they live amongst their kind. They'll be more comfortable that way."

No one stirs as I move through the shanties, but I stop anyway when I come to the whirlpools that separate our world from that of the Sea Witch: a wall of pounding, swirling water twisting from seabed to the surface. I look back, my breath uneven. Half expecting to see an army of men led by Zale, charging towards me. I have never been this far from the palace before, not once in my near-sixteen years. And to move past the whirlpools, to swim through the chewing currents and allow myself to be spat out on the other side, is strictly forbidden by Sea King Law. His people are not permitted to travel beyond the Outerlands, especially not to the Shadow-lands. If I do this, I remind myself, there is no going back.

"If I do what you're suggesting, there is no going back," I said to Cosima tonight.

A knock on the door. Grandmother had just left and I assumed it was her again. I knew it was not Zale; he never knocks.

"Come in," I called. It was Cosima.

"Crying, sister?" she asked.

"What are you doing here, Cosima?"

She sat next to me, adjusting her tail in line with mine, and I knew she was comparing them, my dark green against her royal blue, searching for a flaw in my scales that would mean she had won, for once.

"I heard you," she said in a strange sing-song manner. "I heard you talking to Grandmother." My chest tightened, squeezing all the air out of my lungs. What had she heard? And, if she had heard the worst of it, what would she do?

"So, that was you earlier," I said, as nonchalantly as I could manage. "I knew it wasn't just a fish, no matter what Grandmother thought."

Cosima picked up a mirror from the squat wooden cabinet beside my bed. A relic from a storm seven years ago. Vicious winds, a starving sea, Salkas screaming for flesh-revenge with wild, unfettered abandon. Calling the names of men who were long dead, men who broke their hearts or their bodies, and sometimes both. Corpse after corpse after corpse. It was raining humans for months afterwards.

Cosima gazed at her reflection in the mirror, tousling her golden hair. "Don't try and deny it," she said. "I heard everything you said to Grandmother. You love him. You love a human man." I thought of Oliver, spewing seawater out of his mouth as if it were something poisonous. How beautiful his face was, even when pallid and cold. And then I thought of him calling her name, *Viola? Viola?*

I didn't say anything. It was too dangerous a thing to admit, especially to Cosima. I just focused on catching my breath, *one in* (You'll be fine, Gaia), *breathe out* (Stay calm, Gaia). "What's *wrong* with you, Muirgen?" she said when I remained silent. "It's not fair to Zale. You are to be bonded in two months, and this is how you repay him for that honor? He should be with someone who loves him, who understands him. Someone more suited to the rigors of ruling the kingdom. Someone who . . ." she trailed off. "Anyway," she said. "Someone else."

"I never wanted any of this to happen." I went to take her hand, but she snatched it back. "Cosima, please. You know this isn't my fault."

"What's not your fault? That you stole Zale from me?"

"I didn't steal him. You and I were such good friends— we loved each other, didn't we?" There was a lump caught in my throat. "I miss you."

"Zale was *mine*," she said. "Everything was perfect before. Perhaps if you hadn't been born, then our mother wouldn't have lost her mind and deserted us." I drew back as if she had slapped me, but she didn't stop there. "And you don't even appreciate Zale. You're so ungrateful that you fall in love with the first human man you set your eyes on. I couldn't believe it when I heard you admit it to Grandmother tonight. The humans took our mother, Gaia."

"You're always saying that she abandoned us, now you're saying it's the humans' fault. Make up your mind, Cosima."

"Don't get smart. Those creatures *murdered* her for sport. Have you forgotten that?"

I had taken a deep breath. "We don't know that for sure, do we?"

"What?" She was astonished at this. She obviously

hadn't heard everything I said to Grandmother tonight. "What are you talking about?"

"Well, we don't know what happened to her after she was captured. We only know what Father has told us."

"And that is enough. His word is law, you foolish girl. Have you completely lost your senses?"

"I just want the truth. That's all I've ever wanted."

"And you're prepared to do anything to get this 'truth'?" she snarled, her face fierce.

"Well." *I don't know. I don't know.* "I think so."

"It's going to take more than 'I think so' to do what needs to be done, Muirgen. Don't be pathetic."

She didn't think I was brave enough, I realized, and I felt something smoldering inside me. "Don't talk to me as if I'm a child, Cosima. Yes, I am prepared to do anything to find out what happened to her."

"Okay," she said, and her features fell clean, as if she had never known anger in her life. "Okay, Gaia." A brief smile. "I understand."

"You do?" I grabbed her hand again, the relief at finally being heard almost overwhelming. This time she didn't let go.

"You've always been such a curious mermaid, haven't you, Gaia?" Cosima was the only one who ever called me that. "Even when we were children." She shifted closer to me, cuddling into my side. "Do you remember?"

Cosima and I, exploring shipwrecks. *I'm tired*, she would complain at the end of the day. *Let's go back to the palace.* I would wave her off, happy to stay by myself. "We used to be such good friends before Zale got in the way," Cosima continued, wrapping a ringlet of hair around her finger. "I miss you, Gaia. And I want you to be happy. And you're not happy down here, are you?"

I thought of my father, lining his daughters up in order of their beauty, his satisfaction in my face and my body. His inevitable disgust when I would begin to age and lose my bloom. Zale, his hands and his tongue, and wanting to scour myself afterwards, excavate my bones to make myself clean again. And then Oliver, and that heat running through me when I remembered his dark eyes, and I wanted to feel like that again and again and again. And I thought of my mother. I will never stop thinking of my mother.

"No," I whispered to Cosima then. "I'm not happy. I will never be happy under the sea."

"There is a way," she whispered back. "A way to escape. To have your questions answered. To walk on land, even. But you must go to the Shadowlands. You must go to *her*."

"No, *no*," I said, when it dawned on me what she was proposing. "The Sea Witch? Are you crazy? She will kill me if I even cross the whirlpools."

"You need legs, do you not? If you want this man to reciprocate your feelings?"

"Yes, but—"

"Your birthday is approaching rapidly, sister, and by then it will be too late. How much do you love this human?" she asked, and I could not answer her. There were no words. Maybe there would never be enough words to encapsulate the true love I feel for Oliver. "That much?" she asked. "A human man whom you haven't even had a conversation with?"

"You don't understand," I said, and she smiled again.

"Well, then," she said. "The Sea Witch has the power to help you. You must go to her."

"But Father is the only person in the kingdom with powers," I said, confused.

"Gaia," she replied, kissing me on the forehead as if anointing me. "You really are naive sometimes." She lifted the mirror, capturing our faces in the glass. Her blonde hair against my red, identical blue eyes and rosebud lips. But when I looked at my reflection, all I could see was what Zale had done to me, what I had allowed him to do, and I pushed the mirror away.

"You are beautiful, Gaia," my sister said. "Even when you have been crying, it's quite astonishing." She tilted the mirror so only her face was shown. "But you have not spent years crying, as I have."

Cosima left me then, to wait for the palace to fall silent. To wait for my chance to escape.

Now the whirlpool separating me from the Shadowlands churns before me. After everything I have heard of the Sea Witch, everything that we have been told since birth, the idea of being in her presence is almost unendurable. This is the woman whose Salka warriors killed my uncle, who scored a shadow so deep into my mother's heart that she handed it over as dowry to a man she could never love. And here I am, come to beg a favor from her. But what other choice do I have?

I think of my mother and I ask the gods for a millimeter of her courage. *Mother, mother*, I pray as I push my way through the whirlpool. For a moment I am suspended in that in-between space, momentarily held safe in the deafening void. (I wish I could stay there forever, safe in the nothingness.) However, I make myself keep swimming until I am in the Shadowlands, *the Shadowlands*, and it feels both impossible and somehow inevitable that I am here. Here, the setting for my childhood nightmares, the place that we mer-babies whispered about when the adults were out of earshot.

My mother says the Salkas take bold mer-boys and mer-girls to the Shadowlands and they break their skulls as punishment.

My mother says that the air in the Shadowlands is poison, that only the Sea Witch and her Salkas can breathe there, for their lungs are made of electric rays and can withstand death itself.

No, no! My father says there are traps made of quicksand, so if you cross through the whirlpools, you are sucked into the seabed and buried alive and you will never see your family ever again and it'll be all your own fault because you didn't do as you were told.

For time immemorial, children have made up games where some of us were the Salkas and others were mer-folk and we fought long battles for control of the kingdom. The mer-folk always won, of course, due to the bravery and genius of the Sea King. *Blessed be us who are born in the time of the Sea King. Long live the Sea King*, we said when we finished. *The kingdom has been made great again.*

But now that I am here, the Shadowlands seem different than I imagined as a child, although no less macabre. The water is solid, somehow, catching in lumps at the back of my throat, while the sand has melted to a bubbling mud. Before me, there lies a thicket of trees and bushes unlike any vegetation I have seen before, above or below the surface. Garbled stems of oily thorns blooming into snake heads, their eyes closed in slumber, grating breath through slit noses. They have arms made of congealed nettle leaves, each grasping a treasure tightly. A silver fork, broken pieces of china, clumps of human hair torn out from the roots, a tiny skull that could only have belonged to a human baby. I pray to the sea gods as I pass them, pray that they will not awaken and claim me as their newest trophy.

Hidden behind them is a hunkering cottage, cobbled together out of bleached human bones and chunks of sludge. Many Salkas surround it, floating in the water, clasping one another's hands. Long pale green hair wilting over their faces. The Salkas carry their pain in their hair; it is laced through the strands like ribbons of the thinnest anemones. And then there are their legs. I long to touch them, to count their toes and run my fingers up their inner thighs, but I know I must not do so.

Eyelids fluttering, slowly, then too fast, and I try not to scream out in fright. A flash of white, a low keening cry.

"Who are you?" a Salka asks.

"I am not a threat," I say, trying to quiet her. "I am here to see the Sea Witch." But she is screaming now and the other Salkas are stirring. She presses her fingers to her flat stomach. "Did you take my baby? Where is my baby? Who are you? What have you done with my baby?"

"Sadhbh." A voice comes from inside the bone-cabin. It is like crackling wood at a beach bonfire, like oil slicking over water, a sky so black that you forget the stars exist. A shiver runs down my spine. "Settle."

The Salka called Sadhbh falls silent, tears trickling down her cheeks, her hands still on her belly, twisting.

"The Irish girls find it the most challenging, this new life of theirs," that voice says. "Always searching for tiny hands that were ripped off breasts the moment they gave their first cry."

The door to the cabin has opened, and something is standing there, waiting for me. My eyes struggle to see in the dim until it becomes apparent that it is a mermaid, but a maid unlike one I have ever seen before. A tail so black that it dissolves into the gloomy sea so she looks like a floating torso. Skin pale, and so much of it— rolling into ruffs of flesh around her neck, spooling around her waist. I have never seen a woman of this size before. Every maid in court has been told that we must maintain a certain weight for the aesthetic preference of the Sea King and his mer-men. I did not know such a body was even allowed to exist. I feel faint, as if all the salt in my veins has rushed to my head.

"You are nervous," the Sea Witch says. Her face is beautiful, something I had not expected. As mer-children, we had been told that her flesh was green, her teeth rotting, her skin covered in sores and pockmarks. We were told that she was jealous of the Sea King's powers, bitter because she was no match for his might. We were told that she did not want to bear children and if she laid eggs, she would eat them before they hatched. We were told many things, much of which is difficult to reconcile with the mermaid before me now.

"No," I lie. "I am not."

"Hmm." She angles her head to one side, examining me. "Unfortunately, little mermaid, I don't quite believe you." She swims back into the cabin, indicating that I should follow her.

"I have been expecting you," she says as she settles in the one piece of furniture in the room, a large wooden chair that rocks back and forth. Her tail is vast, the black flesh punctured with (I count them quickly) thirteen oil-black pearls. *Thirteen?* No, it cannot be. That would mean—

"My Salkas told me what you did the night of the storm," the Sea Witch says, conjuring a tube of red lipstick from thin air, applying it carefully. My father does not allow us to wear makeup; he says it is an artifice used to trick unsuspecting men. We must be *natural*, he says, natural at all costs. "I suppose you are wondering why I did not seek revenge for your behavior?" she asks.

"Y-yes," I stammer.

"I was waiting for you to come to me," she says. "Mermaids like you always come to me, in the end. But I have to admit, it seemed rather a foolish move—risking your father's kingdom for the sake of a human man."

"He would have died if I had not intervened," I protest, and I am shocked at my own courage. "The Salkas are murderers."

"Do not speak about my girls in such a manner."

"I'm sorry," I say quickly, even though what I have said is true. The carcass of my Uncle Manannán was evidence enough of that. But I cannot risk angering her. "I didn't mean to insult them or you." I am curious, though— my besetting sin. "You defend their attack, then?"

"I will defend them," she says. "I will defend them until my final hour. For who else will? Not your father. He would have seen us wiped out in a pointless war, no matter what the cost. No matter how many of his own young mer-men died." She snorts. "The Sea King would have been safe, though. He never did like putting himself in danger. Muireann was far too adventurous to be stuck with an old man like him."

"What?" The water seems to be sucked out of the room at the mention of that name. "You knew my mother?"

"I know everything that happens in these seas."

"Can you tell me what happened to her? Father says that my mother was captured and murdered, but we never saw a—"

"Shhh." The Sea Witch places a finger over her lips. "You'll upset my girls with this talk of murder. It brings up such unhappy memories for them, you know. They can be a tad self-involved. But then young people always think they are the first to experience anything. Heartbreak. Betrayal. Lust." She scrapes the word off her tongue. "Desire. Isn't that why you're here, after all?"

I've never heard a mermaid speak about *that* before. Maids are not allowed to feel in such a way; it cannot be desire that has hunted me to this place. It's love. It must be love. Love is *pure*, and I want to be pure again. I want Oliver to help me forget everything that Zale has done to me.

"Am I making you uneasy?" she asks me. "Is there something about me that disturbs you?" She runs her hands down her own body, caressing it with a touch that is infinitesimally tender. "I am comfortable." She sounds out each syllable clearly. "Do you know what it feels like to be comfortable in your skin? Have you ever known?"

No, I think. No, I do not know what that would feel like. I wonder if I ever will.

"That is not why I am here, Sea Witch," I say instead.

"My name is Ceto," she snaps, pushing herself out of the chair until she towers above me. "It is your father who has insisted on calling me a 'witch.' That is simply a term that men give women who are not afraid of them, women who refuse to do as they are told."

"I'm sorry." My voice drops, weak. What does the Sea Witch do to people who anger her? Has anyone ever lived to tell the tale? "I didn't mean to upset you. Please," I beg her, "please forgive me."

"Do not apologize," she says, sitting back down as if nothing has happened and I am overreacting. "I am not upset."

"Sorry," I say again, glancing at the door to the cabin. If she decides to destroy me, how fast could I swim away? But where would I even go now? I need the Sea Witch's help. She is my only hope. "I'm sorry, honestly I am."

"Goodness," she says, sounding amused. "You do realize that you don't need to apologize for your very existence, don't you? No matter what your father has led you to believe."

"The Sea King's word is law," I say, as if worried that he has followed me and is eavesdropping outside the cabin. It's hard to tell which is greater: fear of my father or fear of the Sea Witch. I have been told that one is all-powerful, the other is evil. Which is which? What is true?

"And here you are, in the Shadowlands, disobeying him. I hardly imagined a mermaid so young would possess such daring."

"I am almost sixteen," I say, irritation spiking through me despite my terror. "I am not a child. I traveled through the Outerlands at night and then crossed the whirlpools into your realm, even though it is expressly forbidden."

"I am quite aware of the route you took, dear," she says, yawning. "No need for the traffic update."

"Yes, well." Frustration gives me courage. "I am in the Shadowlands, am I not? Where no other mer-folk, maid nor man, has ever dared to venture before. I am the first to brave these lands, and I am here because I need your help, so—"

"The first?" the Sea Witch says, mockery in her voice. "Little mermaid, do not be absurd. Many maids pass this way, more than you could conceive of." *Did my mother come here before she was taken? Did she need your help too?* "Some come to Ceto to seek revenge. Sometimes they need help with wounds too deep for your healer to understand, wounds the Sea King refuses to even acknowledge. He never was a fan of 'emotions,' particularly in women. *Hysteria*, he called it." Her jaw tightens every time she mentions my father; it's unsettling. "Some come to me because they're afraid of being cast into the Outerlands for failing to breed," she continues. "Help with virility too. There are so many mer-men who are afraid to be gentle. They are made afraid of their true selves, it is a tragedy. For what happens to men who are not allowed to be afraid? They become angry. Vicious. *Feral.* I believe you may have some experience with such men, do you not?"

(My father, raising his voice or his trident or his hand, blows raining down upon us; but we deserved it; we were too loud and too demanding. Too much. We would be better next time. Next time, he would find no reason to punish us. We would have to be perfect.)

"This can't be true," I say.

"And yet it is, little mermaid. But most who come to the Shadowlands are searching for something a little more"—she flashes her teeth at me—"primal?"

Primal. She can't mean . . . "But it's forbidden for us to enter the Shadowlands." I say. "If mer-folk have come here, then—"

Something cold winds around my tail and I look down to find two fat-bellied snakes leering at me. I scream, and the Sea Witch calls them to her side.

"My darling," she says as one twists around her waist, "and my baby," she coos as the other settles around her neck. "Oh, little mermaid. You would be surprised by how many mer-men come to the Shadowlands, and how frequently too."

"But why would they?"

"So many questions. I'm surprised your father hasn't beaten it out of you; he never did like chatty women."

Was my mother chatty? There is an ache in my chest at the thought of her, and I wonder how I can miss someone so much when I never even knew them.

"They want me. A woman with power. Can you believe it?"

"But why would the men come to you for *that*?" I ask. "You're fat." I regret the words the minute they fall out of my mouth. "I'm so sorry," I say in a panic. "I didn't mean that. I didn't mean to offend you."

"Why would I be offended? Being called fat is not an insult, little mermaid. It is as meaningless as being called thin. They are just descriptions. It is your father who has deemed it to be a negative word, and a negative state of being." She looks down at herself with obvious pleasure. "I like my body. And while I value my own opinion over those of men, it might surprise you to know that some prefer a woman of more plentiful flesh. It is nothing to be ashamed of—we all have our preferences—but they have been forced to feel ashamed even so." She sighs. "And I am a fallen woman because of that shame. It is *their* desire and yet I am cast out as a result."

I can sense the beginnings of a headache, as if my brain is struggling to absorb all this new information. We have been told since we were mer-children that extra weight is revolting. There have been mer-men who gained in stature as they aged, but the men were not born to please the eye, as we were. Maids have been told that being slim is as important as being beautiful, as necessary as being obedient, as desirable as remaining quiet. We must stay thin or we will die sad and alone, spin-maids of the kingdom, cast to the Outerlands because we are a drain on the palace resources. Such maids are neither mothers nor sirens and therefore are of no use to anyone.

Ceto wheezes as the snake around her neck tightens its grip. "Ah, my pretty," she says, stroking its blistered head until it releases its hold. "It is not a punishment to be here with you. I am content with my lot. Which is more than can be said for you, little mermaid. What dissatisfied women the Sea King produces. You are not the first of your sisters to visit me, you know."

I stare at her in shock. Who could have come here? Talia, to find a husband? Cosima? She wouldn't have asked the Sea Witch to curse me, surely? I think of her coming to my room, her insistence that Ceto would be the only one to help me, and dread grits my teeth. Was this just a trap, after all?

"Which one?" I ask.

"Names, names," she waves me off. "The girl was quite distressed. She had come of age and realized her nursery-crushes weren't merely confined to the nursery. *Unnatural desires*, as the Sea King would put it. Really, he is most intolerant, he always has been. I sent her away, the poor thing. I have heard of witches who will perform such rituals as she begged me to do but I am not one of them. Burning. Cutting. The girls will feel relentless pain afterwards, but they will not be burdened with desire either." She chuckles at the expression on my face. "Yes, little one, women can experience both. You will see, in time." She smoothes down her hair and I shrink back at the sudden motion. "Pretty maid, she was," she continues. "A tail of the palest blue. About bonding age, I would wager. The Sapphic girls always come to me when it is time to take their vows."

"Nia," I whimper. "But that is impossible; she is betrothed to Marlin. She will have a natural marriage." I have heard of girls with unnatural urges, cured, of course, by bonding and by having children of their own. But never a princess. Never a daughter of the Sea King.

"Natural? And what is natural? Your father deems my Salkas to be 'unnatural' too, and what are they but drowning girls? He believes that he is all that is natural and right, and anyone with differing inclinations must be deemed perverted in order to prove his point."

"But Nia is a princess." A princess who never joined in when my sisters and I were discussing which merman we found the most handsome, I realize. A princess who is always looking out of the window, searching for something she cannot name.

"And you think such things cannot exist within the palace walls?"

"But—" I am unable to continue for fear that I will cry. *Nia.* What will my father do to her if he finds out?

"Don't worry," the Sea Witch says, as if she can hear my thoughts. "Nia will accept her fate, marry the man your father has chosen for her. She will be . . . well, she will be fine. Nia does not have your *restlessness*." She smiles. "Speaking of which, is it time that we should come to the heart of the matter?"

"What?"

"You are here to relinquish your tail, yes? You want to make yourself suitable for the desires of a man?" *Not just any man. Oliver.* "You desire two stumps of flesh to walk upon, stumps that can be spread open in a manner that no sea-tail will permit." Her head drops as she whispers to the snake around her waist. "All this to satisfy a human who isn't even aware of her existence."

"How do you know all this?"

"I knew this was to be your fate from the moment my Salka told me what happened the night of the storm. I could taste your need."

"It's not just about Oliver," I say. "Yes, it's true that I love him." The Sea Witch laughs at this, and I ignore her. "But this is about my mother too . . . She went up there, and she was captured and we don't know what happened to her, not really. My father says she abandoned us—"

"A mother wanting a life of her own is not the same thing as abandoning her children. You would do well to remember that."

"And," I carry on, "he said it was my mother's fault and we shouldn't care about her but—"

"Your father says a lot of things." Her expression is unreadable.

"I need to know the truth." I am pleading with her now. "I have always needed to know."

"You will find no answers up there, little mermaid." Ceto's shoulders sag. "None that you want to hear, anyway."

"You don't understand," I say, fighting the urge to scream at her.

"You seem to be under the illusion that I understand very little," she says. She fishes a small bone from the floor and feeds it to the snake on her lap. "That is a mistake, I can assure you."

"I'm sorry," I say, swimming back so I am out of her reach. "But I can't stay there, I can't be bonded to Zale, I just can't. He, he . . ." I gag on the acid-burn words that could explain what he does to me at night, what he's promised to do once I turn sixteen. *Only two months left.* "I'm begging you," I whisper. "Please help me. I don't know what I will be forced to do if you don't help me."

The Sea Witch softens. "I am sorry that it has come to this for you." Her gaze falls in the middle-distance, as if deciding something. She sighs. "But very well. I shall brew a potion that will slice your tail in two, casing each part with human flesh." She says it as if it's easy, mundane. "I will give you legs. That is what you desire, is it not?"

"Thank you, Ceto." The relief is swift and sure, as if I didn't realize how tense I was until she said those words. *You will have legs.* "Thank you so much."

"There is no need to thank me just yet. Your legs will be admired by all who see them, as will your unusually graceful movements, but there will be a price. There always is. A sacrifice, and one that you will remember for the rest of your life." She purses her lips. "You will be unable to forget, I'm afraid."

"Why not?" I ask, my palms starting to oil. Somehow, I know that I'm not going to like her answer.

"Every step you take shall be one of torture," she explains. "As if a blade of sharpest metal has shorn through the soles of your feet and broken the bones of your thighs, twisting into your stomach and chafing your organs. I wish I could make it otherwise, but it is a penalty that the laws of magic demand and as such, it is beyond my control. Are you ready for that?"

I don't reply. I am too afraid, or perhaps, simply, I do not know what can even be said to something so horrifying.

"And, of course, once you have taken the potion there is no turning back," she says, an uncanny echo of

Cosima's words to me last night. "The kingdom will be lost to you forever: your sisters, your beloved grandmother. You will never see them again."

"I knew as much," I say, determined not to think of my grandmother, how she will feel when she discovers she has lost another girl to the human world. "I am not a fool."

"My most sincere apologies, Princess Muirgen; I would hate to make you feel like a *fool*. Did you also know that the potion will only last for a month? Did you know that if this Oliver does not profess his undying love for you by the time the sun begins to rise on that morning after the next full moon—well . . ."

"What?" I ask. "What will happen then?"

"You will not see your sixteenth year," she says, looking at me with something akin to sympathy. "Your heart will shatter, cutting your lungs to shreds, carving your brain to pieces. And your body will disintegrate, the waves taking you for their own. It is Sea Law. There is no return."

The Sea Witch doesn't understand that if I do not see Oliver again, my heart will crack in half anyway. I will live my broken life with my broken heart, never knowing what became of my mother, forced to smile while

I sing upon my father's request, becoming a respectable wife for Zale. Any fate is better than that.

"And if Oliver does fall in love with me?" I ask, pretending to be unconcerned about any other eventuality.

"You will live happily ever after," she says.

"And the pain?" I ask. "Will that go away?"

"Oh no," she replies. "But women are meant to suffer. And you will have a husband and a child and a kitchen to call your own. Isn't that what every little maid wants?"

"Yes. That is what I want," I say, and the Sea Witch looks away from me, as though disappointed. "I am prepared to take the risk," I add. Oliver will love me; I know he will.

He has to.

"Very well," she says, sighing. "There is more, though. That is the price that must be paid according to Sea Law. But I must extract my own."

"What?"

The Sea Witch narrows her eyes. "You thought such a potion would come for free? This is powerful magic," she says. "And not something that can be undertaken lightly. I will have to use my own blood to create the potion. You must see that I need a sacrifice in return?"

"What kind of sacrifice?"

The Sea Witch pushes herself up from the chair, the snakes shedding from her and wriggling through holes in the uneven floorboards. She moves towards me, her skin as luminous as a pearl. She touches my cheek, her fingers silk-smooth, tracing them down my throat.

"We have heard tell of your gift here in the Shadowlands," she says. "My Salkas inform me that yours is the loveliest voice in all the kingdom." She presses harder on my neck, and I cough. "In order to make this magic work, I would require your most important asset in exchange."

"You want my *voice*?"

"Why so surprised?" she asks. "Did you presume that I would ask for your face or that magnificent mane of hair? No, it is your voice that I value. You should not underestimate its worth, little mermaid." She swims back from me. "I shall give you legs and you shall give me your tongue."

"How?" I ask, pressing my lips together, as if afraid she will reach her hand into my mouth and pluck it out with her fingers.

"I shall cut it out, my dear. Don't worry." The Sea Witch smiles when I recoil. "It won't take long."

"But, but . . ." I imagine the pain of such an act, the *violence*. "Won't that hurt?"

"Love is supposed to hurt. I thought you would have realized that by now," she says. She means my mother, of course. That void in the center of me that her disappearance has scraped clean, widening into an abyss with every new day.

"But without my voice, what do I have left?" I ask her. "How will I make Oliver fall in love with me before the next full moon?"

The Sea Witch shrugs, her hair floating up in the water and exposing her generous breasts. "You will still have your form, won't you? Men have always been told that slimness is the most important attribute a woman can possess, more important than intelligence or wit or ambition, apparently. Although nowhere near as useful, if you ask me."

"But if I can't talk—"

"What has your father told you, since you were a hatchling?" she says. "Men don't like women who talk too much, do they? Better to be silent."

Viola wasn't silent. Viola was loud and demanding, dismissing her brother with an imperious toss of her head, and Oliver looked at her as if she was mesmerizing, as if he could have spent the rest of his life listening to her voice and never tire of it.

"So," she says to me. "A decision must be made, little mermaid. What is it to be?"

"Yes?" I say, the doubt turning the word into a question, but what else can I say? Either I am silent above the surface, or I spend the rest of my life screaming for mercy down here, the water muffling my cries. "My answer is yes. I am ready, Ceto."

"I thought it might be," she says, shaking her head. "But so be it."

The Sea Witch places her hand over her mouth, making a retching noise as if trying to dislodge something caught low in her throat. A lump blossoms, pulsating as it dances up her esophagus, until a flame spills past her painted lips and dances in the palm of her hands. I stare, fascinated. No mer-man is able to conjure flames, not under the sea. This is magic like nothing I have ever seen before, something my father could only dream of.

She crouches down beside a large copper cauldron in the corner of the room, pouring the fire underneath it as if it were liquid. She picks up a jewel-encrusted blade from the ground and uses it to stir whatever concoction has begun to bubble inside the cauldron. She raises the knife to the surface—a few murmured words, words I do not recognize—and she pulls its edge across her breast, cleavage to black nipple, dripping tar-blood into the mixture. It hisses as it lands, the steam curdling into shapes of cloud so unspeakably eerie that I shiver. *What have I done?* I think as every muscle in my body tenses in shock. *What have I done, what have I done?*

"You have done what needed to be done," Ceto tells me, once again seeming to read my mind. "Isn't that all any of us can do?"

"Wait," I say. "I have one last question for you."

"Tick tock." She wags a finger back and forth. "Time is running out."

"Do you know if my mother is alive?" I ask, wishing I didn't sound so forlorn. "Could she be?"

"The Sea King said Muireann was dead, did he not?"

"Yes, but—"

"Yes, but what? You doubt his word?"

"No," I say automatically. "The Sea King only tells the truth. He wants the best for us. We are lucky to have been born his daughters."

"Then why do you ask?"

"I . . ." *I don't know.* "Wait. Did my mother come to you in search of legs too?"

The Sea Witch runs her fingertips down the smooth

side of her blade. "Your mother did not need my aid in such a matter."

"But she came to you for help? Ceto, did my mother come here?"

"There was no one who could help Muireann of the Green Sea," she says. "Not in the end." Before I can ask what she means by that, she holds out the knife before me. "Now, show me your tongue."

And I do as she tells me.

The blade sinks into the flesh, slashing it in two, and I try to scream with the brutality of it, at how fast it happened, my head thrown back in scorching agony. She saws at my tongue, hacking at the sinews, the flesh obstinate, refusing to let go. I gulp, my hands reaching out in desperation as if to say, *Come back, I made a mistake. I have changed my mind.* But I cannot say it. I have no words.

It is done and I am silent.

It is done and there is no return.

Chapter

9

T HE SUN HAS not yet risen when I emerge from the water, gasping in the moon-glossed air. *What have I done?* I scream silently to the sea gods.

After the Sea Witch plucked my tongue out, I kept trying to speak, becoming more and more agitated with the futility of my attempts. *What have you done to yourself, Gaia?* She handed me the potion. "Go to Oliver's homeland," she told me, "and drink this when you reach the steps to his estate, not a minute before."

I pretended to look around me, hoping to convey that I did not know where he lived, and Ceto groaned. "Gaia, Gaia, Gaia," she said, and I wanted to ask her how she knew my true name. "How much you are prepared to give up for one you know so little."

I was to go through the wood of snake-plants outside ("Wave the potion at them if they threaten you," the Sea Witch advised, my terror of those creatures clearly evident. "They will not touch you once they catch sight of the bottle. They know the power it contains.") and the swamp, pushing my way into the battering whirlpools, back past the Outerlands, and then the palace. The lights were still out there, all my family and servants asleep, and I tried to call out, to tell my sisters that I loved them. But I could not. I refused to allow myself to feel sad; it would only be a waste of energy. This was my decision and I had made it willingly. Even so, I blew a kiss and I prayed for their forgiveness.

And here I am now, staring at the house where Oliver lives. It is vast, made of gray stone and windows that are stained with colorful pictures, a large wooden door that is twice the height of any human man I can imagine. I drag myself up the beach, flopping on the steps to the estate, the marble hard against my back. I hold the draught up to my eyeline, watching as it glitters in the moonlight. *No return*, the Sea Witch's voice says in my head. *No return*.

But there is no return anyway, not since I have given my voice away. I open my mouth, attempt to speak once again, but there is only a deafening silence. It is like a phantom limb, my misplaced tongue reaching for words that are just out of its reach. I uncork the bottle, gagging at the acrid smell. As I hold it to my mouth, it chews at the skin, my lips instantly beginning to blister. I drink it in one gulp.

A halo of flames, searing across my skull and melting down my face, setting my hair on fire and dissolving my skin. Flesh peeling off in strips, drifting in the air around me like snowflakes until the sky is dusty with skin. A blade heaving through my torso, twisting and tearing down, cutting me to pieces. I need to scream, anything to release the torture, push it out of my body and away from me, but there is nothing here for me, nothing but my pain. *Oh, the pain.* It is all that exists and all that will ever exist.

Blades coiling in my pupils until blackness pares holes out of my eyes and everything plummets dark. A pinprick of light, expanding, trained like a spotlight upon my father, demanding my attention. He is beating the palace floor with his trident, like a heartbeat. *Where is she, girls?* he says. *One of you must know!* They plead their ignorance, Cosima a fraction too slow to be convincing. *Cosima,* my father says. *I don't know,* she replies. *I don't know.* He comes closer to her. *Tell me, child. You can trust me.* He pushes her back until she is lying on her bed, her hair spilling on the pillow. *I don't know,* she says again, and he smiles. And he pulls his fist back, driving it into her face until I can hear her nose break with a sickening crack. *I don't like girls who lie*, my father says.

I blink, and I am again on the beach by Oliver's home and it is the night sky above me, still, and I must stay awake, *I must*, but I am dragged under by the knife-burn cutting through my body, my tail hewing apart, and I watch as my scales shatter. I never knew I was quite so brittle. The gushing blood seeps into the sand beneath me, and I—

And then I am falling into the relentless dark. Zale is painting stripes across his torso and over his shaved head. *The time has come*, he yells. He is standing on the balcony in the court room, countless mer-men staring up at him, their faces striped for war as well. *We cannot allow the Sea Witch and the Salkas the freedom they have been afforded up until this point. These "women" must be controlled, and soon. I demand revenge for the loss of my maid. I will have revenge. I will have it. I will have my—*

Gaia, a voice says, so soft. A woman suspended in the air, waves of red hair floating above her. Her body pale, two legs instead of a tail, and yet somehow I know that she is a mermaid rather than a Salka, that she has been born of the sea like me. *Gaia*, she says again. *Gaia, my darling. I tried to save you. I tried to take you all with me, but I couldn't win, not against him. I'm sorry, Gaia. I am so sorry.*

"There. Over there!" a voice shouts. A man. "I definitely saw something."

"What?" another man says, laughing. "I can't see anything."

"Yeah, I can't see anything either," a third voice says. "You've had too much to drink, mate. Let's just head back to the estate."

"No," the first man says, and there is an expectancy there that his companions will listen and do as he says. Only men speak like that, I have found. "Look. Over there by the steps to the beach. Can't you see?"

Footsteps and curses and: "My god, what *is* that?"

"It's a girl," the man says.

Chapter

~ 10 ~

THE THREE MEN have surrounded me, each wearing similar material on their bodies. Navy jackets crusted with sand, large gold circles running down the center, their white shirts cut low and showing chest hair. "Fuck," a man says. *"Fuck."* Their faces are dissolving before me, but I stay awake. I fight the darkness.

"Is she okay?" One of the men asks, biting his fingernails like Talia does when she's worried.

"I don't know."

"How did she get here? And why is she—"

"George, I said I don't know." That voice again. His voice. My eyelids flutter as someone crouches beside me. "My name is Oliver," he says. "What's your name?"

Oliver. I am so relieved that I have found him that I reach out for him. *It's me. I am the one who saved your life,* I want to tell him. But no words can come. All I can do is stare at his face and wonder how I ever thought I would be worthy of him.

"Cat got your tongue?" the tallest man asks, pushing a swoop of dark red hair off his face. He leans against the steps as he inhales on a small stick of some sort, blowing smoke through his nose like he is a demon.

"Here," the man with the bitten nails kneels down too. "Have some of this," he says, offering me a glass bottle. "It'll help."

"George," Oliver frowns. "I don't know if that's a good idea."

"It's medicinal, isn't it?"

I push my hair away and drink, wincing as it burns my throat, still scalded from the witch's potion. The tall man whose name I do not know yet starts to laugh.

"Well, well, well, look at what was hiding underneath all that hair," he says, clapping slowly. "I wasn't expecting a peep show. Not that I'm complaining." And I look down in dread, and I see not a monstrous tail but two legs. I run my hands across the soft skin. *The spell worked.*

"Here," George says, taking off the navy material from his body and handing it to me. "Wear my blazer."

So it is not my legs the tall man finds amusing, but my nakedness. Everyone was naked under the sea, man and maid alike. I didn't understand that my body was something I should be ashamed of before now. The redheaded man's eyes are hungry, like Zale's used to be, and I pull back in fright, crouching behind Oliver's legs for protection.

"Oli, it looks like you have a new pet," that man says. "What will you name her? Gingernut Biscuits?"

"You're one to talk, Rupert," George says, ruffling the tall man's hair.

"Fuck off, George."

"Boys, be quiet." Oliver says. He takes off his own . . . *blazer*, they call it, and wraps it around my shoulders. It is warm and it smells of sand and salt and musk, the smell of him, and I want to breathe it in forever. "Up you get," he says, and we look into each other's eyes. Something sharp in my stomach, a drop, then unspooling slowly. *How is he doing this to me?* I smile and then I put my weight on these feet for the first time. The pain slashes through me, fast and true, as if it might gut my eyes.

"Shit," he says, as my knees buckle. "Let's get her inside. My mother will know what to do next."

We take one step, then another, my eyes watering from the ordeal. I look down at these legs, sure that they must be bleeding. Like Makara and Ondine, the children in the nymph-tale who were left in the foreign seas by their father and their wicked stepmother, dropping sea-shells in their wake so they could find their way home. But all I can see is flesh, ten toes. Feet. My feet.

Oliver bursts through the arched doors of the mansion with George and Rupert close behind, calling for help. I collapsed on the marble steps outside, so Oliver carries me in his arms as if I were a child. He runs into the cen-ter of the room, placing me on a chair made of the softest cushion. I want to pull him down, nestle on his lap, and curl into his body; I want to make us one. But he steps back, staring at me with an uncertain expression on his face. *Oliver. Oliver, come here. I need you to touch me.* I blush. These are not thoughts that a nice young maid should be having about a man.

"My god," a woman says, rising to her feet. She is older, her black hair twisted into thick coils wrapped into a bun at the nape of her neck. "Oli, what happened? Who is this girl?"

The room I find myself in is of considerable size, the ceiling decorated with paintings of plump, winged babies, the narrow windows covered with that same painted glass that I had seen from outside. I am entranced by the sun shining through it and dancing in vivid swirls of reds and blues, ghosts of color on our skin. There are other humans here, men and women dressed in black like the older woman is; dark netting shadowing the women's faces, scraps of white material pressed to blood-shot eyes. They are all staring at me, aghast.

"I found her on the beach, Mother," Oliver explains. "She was, well. She wasn't wearing any clothes."

His mother takes a step back. "You found her on the beach?" Her voice is hushed but I can sense the sharp-edged apprehension in it. "Unclothed? And you carried her?"

"She couldn't walk, Mother. She was too weak, from the shock no doubt."

The woman comes over to me. "Who are you?" she says, and she visibly flinches when she sees my face. "Who are you?" she says again, something else in her voice now, a hand covering her mouth, as if she doesn't want to breathe the same air as me. "Answer me imme-diately." She grabs my shoulders and shakes me savagely, the crown of my head hammering against the back of the chair.

"Mother!" Oliver says, pushing between the two of us. "What's wrong with you?"

"Why doesn't she answer me?" Her face is contorting, but not in anger. She can barely contain her fear, I realize. *Why would she be afraid of me?* She weaves around her son, trying to grab at me. "Answer me, girl!" she shouts. "Where are you from? Who sent you here?"

"What is wrong with you?" Oliver says again. "You're acting like a total lunatic."

"Don't disrespect me. Don't you dare."

"Or what? What are you going to do? Throw me out? That would leave you pretty much alone, wouldn't it, Mother?"

"Okay," George says, one hand on Oliver's shoulder, smiling awkwardly at Oliver's mother, who ignores him, her eyes unfocused. "Eleanor, Oli—let's all calm down. The poor girl is exhausted." He crouches before me. "Can you not speak? Is that it?"

Limp with relief, I nod. Thin sheets of something they called *paper* are brought before me, a utensil (a *pencil*) pressed into my hand. I have seen such items in the remains of wrecked ships but I had never understood their use before now.

"What is your name?" Oliver asks me. "Write your name down so we know what to call you." I stare at him, and then the "pencil," in uncertainty. "She cannot write either," someone murmurs. "The poor child, she must be illiterate."

The others are dismissed (*I'm sorry*, Oli's mother—Eleanor—says to her departing friends. *Please tell the Guptas . . . tell them I sent my sympathies.* Oliver's body tensing at the word *Guptas*, and I try to remember where I have heard that name before.) until it is only me and Oliver and Eleanor left behind. A *doctor* is called, an older man with a gray beard who directs all his attention to Eleanor. He proclaims that I am suffering from "shock" and "possibly amnesia."

"Did you hit your head?" the doctor man asks me, holding a metal circle to my chest, and I wince at the cold. "Was there an accident? Did your boat sink?"

"Boats, boats," Eleanor says under her breath. "This family has never had any luck with boats."

"I never thought I would hear a Carlisle complain about a ship," the doctor jokes, his smile sliding off his mouth at Eleanor and Oliver's shocked faces. "Oh," he says. "I'm so sorry, that was utterly unforgiveable. I forgot myself. Please accept my apology."

"And she is mute?" Eleanor asks him, brushing his excuses aside.

"I'm not sure," he replies, before asking me to stick my tongue out. I do not move. I don't want to do this in front of Oliver. I don't want him to think I am unsatisfactory in any way.

"Are you deaf as well?" the doctor asks. "Show me your tongue."

And I open my mouth, averting my eyes so I won't have to witness his disgust.

There are horrified gasps and, "Bloody hell!" and, "What kind of barbarian would do this?" and, "We must take care of her, mustn't we, Mother?"

"Mother," Oliver repeats when the woman doesn't reply. Her lips are in a thin line, compressing white. "We must take care of her. It is our moral duty."

"Moral duty?" Eleanor says. "Oh, Oliver—you're still recovering after the accident. It's probably best if we get her the best help and allow the professionals to take care of it."

"I have seen what happens to people when you get the 'best help' for them," he says. "I haven't forgotten. I will never forget."

"Oliver, we—"

"We *what*? We don't have the space? We don't have enough servants? What other excuses are you going to come up with, Mother?" He turns to me, and I try to hide my shock that he would speak to a parent in such a way, even if she is only a woman. "You have nothing to be afraid of. You're safe now."

Eleanor calls a servant then, a young girl by the name of Daisy, who is ordered to take care of me. "Watch her closely," she mutters to the girl.

A male servant is ordered to transfer me to a bedroom as I am still too frail to walk, and as he carries me out of the room, I can feel Eleanor's eyes following me. The room I have been brought to is beautiful, and I am told that it is my own for as long as is required. A bed draped in gold silk, an antique dresser with ornate molding, a large box (a *wardrobe*, Daisy says) filled with material (*dresses*, Daisy says) so plush that I shiver at their feel.

"They are all black, because we are in mourning," Daisy tells me as she shows me into an adjacent alcove made of cream tiles that are cool to touch. I want to touch *everything*, make sense of this world through my fingertips, but I am conscious that I cannot behave strangely in front of this girl.

"Do you need to use the toilet?" she asks, pointing at a clay seat in the corner, helping me to sit upon it. Liquid runs between my legs, a warm release from that strange tightness in my abdomen that I was unable to explain until now, and I gaze at it in shock. *What is this?*

"Come on," Daisy says as she fills the container in the center full of water. It comes surging down from silver knobs she called *taps*, and she helps me to climb into this *bath*. The relief as I lie down is dizzying, and I duck my head underneath. For a moment, I can pretend that I am lying in my room in the palace, staring at the hazy night sky above the surface. For a moment, I can pretend that nothing has changed. Then I have to come up for air, panting, my human lungs burning with need.

When I am alone, I find a hand mirror on the bedside table and I hold it to my face, opening my mouth to see Ceto's handiwork for myself. I see a brutal wound, not even a half-stump left behind, just a raw, jagged lesion. I put the mirror away, my hand shaking as the enormity of what I have done begins to fully register. *Remember, Gaia. Remember why you are here.* I stretch my feet out before me, pulling up the nightgown for a better view. I touch one thigh, then the other, running my hands up along the insides until I reach the center, the place where Daisy told me was for the "toilet," and I feel an unaccountable pleasure. Here is something the Sea Witch failed to mention when she said human men preferred legs that were easy to spread.

"Hello?" There is someone at the door. "It's me," he says. "Oliver. Oli, I mean. I was hoping to speak with you before you retire."

I clap my hands. *Oliver.* Excitement courses through me, fizzing rich in my stomach.

"Is that a signal that I can come in?" he says from the other side.

I clap again, and the door opens. His curls are damp, and he smells of those trees that hung ripe with sharp-smelling yellow fruit on the beach where I left him. He is wearing a coat of soft, black material wrapped around him, the same on his feet.

"I hope you don't mind," he says as he sits on the bed, and I am light-headed being this near to him. Why did no one ever tell me that it was possible to feel like this? "I wanted to say hello." There is silence, a silence I try to fill up with my prettiness. For what else do I have now? "Your eyes are so blue," he says. "I don't think I have ever seen a girl with eyes that shade before."

It feels odd to be complimented on something that was so commonplace under the sea. The mer-folk would comment on the flame-red of my hair, or the sweetness of my song. No one would think to say my eyes were blue because what other color would they be? There is another awkward pause. The Sea Witch told me that men like the sound of their own voices, that Oliver would present his opinions to me as if they were a gift; she said all I would have to do in return is smile and nod. Why is Oliver remaining quiet? Have I done something wrong, already?

He stares at his hands, the energy leaching out of him until he hunches over, like an old man. "I don't know why I came," he says, his voice bleak. "I don't know why I do anything these days." He stands up, his fingers brushing against mine as he does so. A shiver of heat runs through me, and I am torn between pulling away and reaching forward and grabbing his hand, moving it to where I need it to be, to this new place that I have just discovered. Is this what the Sea Witch meant when she talked about desire?

"Good night," Oliver says, with a wave.

Come back, I want to say. *I am on fire. I am on fire because of you.*

I turn the light off as I saw the maid do earlier. I lie there in the darkness, in my soft bed, and I do not think about my mother. I do not think of my father, and what punishments he has devised to ensure that the rest of his daughters do not dare to misbehave as I have done. All I can think about is Oliver.

Oliver and the way he might touch me.

Chapter

11

"RISE AND SHINE, miss," Daisy says, throwing open the slatted blinds, the sun chasing the shadows away. I stare out of the window. It is so strange seeing sky instead of water, sharp edges rather than soft blurs. Will I get used to it, I wonder? *Could my mother be looking at that same sky today?*

"You were out such a long time," she says. Daisy is small, shorter than I, with dark blonde hair tied in a neat ponytail, her face more freckles than flesh. No one had skin like that under the sea; it was alabaster white from the moment we were hatched to the moment we dissolved to sea-foam.

I find myself drawn to how different everyone looks up here, how unique. It is far more interesting than the conformity my father prizes. Daisy is wearing the same outfit the other girl servants are attired in, a black dress with a white band around her neck, those odd things on her feet that all the humans wear.

"Did you sleep well?" she asks.

I dreamed of the woman with the red hair again. My mother, it must be, for looking at her is like looking in a cracked mirror: almost the same but not quite. *You have made a mistake, Gaia,* she told me, and I thought I could hear my sisters screaming in the distance. The woman clasped my hands in hers, her eyes brimming with tears. I wanted to catch them, hold them to my lips. I wanted to know if her tears tasted of salt. *You made a terrible mistake, just as I did.*

"Very good," Daisy says, as if I have replied. "But it's time for you to get up now. Mrs. Carlisle and Oliver are waiting for you in the orangery." I place my feet on the cool, hard ground, holding on to the bedpost to pull myself upright, a puffing breath. It feels as if I am dancing on nails.

"I chose this dress," Daisy says as she rifles through the wardrobe, oblivious to my suffering. She holds up a garment for my approval. "Not that there was much of a choice," she mutters as she gestures for me to hold my hands up. She pulls my nightgown over my head, replacing it with this new dress. "Black clothes, and black clothes, and more black clothes," she says, walking around me so she can tie up the back. "There was a storm, you see, and a shipwreck," she continues, sitting me on a chair in front of the mirror. "It was terrible— everyone onboard killed except for Oliver. It's a miracle, don't you think? Sure, what else could explain it?" Daisy bends down to push the feet (My feet. *Mine.*) into the same contraptions that she has on her own. "Do you not wear shoes where you're from?" she asks; I am bent over, one hand pressing hard on her back, my feet lacerated from these *shoes.* "Now, where was I? Oh, yes, the shipwreck. To be fair, miracles always seem to favor the rich, don't you agree? And god knows, the Carlisles are rich. Made their money in shipping—they own half the world's boats and are scheming to take the other half off the Greeks as soon as they can. Not that I know much about business; all I know is that my wages are twice what any of my friends in the other big houses are making, and they're always paid on time." She ties the strings that will hold the shoes on my feet tightly. "The Carlisles are the most important family in this county, you know; my mum was proud when I got the job here."

Daisy is chatty, I notice, with seemingly no sense of propriety. She unpins my hair, ruffling it so that the red curls fan around my face, sighing the word *beautiful* under her breath.

"Ready?" she asks.

"Oliver, please."

"I said no, Mother, and that is final."

"Your father wouldn't have wanted you to—"

"Don't you dare talk about my father. Not after what you did to him."

I hesitate at the door to the breakfast room when I hear the raised voices. Daisy is standing beside me, palms upturned, neither of us sure what to do.

"Oliver." Eleanor's voice is so clear that it pierces the thick wood. "Whatever you might think of me, this is important. This is your *responsibility*. The board has been patient, but they need to see that you're invested in the future of the company. At this stage, they would settle for a sign that you're merely interested."

"And what of me, Mother?" Oliver asks. "Have I not suffered enough? Will you not allow me some peace?"

"Oh, Oli." Her voice quiets. "I am sorry for what has happened; it was a tragedy, and you have seen too many tragedies in such a short life. But . . ."

I cannot hear what Eleanor is saying anymore. "Come on," Daisy whispers. "He seems to have calmed down.

His flare-ups never last that long, thank god." She pushes the double doors open into a round room made of glass, the floor divided into geometric shapes of green and white. Oliver and his mother are sitting at a small table, the white metal carved into whirling shapes, with dishes of blue print so fine that my sisters would gasp to see them.

"Come in, come in," Oliver says, waving at me to join them, even though Eleanor is squinting at me in that strange manner of hers. Daisy touches the small of my back, nudging me forward. These shoes she insisted I wear make my feet feel as if they are covered in seeping blisters, the leather like acid soaking into each open pore. But I hold my head up high, swaying as if I am floating through water.

"She woke late," Daisy says as I sit next to Oliver. "I tried to rouse her earlier, Mrs. Carlisle, but dead to the world she was."

"That's fine, Daisy." Eleanor takes a sip of a pale green-colored drink. "I'm sure you did your best."

"Oh, I did, I know you and Master Oliver like to have your breakfast at the same time every day, and I was sure you would want her to join you, but when I tried to—"

"We get it, Daisy," Oliver says. "You tried to wake her. She was asleep. Anything else you would like to add?"

"No, sir."

"Thank you, Daisy," Eleanor says. "We appreciate your hard work. I know that you are performing your duties with the greatest of care. *All* your duties." Eleanor raises an eyebrow, Daisy nodding silently in return. "You may go now, dear."

She flees out of the room. These humans have such strange ways of walking; there is no lightness to their movements, no elegance. *Ghastly*, my father would have said. *It baffles me to think your mother was so enamored with these specimens.*

"You are so beautiful," Oliver says, and then reddens as if he had been thinking aloud.

"You really are," Eleanor agrees thoughtfully. "I don't think I have ever seen a girl quite so perfect, not in real life anyway. It's almost . . ."

"Almost what, Mother?" Oliver asks, jaw tightening. "If you have something to say, then say it."

"I was just commenting on how lovely our new friend is. It's nearly *inexplicable* how perfect her face is. Like a painting." She gives a small laugh at that, as if she has said something amusing, although neither Oliver nor I get the joke.

"Oh, for god's sake, Mother, would you ever—"

Oliver stops as a man-servant approaches the table,

placing a bowl before me, steam rising off it. I peer at it—creamy white, a milky-sweet smell.

"I hope you like porridge," Oliver says. "Or our chef can prepare kippers for you, if you wish. Or smoked salmon?" I put a hand over my mouth at the thought of putting a fish inside, chewing on it until it died in my throat. So it's true: The humans do eat their remains. "Oh, dear," he says in alarm. "Are you a vegetarian?" *I do not understand.* "Do you eat fish or meat?" he continues, and I shake my head. *No. No.*

"Interesting," Eleanor says, and I don't like the way she says it. "Well, porridge contains neither. Our doctors have advised that it is the healthiest option for breakfast to ensure a long life. How long do your people live for, my girl?"

"Her people? What kind of stupid question is that, Mother?"

"Do you take cream and sugar?" Eleanor continues, pretending she didn't hear Oliver. She nods at the servant, who pours a thick white liquid over the porridge, sprinkling grains of brown crystal on top. I imitate Eleanor, lifting the spoon, and this porridge burns but it's delicious, sweet and good. I take another spoonful and then another, until I notice that Oliver is watching me. I place the spoon down. Perhaps women are not permitted to be hungry in this kingdom either. *I am quite satisfied*, my sisters and I would say after two dainty bites at the dinner table. *No more, thank you.* It was important that we neither ate too much nor too little, and so we often went to bed still hungry, the denial of our appetites a sign of our goodness. It was important that we be good.

"It looks like you enjoyed the porridge," Eleanor says. "What do they have for breakfast where you come from?" I remain still. There is something unnerving about Eleanor, as if she is a shark sniffing the water for blood. "We never found out, did we, exactly where that is," she continues. "If I ask Hughes to fetch an atlas, would you be able to show us on that? You do know what an atlas is, don't you, dear?"

"Mother, you're being unbelievably rude right now."

"Oliver! I am not being rude. Surely you can agree that it would make things easier if we knew more about our young visitor," Eleanor says. *What does this woman want from me?* "What shall we call you? Jane Doe, as is the name given to the missing girls from our country? There are many of them, you know. Girls who simply disappear one day, never to be seen again." She stirs her tea with the spoon, around and around, metal scraping off china, causing my teeth to grind. "Foolish, really—probably following some man who doesn't want to be followed. A man with a wife, perhaps. With children. Not that girls like *that* care about such details."

"What has this to do with anything?" Oliver says, scowling at his mother. "And, no, we will not call her Jane. It doesn't suit her. I will think of something more suitable." He finishes the porridge, pouring more cream and sugar into his bowl.

"I was thinking we could go horse-riding today," he says as I stare at my own breakfast, willing myself to resist temptation. Girls are not allowed to want more. There is silence, and I find him looking in my direction. I point at myself to make sure, and he laughs.

"Yes, you, beautiful one." *He thinks I'm beautiful.* I wish I could tell him that I think he's beautiful too, more beautiful than any man I have ever seen, above or below the surface. "Do you want to come horse-riding with me?"

I do not know what a horse is or how I could ride one, but I smile my *yes*. The more time I spend with Oliver alone, the more likely it is that I shall convince him to fall in love with me. I *must* convince him of it. When he is in love with me, I will be safe. And once I am safe, I tell myself, I will be able to find my mother, if she is still here to be found.

"Wonderful," he says. "I bet George's riding gear will fit you; he is as slender as a girl." He snaps his fingers at the servant. "Call the Delaney house. Ask their butler to send George's riding outfit to the estate, immediately."

"Oli," his mother says, as the servant leaves. "The Galanis people are coming in from Athens to discuss the sale. It's important that you—"

"Enough, Mother," he says, slamming the spoon down on the table. "You can go in my place, can you not? You're better at all of that stuff than I am, anyway."

"Yes, Oli," she says. "Of course I can."

No. No. No.

I shake my head, backing away from these *horses*. They are huge animals, with slobbering mouths and stamping feet, throwing their heads back as an older man with dirty fingernails and two missing teeth tells them to hush. ("This is Billy," Oliver introduced us. "He's the best groom in the country." "She don't got a name?" Billy asked Oliver when I remained silent. "It's a long story," Oliver replied.)

"What's wrong?" Oliver asks now. "I thought you wanted to go riding?"

"Are you afraid of horses, miss?" Billy asks, pulling at the leather strips around the animals' heads. "No need to be; Blaize and Misty are two of the gentlest creatures in the stables."

I turn to Oliver in panic, clutching at his elbow.

"Oh, for pity's sake," Oliver says, clearly annoyed. I've only had legs for a day and already Oliver is weary of me. (. . . *the waves taking you for their own. It is Sea Law.*) I can feel an ache forming behind my eyes. I have so little time to make him love me; I cannot afford to anger him. What would my mother tell me to do if she were here? How did she manage to calm my father when he was in one of his moods? I nestle into Oliver, resting my head on his shoulder until I feel him relax. *That was easier than expected.*

"We'll go on Misty together, Billy," Oliver says. "The lady can hold on to me." He winks. "As tightly as you need."

And I do hold on tight. The leather seat (a *saddle*, Billy had called it) is solid between my legs, rubbing against that new center in a way that makes me feel uncomfortable and restless all at once. Misty runs faster, Oliver urging the animal to pick up speed as we jump over holes in the earth, broken-down fences, and trickling streams. I have my arms around his waist, pressing my body into his back, the country air roaring past my ears until I am becoming frenzied with the thrill of it. I never imagined such a thing when I was under the sea.

"Whoa, Misty," Oliver says, pulling back on the straps (*reins*), the horse slowing until we come to a standstill. We are at a clearing in the woods, sunshine dappling through the leaves and falling on the ground in shards of light. Oliver jumps down, his thighs muscular in those tight cream trousers (*Impure thoughts*, my grandmother would have said, *those are not for good girls*. Why does being a good girl always have to be such hard work?), and he ties the reins around the stump of a tree. Misty steps back, snorting, but gives up when he finds he cannot escape. Do all creatures who find themselves in captivity surrender so easily? Oliver reaches up and places a hand on either side of my waist, lifting me down.

"There you go," he says as I stand before him, swallowing down the excruciating pain that my feet are subjecting me to. He points at a mountain ahead, steep, a daunting prospect at the best of times, let alone with serrated knives for bones. "Ready for a climb?"

He insists that I walk ahead of him. "Just keep to the path," he says, and I do, each step feeling as if a steel trap is opening and closing upon my toes, the metal teeth tearing through and chewing on my bones. But I keep walking, the boughs of the trees grazing my shoulders and the top of my head. I reach down to pick one of the flowers blooming from the ground, pressing it to my nose and inhaling its scent, the strength of which I could never have imagined beneath the sea.

"Christ," he says when we reach the top, wisps of clouds drifting below us, obscuring our view of Oliver's kingdom. I sit down on a rock as quickly as I can, fighting the urge to throw my head to the sky and scream for oblivion, for a mercy of any kind. "I have never seen anyone move like that. Were you a dancer where you come from? You have such grace—" He snaps his fingers. "That's it. That's what we shall call you. Grace. It is a fitting name for one so beautiful." He sits beside me, taking my hand in his, sweat beading his brow. "Is that okay? Do you like it?"

I will like any name you choose for me.

"Grace," he says again. My hand is still in his, and I hope he never lets go. "The beautiful Grace."

Later that night when Daisy pulls the riding boots off, she sees the blood spilling from the soles of my feet, and there is so much of it, this human blood, smearing on the carpet and on the sheets and all over Daisy's hands until her fingernails are encrusted with my pain. I stare at it, fascinated, and yet I do not feel afraid.

"What is this?" Daisy asks, her eyes huge. "What have you done to yourself, miss? We have to call the doctor, miss, we *have* to."

I place my finger to my lip.

"But—"

I take her stained hands in mine, urging her to keep my secret.

"Okay, miss," she says, and she's confused, as if unsure as to why she is agreeing to my demands. "I won't tell nobody." And somehow, despite how chatty I have found Daisy to be, I sense that I can trust her.

And I smile. Oliver will be mine. It is worth it. All of this will be worth it.

Chapter

12

THE NEXT MORNING, Daisy brings me a draught; a "special drink," she calls it.

"It'll help with the pain," she says, as she places a bronze goblet on the dresser. She nods at my feet she so carefully bandaged the night before, already soaked through with blood. "I should tell the mistress, we should get the doctor. Mrs. Carlisle said I was supposed to watch for anything odd—"

I sit up straight, clutching at Daisy. I have learned since my arrival that doctors means scientists and scientists means experiments and tests and medical studies, like my grandmother warned my sisters before they traveled to the surface. *Don't get too close*, she told them. Is that what happened to my mother? If they allowed her to live, did they use her for scientific research, her body torn apart to help with their "enquiries"? I don't know, of course; that's the problem.

"Okay, okay," Daisy says, rubbing her arm. "I get it. No doctors." She picks up the goblet again and hands it to me. "Hopefully this will help." She wavers, as if deliberating whether to continue or not, her skin flushing. Daisy's feelings are so easy to decipher, mapping themselves scarlet onto her skin. "And I haven't told Mrs. Carlisle anything either. Don't worry about that."

There is no smell off the clear liquid and only the slightest aftertaste of something too sweet. "Aniseed," Daisy says when I grimace. After ten minutes, she urges me to try standing and I do so, feathers rushing up through my throat and into my eyes, turning my vision hazy. But the throbbing in my legs has stopped. I cannot feel my feet. I cannot feel anything.

"Better?" Daisy asks as I stare at her in wonder.

Are you a witch too?

We begin to establish a routine, Daisy and I. She wakes me in the morning, unwrapping the bandages from my feet, shuddering as she mops up the crusted blood that has gathered there since bedtime.

"Oh, Grace," she says every time, unpicking clumps of peeling flesh between my toes with a small brush.

"What are we going to do with you?" She draws a bath, handing me the magic potion to drink while I soak in the water—oh, and the holy relief of both. Once I have been dressed, my hair wound into braids and red powder dabbed on my cheeks (*It'll make you look a little less lethargic*, Daisy explains, and I speculate as to what my father would say if he could see me with paint on.), I take breakfast with Oliver and his mother.

A bite of porridge or toast and that is all; I refuse offers of any more food.

"What a tiny appetite you have," Oliver says every day, and I ignore the sound of my stomach rumbling. "Like a little bird."

"Yes," his mother agrees, buttering a bread roll and stuffing it into her mouth, as if she is taunting me. "Don't you ever get hungry, Grace? It is most unusual for a girl your age."

Then a variation on this: "Oliver," Eleanor will say, turning away, bored with whatever game she has decided to play with me. "I was hoping to speak to you about—"

"Maybe later, Mother? Grace and I are going riding again, it's such a pleasant morning. We should make the most of it while we can, don't you agree?"

And on it goes.

"But, Oli," his mother says the following day, "It is imperative that we deal with—"

"I'm so sorry, Mother. I've decided to take Grace into the village, I want to treat her to croissants. Will we finish this conversation later?"

And on.

"I beg of you," his mother says the day after that when Oliver has dabbed his mouth with a napkin, pushing a nearly empty bowl away from him. "I cannot make any more excuses for you, Oliver. Petro Tsakos is meeting with the Galanis people too. If Tsakos-Co secures this merger over us, they will control more than a quarter of the world's fleets, and it will be next to impossible for us to catch up. You are twenty-one now and—"

"Mother, I know I've been distracted this week," Oliver says. "But Grace and I have plans today that cannot be changed. I'm sure the board will do whatever you tell them to do. Most people do."

I sneak a look back at Eleanor as we leave, slumped in her chair. Her life seems such a struggle, continually trying to get all these men to respect her, to give her the keys to their kingdom. Perhaps they never will. Perhaps she should just build her own, like the Sea Witch did.

I want to tell Oliver that he should go back and speak with Eleanor, that the matter is clearly of great importance. I wish I could tell him how lucky he is to even have a mother.

"Oh, Grace," he says, as we walk through the front doors, servants scurrying out of his path. "That's what I like the most about you. You never judge me."

"We used to have parties here," Oliver tells me, linking arms with me. Adrenaline courses through me as his skin meets mine, and I shiver. How can one man have such an effect on me?

We left the mansion and he led me down the marble steps, but not to the sea. A sharp bend to the right, through a thicket of tangled roses, thorns catching on the ends of my dress as we fought our way into this secret garden.

"There'd be a band in the gazebo." He points at a wooden structure in the corner, tangled weeds creeping around it. "And everyone would dance in the middle of the lawn until the sun rose. There was music and drinking and people kissing, which I thought was disgusting at that age, of course. Little did I know how my opinion would change within a few years." He sneaks a look at me and I blush. "I wasn't allowed to stay at the parties for very long. They just rolled me out to charm the guests, then my nanny would come and take me back to the playroom. I was the only one of my friends with a live-in nanny, you know. Mother was too busy working. Working, working, working, that's all she ever cared about."

Where was Oliver's father in all this? I wonder. As though he heard me, Oliver continues.

"My father would come if he was feeling well enough," Oliver says. "Everyone would have been inquiring about him. *Where's Alex?* they'd ask, and my mother would promise that he would be there soon. The party couldn't start until Dad arrived; he was the life and soul of every event. But towards the end . . . Dad just looked sad all the time. Then he would become bothered, and my mother would be embarrassed, apologizing for his behavior. *My husband isn't himself these days,*" Oliver mimics in a mocking tone. "He wasn't well; he needed help, and she just . . ."

She just what? What did Eleanor do?

"I'm feeling tired," he says abruptly. "You'll find your own way back, won't you, Grace."

It isn't a question.

Every night, I dream of that woman who looks like—who must be—my mother. *Gaia*, she says, and she starts to cry. *Gaia.* And every morning, I awake determined that today will be the day that I find out what happened to her, discover the humans who betrayed her and locked her away. Even if she is dead, I need to know for certain.

Then Oliver does something to distract me, or he simply looks at me with those dark eyes of his, and I forget my mother. I had thought that impossible; her name has thrummed its beat down my spine every day since she disappeared, making a home out of every vertebrae. But Oliver makes me forget everything. I want him to look at me, I want him to touch me, I want him to make me feel things that I had never thought appropriate for a girl to feel. I want him to make me his.

But I do not have that much time. I count the moons and the sunrises, scoring them across my heart in order to keep track of the days that are falling away from me. How do I make him love me? My grandmother said bonding was about anticipating your husband's needs and meeting them, and I have been trying to do that but my very existence is now at risk. The ticking of the clock, the light changing its skin in the sky, and then another day is done. It is hard to admit this, but I am beginning to wonder what death might taste like.

At breakfast every morning, Oliver asks me to accompany him on today's "adventure," and at first I had presumed I would shadow him while he went to work as Eleanor does. She is unceasingly busy, always leaving the house for meetings, every available space in her office piled with papers and files as she talks into something called a *telephone*, rattling off lists of numbers and figures off the top of her head. "Have you taken a look at those reports I sent you, Oliver?" she asks him. "Did you look at the spec for that new ship? Oliver, are you listening to me? *Oli?*"

But instead of boardroom tables, there are more horse-riding expeditions for her son, more mountains to climb. Cricket on the lawn, birds falling to the earth—*thud*—as the boys stalk the fields with weapons called *guns* clasped in their hands.

"Look at Grace," Rupert says as he reloads bullets. "She's horrified. Are you one of those animal rights freaks?"

"You're vegetarian, aren't you?" George asks. He is the only one who ever seems to pay any real attention to me.

"Vegetarian, what nonsense," Rupert harrumphs. "You don't *always* have to come with us, Grace, you know."

But I do have to. I have to spend as much time with Oliver as possible. So I sit on the sidelines, watching as

Oliver plays tennis or polo with his friends. I notice that George always cheers when Oliver scores a goal, holding his mallet up in delight and yelling, "Well done!" I notice that Rupert turns away at the same time, hair slicked back with sweat, teeth gritted rather than congratulating Oli. You notice a lot of things when you are forced to stay quiet.

"Fuck," Oliver says now, as I touch the space between his shoulder blades to remind him that I am here. We are in the games room. George and Rupert and a few other men are playing something called poker in the corner; occasionally Rupert shouts that George is "cheating." Oliver had been sitting in an armchair by the window, staring vacantly out at the sea. I did not like to see him alone, so I decided to keep him company.

"Don't do that, Grace," he says. "You frightened me."

I'm sorry. I didn't mean to upset you.

Oliver's breathing is labored, one hand to his chest as if to remind himself to inhale. He grabs at the glass at his elbow, draining what's left in it. I do not like this time of the evening, when we all retire to the games room and a cabinet full of shining bottles is opened and the men fall on them as if dying of thirst. Their laughter grows louder and more meaningless until they find everything funny. I am not enjoying myself; not that it seems to matter to anyone except for George, who occasionally asks if I'm all right, if I want a drink, if I'm getting tired. The magic draught that Daisy has given me is beginning to wear off, pain crashing over me like waves tipped with shining blades.

"What's the matter, Grace?" Oliver asks, his eyes suddenly on me.

I look over at Rupert, tormenting the young servant girl who is unlucky enough to have the night shift. I met this same girl a few days ago; she and Daisy found me in the rose garden, sitting on a bench hewn from stone. I wanted to look as if I was enjoying the sunshine, turning my face up to meet its warmth, but truthfully, I had been compelled to sit until the throbbing in my feet subsided.

"There you are," Daisy said. "Gorgeous weather, isn't it? We decided to eat our lunch outside to make the most of it, don't get too many days like this. This is my friend, Ling." The other girl half waved at me. "And this is Grace," she said, Ling's eyes widening in recognition. They settled on the bench with me, Daisy offering me some of her sandwich (*Don't worry*, she said, *it's only cheese.*) while Ling told me about her family, about her father who had been a doctor but who'd died last year, forcing her and her younger sister to find summer jobs in the Carlisle house to help their mother pay the bills. (*It's fine*, she said, clearing her throat. *We'll be fine.*) "Ling is a traditional name in my father's homeland," she said, as if this was something she'd had to explain many times before. "It means clever. Intelligent. Dad chose it for me." I could not imagine the Sea King ever finding such a name appropriate for a girl-baby. *It will only give them ideas*, he would have said.

Ling is tiny, so small that Rupert has to crouch down to whisper in her ear. She wants to escape, I can tell, but she has nowhere to run to. I am very familiar with that feeling.

"Rupe, come on," George says, placing his cards on the table. "Leave the girl alone."

"Shut it, Georgie Porgie."

"I mean it, Rupert." George gets to his feet. "Get away from her."

"She doesn't mind, do you, sweetheart?" I can see the tip of his tongue darting into Ling's ear, her barely perceptible shudder. I should go over there and help, like I wish someone had intervened when Zale put his hands on me. But is it my place to do so? But maybe this type of behavior is simply what women must withstand in order to exist in the world? We are trained to be pleasing, and to crave male attention, to see their gaze as a confirmation of our very worthiness. Are we allowed to complain, then, if the attention is not of the type we like?

"Are you tired?" Oliver asks me. "I understand, it's getting late." He sways as he stands, brushing up against me. I want to beg him to touch me again, and again. Is there something wrong with me? Could Zale smell this *want*? Is that why he did what he did?

"Where's George gone?" Oliver asks, watching the men playing cards.

"Gone off in a huff," Rupert says, and Ling glances at the open door behind her. "He's so boring these days."

"Leave George alone," Oliver says, losing interest. "Grace is tired, so we're going to call it a night."

"Of course, mate," Rupert says. "Whatever you want." He smiles at Ling, tucking a piece of hair behind her ear. "I have a few ideas about how I can spend the rest of the night, anyway."

"Ready, Grace?" Oliver says, and I nod my head.

I leave that room.

I leave Ling with him.

"Apologies," Oliver says as we climb the red-carpeted stairs to my bedroom. My feet are sinking into the fabric, and yet its luxury grants them no comfort. "I know

I wasn't much fun tonight." The walls of the corridor are lined with images of his family, *photographs*, they're called. Oliver as a child, always holding his father's hand, his mother smiling too brightly. Alexander Carlisle, a handsome man with broad shoulders who becomes smaller with each passing year. "I'm tired."

He tires easily, I have noticed. Daisy said his valet told them downstairs that Oliver hasn't slept properly since the accident. Maybe he's afraid of the darkness, the weight of an endless sleep pressing down upon him. Maybe he's afraid he will never wake up. Maybe he's secretly hoping he won't. *I could make you happy, Oliver. I could save you for the second time, if you would allow it.*

"You are beautiful," he says. He rests his forehead against mine, so close, and I find myself short of breath. This is it. *Please, Oliver. Please kiss me.*

"Is it okay if I . . . ?" he whispers, moving his lips to mine. It feels so different to when Zale forced his tongue into my mouth that my eyes prick with tears. This is how my first kiss should have felt like. *Oliver will heal me.*

He pulls away, a hand against the wall to steady himself. *Oli.* I reach for him. "No," he says. "I shouldn't have done that. It's too late and I've had too much to drink. And it's too . . ." His face pinches. "It's too soon, don't you understand?"

He leaves me. And all I understand is that I am buzzing, as if every nerve ending in my body is being kissed by bees. *I am alive.*

I sit on my bed, relive what just happened in graphic detail. His thigh nudging my legs apart, his fingers on my throat. That heat rising. I pull the dress up around my waist, my hand drifting to that new place, that part of me that I had not known would exist when I struck a bargain with the Sea Witch for human legs. I am made wild with longing, my fingers dipping inside the wet heart, imagining Oliver's body on top of mine. Something akin to bliss, or maybe agony, teetering on the knife-edge in between, shivers from my very center to my toes, an overwhelming relief knocking me drowsy.

I did not know such ecstasy could exist for women is my second-last thought before I fall asleep.

I am running out of time is the last.

Chapter

13

WHERE'S OLIVER?

He is not there the next morning when I go to the orangery, my skin flushing as I remember what I did in his name last night. Eleanor is at the breakfast table by herself, folders piled beside her plate as she discusses today's schedule with her assistant, a fair-haired young man called Gerald.

"And there is that museum opening at—" She breaks off when I walk in, and Gerald pauses his incessant scribbling in that notebook he carries everywhere with him.

"Grace, there you are," Eleanor says. "How did you sleep? Gerald happened to be passing your room last night and he said that you were thrashing around in your bed. Like a woman possessed, he said. Not bad dreams, I trust?"

I was dreaming of Ceto, sitting in her chair in the Shadowlands, counting the pearls in her tail. *One, two, three*, she began, touching each pearl in its turn. *Thirteen*, she said, staring at me. *Remember that, little mermaid.*

"I want to be sure that my guest is happy, while you are here," she says. "And we don't know how long that will be, after all. Not too long, of course. I'm sure that you have your own family to return to. Do you have family, Grace? Brothers? Sisters? A mother who misses you? I bet your mother looks just like you, doesn't she?"

Eleanor waves a hand at the seat beside her, gesturing at me to sit. "You'll be wondering where Oliver is," she continues. "He's in his room, I think, but I wouldn't disturb him when he's in one of these moods. So like his father, that one. Best leave him to it."

And so it goes. Day after day. Did Alexander Carlisle also spend days disappearing from sight, turning into a ghost, slipping away before anyone could catch him? Oliver's crumpled napkin is on his plate when I arrive to the orangery for breakfast, no matter how early I wake up. Eleanor and I, side by side, and she always has so many questions.

Where are you from? Who are your people? Blink your eyes once for yes and twice for no, Grace. We must be able to communicate in some manner, since you can't read or write. Most unusual in this day and age. If Oliver were here he would say, *Stop it, Mother, there's no need to interrogate Grace.* But he's not here. He's never here anymore.

At lunch he has always gone out with "the boys," hunting or riding, servants following with picnic baskets of food and drink. I am not invited. "Boys will be boys," Daisy says, attempting to reassure me as I stand by my bedroom window, watching them leave. "It's nothing personal, Grace."

And maybe it wouldn't feel so personal if my life wasn't resting in his careless hands. It wouldn't feel so personal if I hadn't made the sacrifices I have in order to be with him. Why is he punishing me? It was he who initiated the kiss, not me.

The only time I catch a glimpse of Oliver is at dinner, but he doesn't sit with me now. It is always a grand affair, the guests are businesspeople and members of this country's parliament, others in dark sunglasses that they refuse to remove, even indoors, as if disguising their unusually attractive faces. Tonight, there is a man on either side of me, the duke of something on my left and a Mr. Large Gold Watch on my right. "Gosh, you're pretty," Gold Watch says, openmouthed, his wife opposite him frowning at me, as if it were my fault.

During the course of the meal, Oliver drinks glass after glass of red wine, signaling to the waiter once the bottle is finished. "Another round, *garçon*," he says, snickering, and Eleanor leans over and touches his arm.

"Maybe you've had enough, dear?" I can see her whisper to him, glancing nervously at the rest of the guests. "Remember, we have company."

Oliver shakes her hand off. "You can't control *all* the men in this family, Mother." He speaks loudly and a hush falls over the table.

"Oliver, that's not fair. I didn't try and—"

"Oh," he says, ignoring his mother's pleading expression. "Oh, I think you did."

After dinner, Eleanor has invited a few guests to accompany her to the drawing room. I have joined them because I have nowhere else to go; Oliver left before pudding was served, beckoning Rupert and George to follow him. I tried to look like I didn't mind.

The drawing room is Eleanor's favorite place in the house; it is where she spends the most time, besides her office. It is floor-to-ceiling glass walls overlooking the sea, curtains and chairs in a primrose silk with the outline of roses picked out in cream thread. The handful of guests remaining after dinner include Henrietta Richmond, a woman with skin stretched tight across her bones, and her husband, a balding man called Charles. "New friends," Eleanor crowed when they agreed to stay for a nightcap. I had heard her tell the assistant earlier to ensure these two guests were particularly well cared for. ("Wine, Gerald," she said, "and lots of it. I want the Richmonds feeling very merry and *very* generous.")

Charles owns a company Eleanor wants to acquire, and she is determined to have it. This world of money and business that Eleanor thrives in seems so complex, full of knots that must be untangled, never-ending problems to be solved. Eleanor is half-nursemaid, half-warrior, manipulating, flattering, and bullying those around her to get her own way. It is most bemusing.

They clink glasses, ignoring me, then Eleanor reaches over to say cheers to the man they call "Captain." He is sitting by the fire, hands in his lap, while the two women are cuddled on a chaise longue. I am in an armchair opposite the Captain, Charles standing at the drinks trolley, examining the labels carefully.

"Charles," his wife says. "Maybe you shouldn't have any more."

"It's a party, Hen. Relax."

"Come now, Captain," Eleanor says quickly as Henrietta's lips disappear into a thin line. "You must have some tall tales for us, good man. The Captain is one of this country's most renowned sailors," she explains to the others. *Sailor?* "Well, he is more of an explorer, really, aren't you, Captain? Going places where no other man dares to go." I look at him more carefully, this captain, this man who takes to the seas in search of adventures. What could he have seen on his voyages? "He is famous for his storytelling," Eleanor continues. "And he is most sought-after company because of it. The last time he came for dinner, he gave the most wonderful account of his trip to Antarctica." She smiles at the older man. "Where have you been these last few months, Captain?"

"I do love a good tall tale," Charles says, throwing back his drink. "The more outrageous the better, if you please, kind sir."

"They're not tall tales," the Captain says. His voice is deep, and so low that each of us has to strain to hear him. I have seen him at Eleanor's dinner parties before now, but I have never heard him speak until this moment. He always seems to be on the periphery, watching everyone else. Watching me. "I only tell the truth. The things that I have seen are beyond mere exaggeration."

"Oh, how exciting," Henrietta says. Her face is beginning to perspire from the heat of the fire, and she wipes sweat away from her upper lip self-consciously. "Like what, Captain?"

"Things that cannot be explained," he says, without moving his gaze from the fire, as if he doubts Henrietta's ability to understand. "Things that do not make sense to the rational mind, but which I have seen with my own eyes and know to be true. Things that can never be proven, so scientists dismiss them as fanciful delusions, the ravings of men spent too long at sea, the salt melting their brains." I shift in my seat, leaning forward so I can listen better. *Go on*, I urge him. *Tell us what you have seen. I need to know.*

"Come now, old chap," Charles drawls. "Don't keep us in suspense. What's the weirdest thing you've sighted at sea?"

"That depends on your definition of *weird*, I suppose."

"Perhaps this was a bad idea," Eleanor interrupts, holding her wine glass so tightly I'm surprised it doesn't shatter. She looks curiously pale, as if she has suddenly taken ill. "It's not fair to expect the Captain to entertain us. He's probably tired anyway—it's getting late . . ."

"Now, now," Charles says with a wink. "You started this, Eleanor. I was promised *extraordinary* stories and I want to hear them."

"Okay," Eleanor says, her lips white. "Carry on, Captain."

He grunts. "I have seen creatures that are half-human and half-fish, flesh and scales made one," he says, and my heart lingers slow, anticipating what he will say next. There is a high-pitched ringing sound in one of my ears, and I rub the lobe roughly to make it stop. "I have seen them swimming past my ship, waving at my men," the Captain continues. "Calling to them. Tempting them. Trying to lure them to their deaths."

"Wait," Charles says. "Do you mean *mermaids*?" The Captain doesn't respond, and Charles bangs his fist off the table with glee, causing Henrietta and Eleanor to jump. Eleanor doesn't look at all well, and I wonder what is wrong with her. "You *do* mean mermaids," Charles says, and time winds down, the clocks softening their ticking.

All I can hear is my breath, shallow. *Mermaids don't lure men to their deaths*, I want to say. *We are not Rusalkas.* And then I think, *Maybe this man knows about my mother.* Maybe he was on the boat that captured her. I look at his strong hands and I picture them knotting around Muireann of the Green Sea's neck—so thin, so pale—and I shudder.

"Tell us more, Captain," Charles says, perching on the armrest of the chaise longue. "Are they very beautiful, as the legends always say?"

"Some of them are," the old man says. "Some of them possess beauty of an inexplicable nature, beauty that would never be seen on earth." He looks at me as he talks, his eyes narrowing, and I edge back into my chair to make myself inconspicuous. Could he know my secret? I should rise, indicate tiredness and go to bed, but somehow I feel unable to do so. This is the closest I have ever been to discovering the truth about my mother. I cannot leave. "And then there are others who are plain eerie," he says. "Green hair and jagged teeth, wild eyes. Hungry, those ones are. Ravenous."

"Interesting," Charles says. "Of course, stories about mermaids have been around for centuries, and in many different cultures around the world, do you know. I read a *marvelous* book a few years ago, and it said the first mention of these creatures was in Greek mythology and it dates to around fifty BC—"

"One thousand BC, darling," Henrietta says.

"—when a goddess called Ataractic fell in love with a—"

"Her name was Atargatis, darling."

"All right, Hen," Charles continues. "I just thought everyone might like a bit of background. It's all guesswork anyway, really, what would happen if cross-species, eh, copulation took place." He chuckles as if my kind are nothing but a fanciful joke to be bandied about at parties. "Shouldn't make such rude comments with young girls present, now, should I?" he says, and looks at me. I wish he wouldn't. I need the Captain to keep talking, to tell a story of a mermaid caught many years ago. A mermaid who looked just like me.

"Yes, Charles," his wife says, rearranging her skirt. "I wrote my thesis on folklore and fairy tales, don't you remember?"

"*Interspecies copulation*, this book said," Charles repeats, as if Henrietta hasn't spoken. "I wish I could tell you all the author's name; he sounded a terribly clever chap."

"Rachel Conlyons."

"What?"

"The author's name was Rachel Conlyons," Henrietta says again. "And it was *my* book, Charles. You took it from my nightstand."

"Hmm, yes. But it would make you wonder, wouldn't it, Captain?" Charles says. "Bit of a coincidence, the similarities between all these myths. So, you think there could be some truth in it, then?"

"I don't know anything about coincidences, sir," the Captain replies, back to staring into the fire. The humans do this, I've noticed, with fires and with water. They stare into the elements as if they hope to find a missing piece of themselves within. "There have been stories, but none proven as no mermaid has ever been caught, not in living memory."

No mermaid has ever been caught? My breath catches, elbowing the sides of my throat. *But what about—*

"I have heard of men who have fallen in love with the maids from the sea," the Captain says. "But it does not last very long. How can it? These creatures will always pine for their homes and, one day, the lure of the sea will prove too much for them. They will abandon husbands, children—it does not matter what attachments they have formed; they will throw them aside for the trace of salt upon their skin. These beings are not the same as you or me."

"No," Eleanor says, standing up. She places the wine glass carefully on the table. "They are not."

"Eleanor," Henrietta says. "Are you quite all right? You're as white as a ghost."

"I'm tired," Eleanor says. "I do believe it's best we all retire now."

Another two days pass.

No mermaid has ever been caught, not in living memory.

The Captain's words sharpen in my mouth, seizing in my gums. They are all I can taste now.

No mermaid has ever been caught, not in living memory.

Then it is three days since the dinner, and the last time I saw Oliver.

I try to sleep but my sisters whisper in my ears as I drift into unconsciousness. I see Cosima and Zale, my father wrapping black seaweed around their wrists, bonding them together. *Come back, Muirgen,* my sisters cry. *Help us, Muirgen.*

I wake, sweating, unwilling to go back to that state, down in the depths of my dreams where I have no control over what I will hear and see. Instead, I have begun to walk to the sea at night, my heart thirsty for the salt water. This world is awe-inspiring to look at, that cannot be denied. Every day there is something new to see, to smell, to hold between my fingertips to make real. But I had not realized that this world would be so loud. It seems as if people surround me constantly, wanting to touch my hair, to comment on my dresses, to tell me that I am beautiful. Their piercing voices scratch at my ears, and before long I am tired of all this *newness*. And so I go to the sea. The sea is familiar. The sea is easy. The sea is *quiet*. I sit there and I watch the moon track the sky, warning me. *No time. No time. No time left, little mermaid.*

One night, as Daisy untangles the day's complicated hairstyle, I find myself rushing to the toilet to vomit. There are black spots bursting in my eyes as I heave over the toilet. It is like I am trying to dislodge some of this torment and spew it out of me. Daisy rubs my back, murmuring, *shush, shush, my pet.* I slump on the bathroom floor, watching my feet warp, as if my eyes were made of flawed glass. The Sea Witch's spell is falling apart, taking chunks of my flesh with it.

"We need to call a doctor," Daisy says. "This is too serious, I can't—"

I rear away from her, shaking my head. "Okay," she says gently, as if taming a wild beast. "But it doesn't feel right, Grace. I've never seen anything like this before and it's getting worse, not better. I could lose my job. If Mrs. Carlisle finds out I kept this from her . . ."

We both start at the sharp knock, Daisy kicking the basin of bloody water under the bed.

"Grace?" A voice from the other side of the door. A woman's. "It is Mrs. Carlisle. May I come in?"

Did she hear what Daisy said?

Daisy manages to pull the duvet over my legs just as the door opens. "Good evening, ma'am," she says.

"Thank you, Daisy," Eleanor replies. She is dressed in the violet dress she wore to dinner. (Spindly candles in silver candelabras, flowers blooming through the center of the table, but no Oliver . . . "Busy, I'm afraid," Eleanor had told the guests, and they waited until the president of a neighboring country engaged her in conversation before they started to gossip. "I mean, really," they whispered. "How can Eleanor Carlisle be trusted to run an entire company if she can't get her own son to attend a dinner party? The market is so volatile right now, did you see that latest report from . . ." These people have no uneasiness about speaking this way in front of me, of course. No one is wary of a girl who is mute.)

"You may leave," Eleanor tells Daisy now. "I would like to speak to Grace before bedtime."

Daisy doesn't move, standing by my bed as if she is

my guard, like the armed escort that flanks my father on the rare occasion he leaves the palace.

"Daisy," Eleanor says. She sounds like Oliver, the same imperious tone, barely masked irritation at not being instantly obeyed. "I asked you to leave so that I can speak to Grace in private."

"Yes, Mrs. Carlisle." Daisy backs out of the room, widening her eyes at me in warning behind Eleanor's back. What is she trying to tell me?

"So," Eleanor says when we are alone. "May I?" She gestures at the bed and I nod in acquiescence. It's oddly intimate when she settles beside me. When we are this close, I can smell her perfume, floral with a hint of something woody, can make out the crisscross of fine lines around her eyes and mouth.

"I see you, you know," she says. "Night after night. I see you going down to the water. What is it about the sea that fascinates you so?" I shrug, the very picture of guilelessness, for how can I tell her that I need the sea? I need a respite from all the noise and the clamor of this world. She catches hold of my elbow. "You really are astonishing to look at," she says, but there is no emotion in her tone. She doesn't say it the way others have said it, as if beauty is something I should be celebrated for, as if my face is all I need to be deemed worthy of love and respect. She doesn't say it like Oliver does either, like he's blaming me for making him feel something he does not want to feel.

"I have heard tell of another woman with eyes so blue and hair so red," she says, twisting her wedding ring around her finger. "One whose beauty could rival your own. It's quite some time ago since I first heard of her, I never actually saw her. Not in real life, anyway." She laughs, a dry humorless sound, like the cracking of a whip, and I feel very cold. *Is she talking about . . . ?* "But her face, oh, her face haunts my dreams." She peers closely at me. "And sometimes I cannot tell the difference between her face and your own. Isn't that peculiar, Grace?"

I shrug again, surreptitiously wiping my sweating palms on the bedcover.

"I've seen the way you look at my son," she says. "There's no need to be embarrassed." She reaches out to take my hand in hers, and grips it too tightly, rubbing at my knuckles as if she wants to wear the flesh away. "Oli is a handsome boy, and charming when he chooses to be. But I don't want you getting hurt, Grace. You don't want to know what it's like loving a man who is in love with another woman. It can send you . . ." She laughs in that strange way again. "Well, it can send you quite mad." I stare at Eleanor's hand, the heavy jeweled rings on her fingers. All paid for by Eleanor, with Eleanor's money. Everything in the house belongs to her.

"Oliver's girlfriend died," she says. "Did you know that?" Viola, with her blunt haircut and those long legs. The way Oliver looked at her . . . he has never looked at me like that. "Oliver and Viola were childhood sweethearts," Eleanor continues. "The Guptas are an important family in this county, and Viola was much sought after, beautiful as she was." She *was* beautiful, Viola. I wish I had her brown skin and her brash laugh. I wish I had her voice. *I wish I had any voice at all.* "Oli and Viola would have been married within a few years, and we were all delighted. A very suitable match; it's not like Oliver Carlisle could marry any old stranger he picked up on the street. Or the beach, as it were." I bite my lip to stop its tremor. "But I do not tell you this to hurt you. I tell you this for your own good. My son is grieving, more deeply than you could ever understand." *And what do you know of me?* I want to ask her. *What could you ever know of the sorrow that I have endured?* "Oliver does not see you in that way," she says. "Not now, not ever. It's important for you to retain a little dignity. That is all I came here to say."

Eleanor stands in a rustle of silk, placing a hand to my forehead as if she's blessing me, like Cosima did on the night before I left the palace. Maybe they were both secretly cursing me.

Then she's gone. I take a huge gulp of air, as if I had forgotten to inhale for the duration of her visit, and I pick up the hand mirror on my bedside locker. The face in the glass: the eyes so blue, the hair so red. And I see the woman who haunts my dreams. I see my mother. *Was Eleanor talking about—* The sea, I think. I need the sea.

I throw the covers away from me, dragging myself out of bed and tiptoeing down the stairs on these broken toes. Each step is white-heat, acid in a gaping wound, licking the edges with a caustic tongue. The front door thrown open. The marble steps. And then the sea, oh, the sea.

It is calling me, but it doesn't speak to me, it doesn't call me daughter anymore. Its voice is as lost to me as my own, and I'm not sure which hurts more. I soak my feet in its waters, the pounding solace, throw my head back to show the night sky the gaping hole where my tongue used to be. I wish I were able to talk to someone, that I had someone to hold my hand and tell me that they cared about me. I realize at that moment I am lonely, and I have been so for as long as I can remember. I realize that a part of me broke the night my mother left, that night of my first birthday. And I am not sure if I know how to put myself back together again.

My father told us that she abandoned us that day, that she chose to indulge her selfish obsession rather than stay close to home with her children. She was dead, he said, she was captured by the humans. He said that he would have saved her if doing so hadn't meant endangering the entire kingdom. (*But I think we should remember, girls, that maybe she didn't deserve to be saved*, he would say, waiting for us to nod in agreement. He needed proof that we loved him the most.) And yet the Captain said a mermaid had never been captured in all his time at sea. He would have heard tell, surely; it would have been the talk of the county.

I promised myself I would discover the truth about my mother's fate, but I have been so consumed by Oliver, by my determination to make him love me, that I forgot about Muireann of the Green Sea. And for what? Oliver makes me feel something that I do not understand, something that I cannot name. But . . . but he does not love me, his mother says—and he never will. He loves a girl called Viola, and she is dead. What am I doing here?

I look at the star-smeared sky—only two weeks to full moon, two weeks, and how am I supposed to make this man love me if he's never here to see me, to witness my beauty? I thought I knew despair when I was under the sea. I thought I knew true loneliness. As a tear trickles down my cheek, falling salt on my lips, I realize that I was wrong.

Chapter
14

*D*AISY'S DRAUGHT WEARS off quickly now, pain eating through its relief with jagged teeth, licking its lips and looking for more flesh to devour.

"Please let me get you help," Daisy begs one evening. The bleeding had gone on and on after she removed the bandages, and I must have fainted with the weakness, regaining consciousness to find Daisy's stricken face staring down at me. "This has gone too far. I'm afraid for you," she admits, and I am ashamed for what I am putting her through. "Let me just get the doctor. Mrs. Carlisle never has to know," she says.

Daisy has warned me about Eleanor, told me to be careful. "You can't trust her, Grace," she said one night after everyone else had gone to bed. "She asked me . . .

she asked me to keep an eye on you. To report anything strange back to her. If she found out that I kept this from her . . ." Daisy blanched. "I need this job, Grace. My family depends on my wages to pay our mortgage."

I don't know what a mortgage is, but I know that Daisy has been kinder to me than any other person above the surface, and still I give her trouble. I am like the kitchen's cat, bringing in dead mice and laying them at the servants' feet, expecting them to be grateful. Why must I always cause problems for the people I love?

"Grace?"

An insistent voice and a nudge to my ribs, and for a moment I expect to see my father looking at me, at his dreamy youngest daughter, with an expression between indulgence and irritation. But it is Eleanor awaiting my response, and it is not Sophia trying to keep me out of trouble, but George. He smiles gently at me, showing slightly uneven front teeth. *Eleanor*, he mouths.

"I said, you look tired, Grace. Are you sleeping well?" Eleanor says. She turns to Daisy, who is waiting tables tonight. "Daisy, has Grace been sleeping well?" Daisy doesn't reply, dropping a salad spoon to the floor. "Daisy," Eleanor says. "I asked you a question."

"She has been sleeping fine, Mrs. Carlisle."

"She doesn't look like she's been sleeping fine," Eleanor says. "But you wouldn't lie to me, Daisy, would you?" All the guests titter politely at the thought, Daisy's blushes betraying her discomfort.

There is an empty seat at Eleanor's side. Oli has not come to dinner this evening; he and Rupert had "duties to attend to," Eleanor informed us before dinner began. What duties could Oliver have at this time of night? Duties that involved Rupert, but not George?

I have been stuck here ever since, listening to the men talk to one another about politics and war over the heads of their female companions. I had not expected there to be so many similarities between this world and that of my father's. War and money are still the domain of the men—serious, muttered conversations in private rooms, waving cigars—while the women are expected to adorn themselves with jewels, ensure they are pleasing to the eye. Men talk, women listen. All the women but one . . .

"And that, my dear lady," an older gentleman in a bow tie says to Eleanor, waving his fork at her, "is why the Carlisle Shipping Company has been such a success."

"Yes, I am aware of that," she replies, unsmiling. "I am the CEO, after all."

I rise from the table.

"Leaving so soon?" Eleanor asks, and I nod. One foot hits the ground (a blade slicing through it, making ribbons of my veins for fun) and then the other (a flame mouth, licking flesh to ash), but I keep my face very still. No one likes to see a woman's pain, my grandmother always told me.

"What elegance that girl has," I hear a woman murmur as I close the door behind me. "She's like a prima ballerina. Could she be from Russia, do you think?"

"We don't know where she's from," Eleanor replies. "But we will find out."

A threat, not a promise.

In the hallway, I stand at the bottom of the stairs to my bedroom, imagining climbing each step. My feet would collapse in on themselves, sawing through skin to show their bone-trophies to the world. I turn away. I turn away and I go in search of relief. Down the steps, screaming soles against cold marble, and there it is. My sea.

Thank you, I whisper silently as I duck my toes in its waters. I have been so fearful of dying, but it might be a relief, after all of this.

"Grace?" A voice from behind me. It is Oliver, and when he comes closer I see that his eyes are red-rimmed.

I did not know that men were allowed to cry. It seems weak—*womanly*, Zale would no doubt say.

"What are you doing here?" Oliver sits beside me, banging his boots off the side of the steps. "Fuck, what happened to your feet?" he says, peering into the water. "Grace, are you okay? That looks awful. Shall I call the doctor? Are you in pain?"

I shake my head. *I love that you worry about me, Oliver, but I am fine.*

"Are you sure? That doesn't look normal."

I look away from him. Sometimes I wonder if I will ever be normal, above or below the surface.

He shrugs. "Whatever you want, I guess." We sit side by side, facing the ocean, neither of us saying a word. He is silent because he wishes to be, while I am bursting with words I cannot say. I feel as if they are filling every vein and artery, the alphabet carving itself into my bones, swirling letters across my body. It's amazing how cavalier I was in relinquishing my voice; how little importance I gave it. Since I have been silenced, all I want is to be able to talk.

"It's beautiful," Oliver says, still staring at the view. I had never thought of the sea as being beautiful before. It had just been home, and more than that, it had been the place I wanted to escape. The sea meant Zale and his eyes on my body, and then his hands. It meant my father demanding I perform for his pleasure. It meant Cosima weeping into her pillow. Questions about my mother, and answers that would never be given, no matter how much I begged. And now I only have two weeks to figure it all out. I don't want to die with my mother's name frozen on my lips.

"We used to go out sailing all the time . . . before," Oliver says. "My father loved to be on the water."

Yes. Go on. You can trust me.

"You'd have liked Dad," he says, running his hands up his bare arms as goose bumps form on them in the cold air. "He was funny, you know? And he always had time for me. It didn't matter how busy he was, he would play games with me and tuck me in at night. Not like my mother. The only thing *she's* ever cared about is that stupid company. She drove Dad away. None of this would have happened if it wasn't for her."

His gaze is distant, abstracted. I put my hand on his forearm and he jerks away. "Shit, Grace. You scared me."

My touch scares him?

"I'm scared all the time now," he says under his breath. "I haven't even gone sailing since the accident; I'm too much of a fucking pussy. And I practically grew up on boats. Sailing is in my family, on both sides, even though it was Great-Granddad Blackwood who started the company. My mother changed the name to Carlisle when she and Dad got married, trying to make him feel included or some crap." He juts his jaw out, like he's spoiling for a fight. "Would have been better off actually spending some time with her family. That might have made Dad happier."

I squeeze his arm, and he relaxes. "Sorry," he says. "It's just . . . I hate the fact I haven't gone back out. My dad would be disappointed in me. We used to sail the boat together in all kinds of weather, and I never felt afraid then. Whatever was out there. I saw some strange things, Grace."

I widen my eyes, even though I know more about what the true depths of the sea have to offer than he ever will. I think that he likes to explain things to me. I have found this to be true of most men.

"But the sea takes things from you too, no matter how beautiful it is," he says. "It sucks people in and spits their bodies out. Dad. All my friends. I don't know why I didn't die too; I should have died that night." *You lived because of me, Oliver. I saved you.* "It took her too," he continues. "Jesus. I still can't believe it."

I lean my head on his shoulder, but he doesn't seem to notice. "We weren't even supposed to go out that day. Rupert said it wasn't safe; he thought there would be a storm. Begged her not to go either, Viola told me. That just made her more determined." He swallowed. "George wouldn't go, not when he heard 'storm'; he doesn't exactly have sea legs. But Viola," Oliver's voice cracks as he says her name and my heart cracks a little too. "She didn't give a damn. She wanted to go out anyway. *Don't be so uptight, Oli*, she said." He rubs his hands against his eyes, calms himself before speaking again. "I'm sorry, Grace, I know this is a lot to dump on you. But you're such a good listener."

He looks at me and his eyes are soft and something inside me melts too. I think he's going to claim my mouth with his again. I lean in, just a fraction. "And I'm sorry for kissing you the other night," he says.

No. That's not what he's supposed to say. "It was wrong of me. You looked beautiful, and I—I got carried away, I guess. I'm sorry." He groans. "I'm embarrassing you now. I'm embarrassing myself." He watches me. "I wish I knew what you were thinking right now," he says. "It would all be so much easier if you could talk."

I watch him stand. He reaches down to ruffle my hair as if I am a child, or a pet. "Good night, Grace."

He walks away from me. And whatever hope I had breaks inside of me.

Muirgen.

My spine straightens at the sound of my old name, as if on reflex.

Muirgen.

I push myself forward, as if to propel myself into the water, dive in to find whomever is calling my name. But I cannot do that, I realize. I would drown, these weak lungs howling for forgiveness. I have seen what becomes of humans who have tried to find mermaids.

Muirgen. Come back. We need you.

I think I see a hand stretching from the water, urging me to approach. *Grandmother?* Sorrow cuts through me, like a scythe through kelp.

I must run from the sea, before I give way to temptation and annihilate myself beneath the waves. My desire to taste salt is too strong.

I try to stand but I fall, the ground tearing my knees open, more blood spilled, washing the stone bright. And I cannot call for help. When the Sea Witch asked for my voice, I did not think of an eventuality where I would need to scream for someone to save me. I crawl up the steps, pulling these decaying legs with me. I can hear the sea behind me, someone calling me, my name, begging me to come home.

But how can I? It is no home for me anymore.

Chapter
15

I N MY DREAMS, I go to the sea again.

I was naked there but I wasn't ashamed, not in the way the humans have taught me to be. *Gaia*, the water whispered, and I could hear its voice again. *Gaia, come home.*

I saw my sisters. My grandmother too, a shadow bleeding black around one eye as she sank beneath the surface, like she had forgotten how to float.

And I saw the Sea King. He was farther out than the others, Zale by his side, an army of mer-men behind them. They were armed with spears, slain Rusalkas spiked upon them, their swollen eyes shot through with veins of scarlet. *We are coming for you*, my father said. *I promise fire and fury the likes of which the human world has never seen. And I shall kill that man if he has dared to place one finger on the daughter of the Sea King.*

No, I said, and in the dream I could speak again. My voice was clear, strong. I had forgotten how good it sounded, and I cannot believe how easily I allowed myself to be silenced. *You cannot harm Oliver.*

She loves him, Father! Cosima cried.

Love? my father said. *Do you know what I do to little mermaids who fall in love with humans?* A baby herring scurried away from the shoal, and my father didn't break eye contact with me as he thrust the trident deep into the fish's back. *Be careful*, my father said as he cracked its wriggling head off. And I watched it die.

I woke then, trying to call out. I clutched my throat, forgetting that I had lost my voice, that I will never be able to say my mother's name ever again. I folded my knees into my body, pressing them against my heartbeat. I was sure I could hear it faltering inside my chest.

Something shifts after that night by the sea. Oliver becomes comfortable in my company again; he stops hiding from me. And as hope, oh that treacherous hope, rises in me again, I realize that I need to work harder if I am going to win his love in time.

I begin to smile at all of Oliver's jokes, whether I understand them or not. I laugh with bright eyes, the way I see ladies at dinner do.

I wait by his door in the morning, holding a glass of fresh juice for him. "Thanks, doll," he says, as if he can't quite decide if I am a sister or a servant. Too pretty to be ignored, too silent to be enjoyed. Thus, I must become indispensable.

"Grace," he says in surprise when he opens his bedroom door one morning and finds me waiting for him. I nod at the stairs. *Will we go to breakfast together?* I walk with him to the orangery, where Eleanor is detailing the seating plan for that night's dinner. "No," Oliver says when he sees the chart in her hands. "Grace is to be by my side."

"But—"

"Mother, if you want me to attend this thing, then Grace will be sitting next to me. If not, I can easily find other ways to occupy my time. What will it be?"

Eleanor nods, but I see her jaw clench in a way I know means she is furious. She has always watched me, but I have begun to watch her in my turn. *What do you know about my mother, Eleanor Carlisle? What do you know of a woman with hair as red as mine?*

Oliver has allowed me to rejoin his afternoon excursions, insisting that I accompany "the boys" to their parties. This time I don't get tired, no matter how late they finish up.

"Does she always have to be here? She can't stop *staring* at you, it's creepy," I overhear Rupert complaining as he and Oliver saddle their horses in the stables. "Besides, I thought this was a girl-free zone."

"You never minded when Vi joined us," Oliver says. "Anyway, Grace is different," he continues when Rupert doesn't respond. "She's not like other girls."

I know enough of this world to realize that this is a compliment, but it doesn't appease my fears. Other girls might be high maintenance and demanding, insisting that their needs are as valid as Oliver's are and should be treated as such, but the other girls can run and walk and dance for hours. Other girls can laugh. Other girls can talk, tell Oliver all that he needs to hear. I have to be *better* than the other girls if I am going to live.

Sleep is still elusive. Each night, the water calls me, promising me respite from these clamoring doubts. And each night, Oli and I find each other again on the beach.

"Fancy seeing you here," he says, then starts talking immediately, as if he has been holding his breath all day. All his life, maybe.

"People said my father went crazy," he says, "but he was just under immense pressure. My mother never gave him any peace." He cracks his knuckles, one by one. "Always nagging him—how to dress, who to talk to. *Look at these figures, these accounts.* That bloody company. And now she's doing the same to me, Grace. I don't want anything to do with it—to obsess over numbers and forecasts and profits. I don't know why she can't just run the whole thing like she wants." *Because she can't. They do not trust Eleanor because she is a woman.* If I can see this after so short a time, then why can't Oli? But if this is the way it has always been, who am I to challenge it? And how could I? If I cannot speak, I suddenly realize, then I can change nothing.

"I just wish," Oliver says, interrupting my thoughts, "that things would go back to the way they used to be, way back when. Before Dad's accident." I raise my brows into a question. "There was an accident," he explains, his face so stark that it is hard to look upon. "Dad's boat was wrecked; he was found thrown on a beach. It was a miracle, they said, that he was alive at all—but he was never the same after that. He wouldn't take me out in the boat anymore. He would go to the beach alone—back to the place where he was found, swimming out to sea and going farther and farther each time." Oliver presses the heels of his hands into his eyes. "And then he stopped," Oliver says. "He took to his room, and I wasn't allowed in there, so I would sit outside. That's all I can remember from then, the locked door and the smell of fresh paint from inside. I was only little at the time; I didn't know what was going on. We should have kept him at home," he mutters to himself. "I told her, Dad would have preferred to be at home but . . ." He sniffs back tears again, and I pretend that I haven't noticed. "I would never have survived if it hadn't been for George and Rupert," he says. "And Viola." *Viola, Viola.*

Another night, he tells me more about her. It's a good thing, I tell myself, even though it hurts to hear him speak of her in such an intimate fashion. But it means he trusts me. "We were kids when we first met," he says, lying on the ground. The sky seems so close tonight, as if you could fill your mouth with stars if you so desired. "Five, maybe six. It was around the time my father died, anyway. I needed to have some fun, you know?" He looks pleadingly at me, as if asking for my absolution. "And Viola *was* fun. She was always first to climb a tree, no matter how tall, or to take a dare to dive off the cliff edge, or to sneak out of the house when she had been punished. She was fearless. She was my best friend."

Fury seethes in me, like scraps of smoldering coal. Did Viola give up her family for him? Her voice? Did she change her body in order to please him? *Why must it always come back to Viola Gupta?*

"Thank you," Oliver says at the end of these conversations. "You are such a good listener. I can't talk to anyone else about this."

He trusts me, I tell myself. He confides in me. Daisy tells me what his valet says: that his nightmares have stopped, that he no longer calls out for Viola in his sleep. That has to be significant. It has to mean *something*.

And yet, he still does not kiss me.

We are by the sea again. Oliver staring at the water as he talks. I have never known anyone to talk so much. Black night stroking black sky, softly. No moon to show us the way.

"Here," Oliver says, holding a seashell to my ear. *A queen conch*, I want to tell him when I see the peach-and-opal husk. *Lobatus gigas*. Unusual to find it in these waters.

"Listen," he says, and I find the sound of home captured in its skull. "Can you hear that?" He takes it away, pressing it against his own ear, and it is all I can do not to wrench it from his hands. "My father showed me that," he says, throwing the seashell away from him onto the sand. "Before he went mad."

I listen to Oliver breathing, in and out. I want to hold him like a seashell and listen to his heart. Listen to his home. "And he did go mad, Grace," Oliver says. "We used to find him here, in the middle of the night. Knee-deep in the water, screaming at the sea. *Come back*, he kept shouting. *Come back*." Oliver allows the silence to blanket us both. *Who was his father shouting for? Who had left him?*

If I had my voice, what would I say to him now? Would Oliver even want to listen? Or does he just see me as a wishing well, a cavern that he can throw his words into, waiting till they hit the bottom?

"I miss him so much," he says. "I miss all of them." He stands, head thrown back to the sky. *I used to look up*, I want to tell him. I looked up because I thought it would be better here.

"But," he says, and he holds out a hand to pull me up, before turning for the house, "perhaps it is finally time to let them go."

Chapter

16

OLIVER WALKS ME to my bedroom, and I do not
limp once. He cannot see me as anything less
than perfect. Inside, I sit in the armchair by
the window, a gray-and-green tweed shawl pulled up
to my neck. Watching the waxing moon. It will be full
soon. And then my time will be up.

The house is eerily quiet, as quiet as the night when I
crept away from my father's palace. I lean my forehead
against the pane, breath fogging up the glass. I do not
want to think of the time slipping through my fingers. I
pull myself to standing, balancing on the sides of my feet
so I shuffle forward like a crab into the corridor outside.

I can examine the photographs more intently now
that there is no one here to catch me in the act. There
are many to examine. Most of them were presumably

taken by Eleanor, as it is just Oliver and his father in the frame. The exception is a photo of the couple on their wedding day: Eleanor beautiful in a simple slip dress, her hair a halo of tight curls around her head. She is gazing at her new husband with adoration, but he is laughing at a joke an unknown person has made, pointing at someone off-camera. The famous Alexander Carlisle. He looks like Oliver; the same chiseled features, that glint of mischief in his eye. I wonder what he would think of me, were he still alive. Would he view me with misgiving, like Eleanor does? Or would he be more welcoming? My charms might be more persuasive with a man.

I pause outside Oliver's room, pressing my ear against the wooden door. A loud rumbling sound comes from within, a scrape as a breath whistles through his nose. No difficulty in sleeping, as I have.

I walk on, through the house. It's much more pleasant at this time of night, without the hustle and bustle of the servants and Oliver's friends and Eleanor, watching me. Waiting for me to make a mistake. It can be very draining, pretending to be something you're not. I limp on, moving farther along this winding corridor than I have ever been before. At the very end, there is a turn to the left. The photographs have disappeared, the carpet becoming frayed, threadbare in patches. There is just a door ahead of me, the cream paint peeling off its wood as if scratched off by sharp fingernails. A musty smell is wafting from its heart and there is a recording playing, seemingly on repeat, a melancholy voice humming over the sound of waves crashing open onto the patient sand. I find myself inside then, as if against my own will, like a current has caught hold of me and is dragging me through the door.

The room is empty of any furniture, the blinds drawn, dust gathering on their thick slats. The walls are painted to resemble waves, but those in the grip of a storm, fish whirling in panic, seeking the ocean floor. There are canvases strewn in every direction, roughly drawn with no real skill, but it is clear they depict the same face. Eyes so blue and hair so red. A woman so beautiful it is almost unnatural. I reach out to touch one, my fingers caressing the paint. I am moving through dreams as I stare at that face, swimming through songs of my childhood. It doesn't feel real.

It is my mother.

"What are you doing in here?" My heart hurtles against my rib cage and I put a hand to my chest, as if trying to hold it in place.

"I asked you a question." It is Eleanor. How long has she been there? Did she follow me from my bedroom?

Did she see me walking in such a peculiar manner? "What are you doing in here, Grace? How did you open that door?"

She is in a cream lace nightgown, her hair protected with a silk cap. Her face is bare of makeup, and she looks younger than usual, even with the ashen shadows beneath her eyes.

"Oh," she says. "You can't explain because you have no voice. Most convenient." She looks around the room, her mouth tightening. "Look at these monstrosities," she mutters, moving from one painting to the next. "This was Alexander's room," she continues, as if she's giving me a tour, ever the polite hostess. I stare longingly at the open door. "I kept it just the way he liked it, or the way he left it, anyway. He was holed up here for months, Grace. *Months*. The smell." Her face curls in disgust. "If it was up to me, I would burn everything in here. I can't do that though, can I?"

I don't move. "No, I can't. I can't do that because Oliver would be angry with me and he's angry enough these days, isn't he? It's *all my fault*, you see. I'm sure he's told you that. His bitch of a mother . . . All my fault for getting Alex appropriate care." She runs a finger across my mother's face. "I couldn't take care of him, Grace, not here, and I had a business to run. We had bills to pay, all these servants; they depend on me for their livelihood. Not to mention the shareholders. Oliver likes his luxuries, my god, the *bills* that boy can run up. He's less interested in where the money comes from. He prefers to blame me for everything while he continues to spend everything I earn."

I don't like this version of Oliver that she is describing. Someone who is selfish, weak. A man who is prepared to abuse his mother while still using her for all that she's worth. That isn't the Oliver that I know; my Oliver is kind and decent and— (*Is he, Gaia?* a little voice whispers inside me. *Is he?*) I wish I could put my hands over my ears, making myself deaf to her revelations rather than merely mute.

"Look at this," Eleanor says, when she is in front of one painting. That beautiful woman (my mother, *my mother*), her hair standing on end as if floating in the sea. "It was my fault that he went mad, apparently. That's what Oli thinks, anyway. I *emasculated* him."

She squats on the floor until she's eye level with the painting. "The women always get blamed. Have you noticed that? The wives are nags. The mistress is a bitch for betraying the sisterhood. And the men just fall through the cracks in between. We expect so little from our boys, don't we, Grace?"

The room seems to be shrinking, as if there is less oxygen for us to share. The smell, the sound of the water, all of these paintings with my mother's face . . . I need to leave, and soon.

"We were childhood friends, Alex and I," Eleanor says, standing again. "And he was captivating, even then. Everyone loved him. They tolerated me well enough, although clever girls are never much appreciated." I don't know why she is telling me all of this. People feel so free to tell me their stories now that they can be sure I won't repeat them. I shall grow fat on all of these secrets. Eleanor cracks her knuckles, just like Oliver, but she does it slowly, each snap deliberate, echoing in this room. "His family was very grand but had no money left—gambling debts. Well. I needed Alex, and he needed money—and god knows if my family had anything, it was money. And I was in love with him." She turns to me, her eyes bright. "It didn't matter what my father said—that Alex was lazy, that all he cared about was having fun. Well, I wanted to have fun, for once. Fun, I could appreciate. I've never cared for beauty. Beauty fades, there's no *loyalty* in it. My mother told me it was better to cultivate my wit, my intelligence. If I'd had a daughter, I would have told her the same. I would have made her strong. A woman needs to be strong to survive."

I imagine what it would have been like having Eleanor as my mother. I imagine what it would have been like to have any mother at all.

"Alex and I were happy until that accident. Until he came back from the sea, changed. I loved him . . ." She's whispering now, pacing back and forth. "I loved him, I loved him, I loved him. *I loved him.* I loved you, Alex. Why did you want to leave me? You can't leave, I won't let you go. What will people say?"

I'm dizzy as my eyes follow her, sweat breaking out under my armpits. A chill climbs up my spine, bone by bone. Is this what unrequited love looks like? Is this what worshipping a ghost does to you? Is this what my future holds if I can make Oliver choose me? Lying awake at night in case he calls out Viola's name in his sleep?

I gingerly back away from her, away from this room and all the haunted spirits it contains.

"Grace," Eleanor says, her head snapping up. I freeze as she points to the painting in front of her. "That woman. Who is she?"

I forget how to breathe. "Grace. Gracie," she says in a peculiar voice. "Look at her. Look at her, I said. Why does she look so much like you, Grace?" She steps closer to me, eyes burning as if she has a fever. "Who are you?"

I shake my head. *I don't know.* I don't think I have ever known. *Please leave me alone. Leave me alone.* "Who are you?" Eleanor screams, the sound piercing my eardrums. *"Who are you?"*

And I run from the room, my feet breaking beneath me. I run away from this mad woman as fast as I can.

Chapter

∼ 17 ∼

U P YOU GET." Daisy shakes me awake. "Come on, Grace, you'll miss breakfast."

I'm barely listening to her ("Exciting . . . It's been . . . dancing . . . do you think?") as she bathes my feet. I sit on the bed while Daisy rifles through my wardrobe, trying to find the perfect outfit for the day ahead. ("Don't you think . . ." Daisy keeps babbling, "it would be really great if . . . I can't wait . . .")

Did I imagine last night? My dreams have been so vivid recently. Does that room even exist? How can I be sure?

If last night happened, then what does it mean? Was my mother in love with Oliver's father? Did she abandon the kingdom to create a new life with him, one without her children? Is that why she called me Gaia, a name meaning "of the earth"? Muireann of the Green Sea cursed me with wanderlust and a thirst for dry air that could not be quenched. And then—what happened? What happened to make my mother vanish, and drove Alex Carlisle mad searching for her? *Where is my mother?*

"Grace." A gentle tug at my hair as Daisy runs a brush through it. "I don't think you've listened to a single word I've said this morning." I stare at her blankly and she sighs. "Never mind," she says. "You'll hear the news soon enough."

I steal along the corridor to look at that room again, but the door is locked. There is no sound of waves creeping under the floorboards, no musty smell.

"What are you doing down here?" Daisy asks. I hadn't realized she had followed me. "That door hasn't been opened in years. And, my goodness, they need to re-carpet those floorboards, it's unsightly." She glances at her watch. "Now get a move on, you're going to be late."

Downstairs, I find the house bustling with activity, busy in a way that I have never seen it before. I take a deep breath, praying that none of them will look my way. *Why must there always be so many people here?* Dozens of servants weave around as I walk slowly, oh so slowly, feeling blood between my toes.

"Are you all right, miss?" one of the female servants stops to ask me in concern. I must be showing my misery. How unbecoming of me.

There are servants on their hands and knees in the hall, polishing the wooden floor until it gleams. More servants on ladders, buckets of soapy water in hand as they wash the stained-glass windows. To and fro, they dash, carrying huge arrangements of flowers and silver serving trays and cut crystal glasses. *Coupe, flute, cocktail, wine, short.* I recite their names silently, recalling my lessons with Daisy at the beginning, when I would point to an object and wait until she told me its name. I had so much hope, then, that I would need to know what everything in this world was called.

"Hey, watch it," a servant says to a girl tracking mud in from outside, wandering into the entrance hall as if amazed to find herself there.

"Sorry," the girl says listlessly. It is Ling, I realize, the servant girl. I remember Rupert's hand closing around her arm. She is pale, so thin now that her uniform is at least two sizes too large for her. I shiver. *Here is another Rusalka made.* Another human woman set on fire by an insatiable man, needing to swallow the sea so she can douse the flames in her heart. She will lament her fate for the next three hundred years. She will sing sailors to their graves for her vengeance. And despite everything that I have been told about the Salkas, despite the fact that they killed my Uncle Manannán and drove my mother into the arms of the Sea King, I would not blame her. We were told to hate them, but how else should they have behaved? The Salkas died with tears freezing in their eyes, sobs choked in their throats, their hearts heavy with treachery. Perhaps my grandmother was correct. Perhaps they are to be pitied rather than despised after all.

The orangery has been overtaken by servants too, rubbing silver and shining cutlery. I limp into the drawing room. Eleanor and Oliver are there, and Oliver is drinking wine. Eleanor's jaw is tight again, but I smile. After all, he likes me because I do not judge him.

"Grace," Oliver says, his voice loose with drink. "You are looking particularly radiant today. Isn't Grace stunning, Mother?"

I take a seat opposite Eleanor, but she doesn't acknowledge me. I watch her closely to see if she will give me any indication that what happened last night was real.

"Morning, Grace," she says eventually. Her face is serene, no sign of stress or lack of sleep. Did I imagine it all? Was it just a troubled fever dream, a manifestation of this nagging need to know what happened to my mother?

"Would you like something to drink?" Oliver asks, waving a decanter at me. "Get you in the party mood!"

Party?

"Oliver," Eleanor says, warning him. "Are you sure that this is the best idea?"

"Excuse me, Mother," he says. "I have decided that we are having a party, therefore we are having a party."

Eleanor stands, smoothing the wrinkles from her dress. She walks to him, placing a hand on his cheek. She looks so sad, so far from the fierceness she displayed last night (*a dream, Gaia, it was clearly a dream*) that I cannot reconcile the two women. "Oliver," she says, and he nestles his hand in her palm. "Oli, my darling. Let me help you."

"Mummy . . ." Oliver closes his eyes for a second then pushes her away. "Don't be ridiculous, Mother. I'm a grown man and I need to live my life. Grace agrees with me, don't you, Grace?"

"Grace?" Eleanor says, going to look out at the garden. "What on earth does *Grace* have to do with any of this? She can't even speak."

"Don't talk about my friend like that," he says. (*Friend?* A blow, but I keep smiling. Good girls must always keep smiling.) "You'd like a party, wouldn't you, Grace?"

He nods as though I have spoken. "So that's decided. We need to move on, all of us. It will be a year next month since . . ." He trails off, his mother still with her back to us. A year since the shipwreck. A year since his birthday, and my own. "A party will be a good distraction," Oliver says. "And we'll invite everyone in the county."

"Everyone? Oliver, our friends lost people too that day. Their *children*. The Guptas lost two. They . . . they have lost a great deal."

"And I have not?"

"Losing a child is different, Oliver. You're too young to understand."

"Do not tell me what I can and cannot understand, Mother. I need this." His voice, rising to a whine. *Oliver can be so*— No. There is no time to criticize Oliver or to wish that he could be different. He is my destiny. My one hope of survival. "I'm thinking a garden party since the weather has been so good these last few weeks. And then . . ." Oliver hesitates. "Then, we're going to move the party onto one of the yachts. It's not like we don't have enough of them." Eleanor's shoulders visibly tense. "One of Dad's old ones."

"Which one?" she asks sharply, and I begin to feel nervous without knowing exactly why.

"The *Muireann*," Oliver says, that name tripping off his tongue as if it was nothing. "It was Dad's favorite boat."

Muireann.

"No," Eleanor says, the blood draining from her face. "No, Oliver, I forbid it. Any boat but that one. It is cursed."

"Don't be ridiculous, Mother."

"Oliver. I'm begging you," Eleanor is so pale now it is as if she is on her deathbed. The *Muireann*. His father named his favorite boat after my mother. Last night was real, all of it; it must have been—the locked room, full of paintings, Eleanor screaming at me. *That room.*

"You can throw the biggest party you want and invite every person in the county," Eleanor begs. "But don't set foot on that boat."

"I want to use the *Muireann*." His gaze lights on me. "Are you okay, Grace?" he asks. "You look strange."

My mother's name, the name that I thought I would never hear for the rest of my life.

My mother was here. This is proof. She was *here*.

"What are you going to wear?" Daisy asks as she throws the wardrobe doors open, grimacing as she rifles through the dresses hanging inside.

"I'm glad Oliver has called a stop to the mourning," Daisy continues. "You would look beautiful in blue, with your eyes . . . No, wait. Green! Green would be spectacular on you."

Oliver has decided to throw the party this Friday because "It's a full moon, so it'll look rather impressive from the boat, don't you agree, Grace?" He is so excited about this party, unaware that it might be the day I meet my end. Would he even miss me? Like his father missed my mother, screaming at the sea to give her back to him?

Oliver has the power to save my life, if he only knew it, and all he cares about is the quantity of champagne they're going to serve. "This has to be special," he tells the event planner, a reed-thin man with a patterned cravat. "I want this to be the biggest celebration that anyone in the county can remember."

It flashes into my mind that Oliver can be petty, with his competitive drinking and now this ridiculous party. And he can be moody and difficult and— But I push away the creeping worry. He is my love, I remind myself, my great love. And my only remaining chance. The minutes are slipping through my fingers like water; I don't have time for regret. Oliver will love me.

And then, at last, maybe I can decide what it is that I want for myself.

"This isn't the right color, but it's a good shape. We could always hire a—" Daisy holds a dress out for my inspection, and then sees my expression. "Grace. What's wrong?"

Daisy is aware that I haven't been sleeping; she assumes it's because of my feet. "You must be in terrible pain," she says to me, and I have no way to tell her about my dreams, how violent they have become.

Seas burned red with spilled blood, my sisters' heads impaled on spikes, eyes bulging. They are dead, all of them, their tails torn from their torsos and thrown to the sharks to feed on. A mirror before me, I am standing there naked. My legs, these legs, rotting, putrefying. Decomposing from the inside out. Then I am back in that room again, Alexander's room, the walls swirling with water, Eleanor's arms outstretched, sucking in the waves then spewing them out of her mouth, washing all those paintings away. Her face, my face, her face, and my face. Over and over again until I cannot differentiate between them any longer.

My mother.

Am I going mad?

"Are you worried about the party?" Daisy says. "Don't be. You'll be the most beautiful girl there. Oliver won't be able to take his eyes off you. This is going to be the night for the two of you, I can feel it in my bones."

Daisy thinks it is easy. She doesn't understand that I am falling apart, that time is eating at my skin, growing mold where my flesh should be. I am decaying before her and she cannot even see it.

A dressmaker is summoned to the estate, a stout woman with a mouth full of pins. Swaths of material are held up to my face, *This color is gorgeous*, and, *Honestly, everything looks simply divine on you. You are so beautiful*, they tell me. But what does it matter in the end? *Beauty fades*, Eleanor said. And what will I have left when that happens?

"Wait," the dressmaker says, holding cloth in her hands. "This is the one." Forest green. Silver flecks. "It could have been made for you." And I am back in the palace, gritting my teeth while my grandmother sewed pearls into my tail for the ball. I thought I knew what pain was then. I had no idea. I wonder what Grandmother would say if she could see me now. *What am I doing here? What have I done?* The panic, like a rising tide. No turning back. *Maybe I could—*

"Are you all right, miss? You've gone a bit funny looking."

"She's fine," Daisy says to the dressmaker. "Grace just gets distracted at times. But don't you think the material is a little dark for this time of year?"

"It looks wonderful on her," the dressmaker argues, taking out a pair of silver shoes in a solid leather. "And I have these to complete the ensemble. Aren't they adorable?"

Adorable—like a child. Men are never called *adorable*. They are hurried into maturity. Whereas we are forced to behave like small girls when we are grown-up, performing youth in our dress and our manner. It is ironic, really, when we spent our childhood years striving to look like adults before our time.

"No," Daisy says, testing the leather between her fingers. "They won't do, I'm afraid. Miss Grace has rather delicate feet. Do you have anything softer?"

Cloth shoes are found, soft as can be. Soft enough even for my broken feet.

"A long dress," Daisy insists, as material is draped around my naked body and pinned in place, even though the dressmaker complains that a short skirt would be more chic and more suitable for summer.

"No," Daisy says. Daisy understands. She knows these legs must be hidden.

"How tiny you are," the dressmaker says, pinching my waist between her hands. "You must take very good care of yourself. What is your diet like? Do you exercise? What's your secret?"

And, "How beautiful you are," the dressmaker says. "You are so blessed."

And then, later, "How perfect you are," the dressmaker says. "I have never worked for anyone with such a perfect face and perfect body. You are so lucky."

Please don't touch me, I want to say, but I know that a woman's body may always be touched if so desired. I am blessed to attract such attention. Everyone says it, so it must be true.

The day of the party is approaching fast, only four days to go, and my stomach is so tight with nerves that I am unable to tolerate any food offered to me. To make matters worse, Oliver never has any time to spend with me. "Not now," he says. "Sorry, Grace. So much to organize." And I watch him with George and Rupert, the three of them bickering about yet another idea they have that will make this party a huge success.

And that night— *Tick tock*, the Sea Witch says in my dreams. She is sitting at a vanity table, applying a bright lipstick. She smiles at me, red lips and white teeth.

Time is running out, little mermaid. Shall I come for you? Are you ready for the help I can give you?

The sheets are dripping with blood by the time the sun rises. My legs end in two open wounds, stringy flesh falling off exposed bone, barely resembling human feet. I stare at them, these battered reminders that I am not human. Daisy is changing the bedclothes every morning and every night now, dry-retching when she spots a sliver of bone needling through the broken skin. I hold her hands in mine. We are so close now that I feel as if she can hear my thoughts. *How beautiful my voice was, Daisy. I could sing so well, you would have wept to hear me.*

She helps me out of bed, picking me up without so much as a cry when I fall to the floor. I lean on her as I hobble into the bathroom. She pulls up a hard-backed chair to sit by the tub as I bathe, collapsing under the water. I could drown myself, but I fear that I would still need someone to hold me down. This new, human instinct to survive is too great to discount. And I don't want to die, not really.

I just want the pain to stop.

"What are we going to do with you, Grace?" I see the fear in her. She knows something is not right. She knows that this is not normal, not *human* in some way. "I wish you would let me call the doctor."

There will be no doctors. What use would they be? The only people who could help me now are the Sea Witch and the Sea King. *Two sides of the one coin*, my grandmother told me; both with powers, but one is celebrated as a great leader while the other is an outcast, exiled to a land of floating girls, angels of death with snarling smiles.

Neither can help me now.

"What's wrong, Grace?" Daisy asks. "You're shaking."

Nothing, I smile.

I sink under the water.

Chapter
❧ 18 ❧

I WATCHED THE sun rise this morning, climbing into the clear sky, and I willed it not to set, never to set again.

"Gorgeous day for a party," Daisy said when she arrived. "Breakfast, Grace? I can bring up some tea and toast if you'd like." I shook my head: *No, I'm not hungry.* The nerves maul my stomach with talons sharp. I stayed in bed until noon. "Best to rest your feet," Daisy had said. "Seeing as you'll be on them for the whole evening."

And then it is time. Stepping into the new dress, clouds of silk cinching my waist. Feet placed into cloth slippers, fingers clenching as my toes start their shrieking beat. But I am relieved that the mutilation has been disguised for this, this which could be the final evening.

"Do they feel comfortable?" Daisy asks, gently tying the laces. "Not too tight?"

They feel like barbed wire, wrapping around and around, piercing deep. Gesturing vigorously, I convince her to give me a second dose of the draught. "It's not safe," she says, but I don't care about being "safe"; I need to be *anesthetized.* The medicine is working its magic already, unraveling the thick clot knotted in my chest, thread by thread, until I am numb; my mother and the boat called by her name, and her painted face after painted face, all drifting away from me. I never realized until I came to the human world how blissful it is to feel nothing.

"We need to cut the hedge back in the garden," Eleanor had said during the many discussions about the party preparations. I kept watching her for a sign, an acknowledgment that our encounter in that room did happen, but she is too busy pretending to be eager for this event she disapproves of. Her rictus grin as Oliver talked of trained doves and ice sculptures ("Won't they melt, Oliver?" she asked. "It is summer, after all.") and singing waiters and juggling clowns and how we "must fly this volcanic water in from the islands, Rupert said it's the best kind and I only want the best, Mother."

"Let's focus on the hedge for now," Eleanor repeated. "It's utterly overgrown."

But Oliver had disagreed. "No, Mother," he replied. "I like it. It reminds me of when Dad was still alive."

"But it's unmanageable, Oli," Eleanor said, faltering at the mention of her husband.

"Just leave it, Mother," he said. "You might want to pretend that Dad never existed, but I don't."

"Yes, dear," Eleanor replied, turning away from Oliver before he can see the devastation on her face. I don't like Eleanor, and I certainly don't trust her, but Oliver's cruelty to his mother is so carelessly done that it's breathtaking. "Whatever you want, Oliver."

The lawn in the secret garden has been cut for the occasion; the rosebushes that Eleanor wanted to trim act as a barrier to any inclement winds the sea might blow our way. The servants are in uniforms, sweating in the midday heat, offering glasses of champagne or portions of food so tiny they can be eaten in one bite.

"Caviar?" a servant asks me in a bored tone. He proffers a silver tray, a bowl with heaped eggs in the center, oily balls glistening in the sun. A silver spoon, all the better to dig in with. "Fish eggs. It's a delicacy," he says, confused, as I back away, bile seeping into my mouth.

"Grace is a vegetarian," Oliver tells the waiter as he approaches. He is dressed in a crisp white shirt and shorts, showing off his muscular legs, Rupert and George following in similar outfits. Rupert grabs a spoonful of caviar from the tray, spreads it on a cracker, swallowing it whole. "That's delicious," he says, eyes never leaving mine.

"You look beautiful, Grace," Oliver says, handing me a glass of sparkling water.

I lower my eyes, as if embarrassed. "It's better not to seem too pleased with one's own beauty," my grandmother had explained to me. "But why do we spend all this time combing our hair and adorning our tails if we don't want to be admired? It doesn't make any sense," I said. "Oh, Muirgen," she sighed. "So many questions for such a little mermaid. You'll find life so much easier if you ask fewer questions."

"Are you having fun, Grace?" George asks, his face as freckled from the sun as Daisy's.

I smile at him in response, and Rupert rolls his eyes.

"What enthusiasm," Rupert says. "Always such a joy spending time with you, Grace; the conversation is truly scintillating." I glance at Oliver, but he doesn't give any indication of having heard Rupert. "God," Rupert says loudly. "I'm so bored." Oliver stiffens. This, he will not ignore. "It's utterly dull," Rupert says, draining the rest of his glass.

"This part is just to keep the geriatrics happy," Oliver says. "Wait until we get onto the *Muireann.*" My heart catches: my mother's name, so casual on his lips. "That's when the real fun will start, Rupe."

Rupert raises an eyebrow, as if in challenge; Oliver grins back at him. They're like schoolboys, the two of them. And this is the man that I need to make fall in love with me by sunrise.

"Ladies and gentleman, boys and girls." A voice is coming from the sky, shaking the leaves from the trees like a deity addressing us through the clouds. I clutch at Oliver's arm and he laughs. "It's just the microphone," he says, pointing towards the gazebo tucked into the corner of the garden. It has been trimmed of weeds since I last saw it, a fresh coat of white paint glistening wetly in the sunshine. "See?" There is a woman standing there, three girls behind her with their musical instruments.

"We are Flora and the Furies," the voice says. "My name is Flora. And these are my Furies. Are you ready to have a good time?" The crowd roars in response. "And a one, two, three," she yells, followed by a sudden burst of music. As it plays, she walks to the front of the gazebo, the sun hitting her face like a halo. She is tall, as tall as

Oliver, dark hair cut to her jaw, a short skirt showing off long, brown legs.

I feel Rupert shift beside me. "Jesus," he says. "She looks like . . ." He takes a deep breath, as if trying to control himself, but when he sees that I am watching him, he stands up straight, swatting his sadness away from him like an irritating insect. "What are you staring at? Why are you always *staring* at everyone, you fucking weirdo?"

I look away. I wish something terrible would happen to this man. *A sudden fall, a snapped neck, a—* I stop myself. These are Salka thoughts, wild and sharp. I must remember my place.

"I've never heard a voice like that before," Oliver says when the song ends. I hadn't even been listening.

"Don't you think she looks like . . ." George trails off.

"Looks like who?" Oliver asks, and neither Rupert nor George answer him. "Bravo," he calls out, raising a glass to Flora. "Thank you," she says, without shame. "Hopefully you'll like this next one too."

She begins to sing again, her voice crystal clear, achingly sweet. Sweeter than anything I have heard since I broke the surface.

That song.

"What is this song?" I hear someone ask. "It's most unusual."

And it is most unusual and I know it, I know it heart-deep. A song that my grandmother used to sing to us in the nursery, a song of mer-men and brave deeds and a war fought that would never be forgotten. A song of necessary death, of the courage that it takes to do what it is right. Trembling notes, hushed by water. *How does she know this song?*

I drift, barely noticing, towards the middle of the garden. Towards Flora.

"What is that girl doing . . ."

"Is she okay? She doesn't look . . ."

"But Oliver seems to like her so I . . ."

And then I am alone and I am dancing and I can't stop. I dance as if I am still beneath the surface, floating through water. The weightlessness of it, even with my pearls on. I did not know how lucky I was. I twirl, my skirt skimming around me in clouds (forest green) of silk (with silver flecks), and if I half close my eyes, I can pretend that my tail has returned to me, imagine that I can travel through the world without being conscious of every scalding step I take. *Why did I not appreciate it when I could?*

"Isn't she graceful . . ."

"I know, it's no wonder Oliver . . ."

"Even though . . ."

"Even though . . ."

Even though I have no voice. Even though my tongue has been torn out of my mouth and swallowed by a hungry woman. Even though I am a stranger who was found abandoned on the beach and there is no telling who I am or where I came from. These people don't care; all they want is to see me dance. So I dance.

The song ends, this Flora reaching the crescendo perfectly. I was the only person in the kingdom who could sing that note; it's beyond most mermaids' capabilities, let alone a human's. I come to a standstill instantly, staring at this woman while she sings my song with . . .

That is my voice.

Ice cold, and a song so sweet and paintings of a woman with a face like my own and a stranger before me with long legs, my stolen voice pouring out of her mouth.

"Well done, little one," the singer says, and I know somehow that only I can hear her. "I am proud of you."

"Grace."

Fingers pinching my upper arm, pulling me away. "Come with me," Eleanor says, pulling me into the bushes. I turn to find that Flora is gone from the gazebo stage, the Furies left playing instrumental music while other guests begin dancing. *I need to find her, I need to—*

"Hello there, Dancing Queen," Eleanor says. Her eyes are bloodshot, pink lipstick smudged on her front two teeth. It's clear that she's been drinking heavily, which is unlike her. She prefers to stay sober at these events, remain in control. *Women can't simply be good enough*, she had said to me one night, when everyone else had left after an exceptionally boisterous dinner party. She wasn't even talking to me, not really; I just happened to be there. *We have to be twice as good as the men just to break even.*

"Are you having fun? Are you enjoying all of this?" She waves back at the party. "I paid for it, you know. Every last thing in here was bought with my money. Not that anyone seems to care. *Ships are boring, Mother!*" she says, mocking Oliver. "No one ever cares about what I want." She is too close to me now, and I can smell wine on her breath. Her hair is mussed, the hem of her cream dress stained by the grass. "This is where I met Alexander, did you know that?" She looks at the garden again, as if remembering. "Right on that lawn. I was only thirteen years old, and I knew immediately that I would love him forever." She points at the sea. "And that's where I lost him." She doesn't say anything for a few minutes, standing with her back to me.

"Where are you from?" she says, spinning on her heel. "Answer me," she shouts when I remain silent, and I put my hands to my throat. *I can't talk, Eleanor. Remember?* "Enough of that." She grabs me by the shoulders, shaking me violently. "I know what you are. I *know*. He talked of a woman who danced like you. Who danced like she was gliding through the air. He wouldn't forget her, he wouldn't—"

I wrench my arm from her grasp. "He wouldn't forget her," she says again, and she begins to sob, a keening sound ripping from her gut, so primal it makes me feel unsteady. "You can't take my son from me too, I can't lose Oliver. I can't. I can't. Please." Eleanor falls to her knees, holding on to my skirt. "You can't take him away from me. I don't want to be alone. I won't survive."

I crouch down, thrusting her hands away from me. She barely notices as she curls up in a ball, heaving with sobs. The mighty Eleanor Carlisle, always in control, is disintegrating before me; she is like a perfect portrait of someone falling apart. Is this what happens to scorned women? *She's crazy*, we used to say about maids in the kingdom who pursued certain mer-men relentlessly, crying and asking too many questions about where their man was and who he was with and if he had talked to any other maid that day. I'm beginning to wonder if, when we call a woman crazy, we should take a look at the man by her side and guess at what he has done to drive her to insanity.

When I get back to the party, Oliver is gone.

And so is Flora.

I try to breathe but I'm beginning to panic. *(I don't have much time left.)* A burning sensation in my chest as if someone has struck a match to my lungs, a dry strike of flint against flint. *(I'm going to die tonight; I am going to dissolve into nothingness.)* I push my way through the crowds and I tell myself I'm searching for Oliver, but I realize that I am actually looking for Flora. *That voice . . .* My voice, it was *my voice.* How did Flora have my voice? And how could I have thrown it away? The only time I was ever happy under the sea was when I was singing, and I sewed my own mouth shut in the hopes that a boy I barely knew could kiss it open again.

I collapse behind a huge tree at the edge of the lawn. Hidden from sight, I rest my hands on my feet for a second. The pain is intense but at least it is real; it is something I can call my own. Night is stirring through the air, thickening with shadows. I can smell a metallic tang, a smell that is my constant companion these days. I touch my feet again, my fingertips coming away sticky. At least it is dark. No one will be able to see me bleed in the dark.

"Grace? It's me. George." A slight figure, the scent of tobacco. I hold my hands out, pleading with him to help me to standing. "What are you doing out here by yourself?" He waves his cigarette by way of explanation. "I'm not supposed to be smoking, my mother will kill me if she sees me. I really wish Eleanor hadn't insisted on inviting her." These humans and their lack of gratitude for their mothers. They seem only interested in women whose legs they can spread. George glances back at the party. "We should hurry. Have you seen the queue for the yacht? It's absurd. Oliver has gone already, he left with that singer. Flora."

Flora, I repeat silently. Flora with the beautiful voice. *My beautiful voice.*

A winding procession of people, snaking from the garden down the steps, a sharp turn along the beach until they reach the marina where the yacht is docked. Young men and women, pushing against us, faces flushed. "I thought Oliver's mother had the *Muireann* burned?" one girl says, then curses as she spills wine onto her cream dress. My heart hurts at the mention of my mother's name, said so offhand. As if it were nothing. "Wouldn't blame her, to be honest," another girl laughs.

The line for the yacht turns around a corner, the sea coming into view. The sky reaching away from us to stitch stars into its surface. I see Oliver. That woman, Flora, standing beside him. She whispers in his ear, looking back at me as if she knew I would be there.

Who are you? She puts a finger to her lips, as if telling me to be quiet, and I trip over the end of my dress. George's hand on my arm steadies me and I wish I could ask him to carry me, to take the weight off these ruined legs. I wish George had been the man I had rescued, that it had been him who I had traded my voice for. I might not love George, but I could live with him and be happy.

"Are you drunk? Is our innocent little Gracie *drunk*?"

"Give it a rest, Rupert," George says, but he takes his hand away from me quickly. "And you just cut the queue, by the way."

"Don't be so wet," Rupert rolls his eyes. He has a half-empty bottle of champagne in one hand, the other around the waist of a barely conscious girl. Her hair is covering her face, her skirt so short that I can see her black lace underwear. He turns to the people behind us. "Do you mind that I've joined my good mate George here, or would you rather be fucking bastards and insist I go to the back?" The two girls nervously murmur, *It's fine, don't worry about it, Rupert. Not a problem.*

"See?" Rupert says to George. He swigs from the bottle, the girl slipping from his grip like a rag doll. She doesn't move as she hits the ground, her legs akimbo, showing her secrets to the world. No one goes to help her.

"What a slut," I hear someone say. "And *what* is she wearing?"

"Oops," Rupert laughs as he looks down at her. "Someone has had too much to drink, haven't you, darling?" He drags the girl up, her head lolling on her shoulders. "Cordelia here and I are going to have a very fun night."

"That girl is comatose," George says. "You can't possibly—"

"You're not my fucking mother, George." Rupert walks away from us, carrying the girl over his shoulder, as if she were a prize he had collected. I remember Ling, her dark eyes, her newfound silence. How she now walks as if she has lead in her bones. Something stolen from her that can never be given back.

"Shit," George says under his breath. "Grace, I have to go after him. I can't let him—not again." He winces an apology at me. "Do you think you can walk the rest of the way by yourself?"

I wave him off, *I'll be fine.* He hurries after Rupert, yanking him back by the shoulder, Cordelia falling to the ground again. George kneels to help her, but Rupert grabs him by the lapels of his jacket, lugging him to standing and screaming in his face.

"Hello?" Fingers prodding into my back. "Hurry up, will you?" Inhaling through my nose when I take the first step without George's help, the pain bitter-sharp.

"Sorry, miss," a man in a peaked cap says when I finally reach the marina. "No shoes allowed on deck."

"Didn't you hear me?" he says when I look around, as if expecting Daisy or Oliver to come to my rescue and explain. "No. Shoes. On. Deck." He points to a container at the side of the ladder. "Put them in the wicker basket and you can collect them after the party, like everyone else."

I cannot take my shoes off, dancing blood across this boat like a seeping shadow, this boat that shares a name with my mother. *Muireann.*

"Come on," someone shouts. "What's the holdup? Get on the boat or go home, for fuck's sake."

I step out of the way. The guests boarding the yacht are all young, in their late teens and early twenties, I would wager, and their excitement is palpable. It is as if an infectious fervor is soaring within them at the thought of the night ahead, at the promise it holds. *This could be the night that everything changes*, you can imagine them thinking. Lovers, hand in hand, trailing kisses and sonnets from mouth to mouth. Young men, eyes hungering: *What about that one? No, look at the one next to her, the dark-haired one.* They estimate the beauty of each passing girl, weighing it up with their friends. Listing pros and cons as if it is their decision to make, that the girls' beauty will be determined by their opinions rather than objective fact, because they are men and a man's word is final. The girls, knowing the men are watching them but pretending to be unaware, performing a calculated innocence they have been told they must possess.

"Hey, you." The man guarding the ship asks me some time later, when I am the only one remaining on the marina. "Are you coming? Crunch time, little lady. I'll have to set sail without you otherwise."

I could go back to the Carlisle estate, limp upstairs and call for Daisy, beg her to give me more of her potion while she bathes my feet. I would try to thank her for everything she has done for me and wave good night, smiling as she leaves me to die in peace. What would she find of me when she came to wake me in the morning?

Bones and tides of blood smeared on the sheets? Or would I simply vanish, leaving no trace?

"Miss?" the man says. "I haven't got all day here."

I must do this. I cannot lose courage before the final test. My mother would have wanted me to be brave. I reach down, shedding my shoes, a soundless scream congealing in my throat when the leather hooks into my feet, stripping flesh with them. It is as if my bones know that these feet are not real, and they are eager to fall away from me.

"Jesus," he says, stifling a gasp. "What have you done to yourself? Do you need me to call a doctor?" *No. No doctors. They cannot help me.* "I can't let you onboard like that, miss," he says. "You need medical attention." I grab his hands in mine. *Please. I need to get on this boat named after my mother. Maybe there will be clues about what happened to her, about her relationship with Oliver's father. I need to know, I cannot die without knowing.* I point at his socks then at my feet. "You want my socks?" he asks, confused, and I nod. "But your feet. Miss, that's not normal." *I am tired of people saying I am not normal.* "You should—"

I sit on the floating walkway, dipping my legs into the water, the blood sizzling-fresh on the waves. I take one clean foot out, then the other, displaying them to him.

With an uneasy glance over his shoulder, he peels off his socks.

"I don't know why I'm doing this," he says as he gives them to me.

Maybe he too is used to doing as he is told.

The man tells me to call him "Captain," although he bears little resemblance to the man at Eleanor's dinner party, the one who believes in mermaids. This new Captain brings me to what he calls the "foredeck hatch," dragging an armchair into a corner where I can curl up, feet hidden beneath my dress. The *Muireann* is much larger than the boat upon which I saw Oliver for the first time. I imagine my mother here. Did she dance on this gleaming deck, smile at the staff in white uniforms, circulating with trays of champagne?

The atmosphere is hectic and overwhelming—do these humans never get tired of so much noise? I can hear the sound of broken glass, and young women are pulling dresses off over their heads so they can dive into the sea, their nubile bodies cutting through it like blades. Heads bobbing in the dark, and they look like Salkas as they wrestle their way up rope ladders, hair pushed back off their faces, dripping salt water. *It's so refreshing*, they say, *warm as a bath*, while their teeth chatter. Girls in their soaking underwear, swaying but not falling. This would not happen in the Sea Kingdom. My father would not tolerate it, especially not for the pure women born of his flesh.

No one is interested in me, tucked away in this corner, so I am free to study them closely. Drinking, dancing. Kissing. Couples going downstairs, the girls pretending to be reluctant. "I don't usually do this," they say, the boys urging them to: "Come on, baby." When they reappear, the girls are flushed, the boys buttoning up shirts with an exaggerated emphasis, looking around to see who has noticed them.

And Oliver. I have been unable to take my eyes off him, and yet I doubt he has even noticed that I am onboard.

He is sitting at the back of the deck, Flora opposite him. He is bending forward, his knees touching hers, but she leans away, as if there is no need to make any effort with him. Oliver looks happy, I realize. He looks the happiest I have seen him since the water claimed Viola for its own. Maybe this was what he needed all along. Someone to talk with, rather than at. The one thing that I could not give him, indeed the one thing I gave up so that he would find me attractive. Flora stands, holding five fingers up; Oliver's gaze following her until she disappears out of sight. He looks dazed, as if he had forgotten the rest of the world had existed until now. Then he sees me and my stomach drops, tightening with that sensation that I cannot name, the sensation that only Oliver gives me, still, *still*. My body is a traitor.

"Grace," he says, walking over to me. "I didn't notice you there. Are you having a nice time?" He takes a glass from a passing waiter, but doesn't thank him. He rarely thanks the staff, I've observed. All the little things that I have ignored about this man in order to make the narrative of true love and destiny fit. I tried to make him as perfect as I needed him to be.

"What a night this has been," he says. "I can hardly believe it. And the band was the highlight, weren't they? I only hired the Furies because one of the servants said that he had seen them at a fête last year. I could have so easily hired another band. And then I wouldn't have met Flora. You know who Flora is, don't you?" he asks me. "The girl with that extraordinary voice." *My voice.* Is Oliver really trying to tell me that he's fallen in love with a girl who has *my* voice? "Tall girl, short hair." *Looks like Viola*, I want to add. *You do remember Viola, don't you, Oliver?* "She's wonderful, Grace. She's so smart and interesting, and she's funny. You rarely meet girls who are funny, do you?"

Maybe because girls have been trained to laugh at boys' jokes rather than make any of their own.

Flora is interesting and smart and funny, whereas all I have to offer is my face and my body. And if he does not want that, then what use am I? I am a shiny ornament to be displayed and admired, but not to be touched. All I have ever wanted was to be touched by someone who loved me.

"And you know what, Grace?" Oliver continues. "I have you to thank for this."

Me?

"It's true." He laughs at my astonished expression. "You've only been here such a short time, but I feel . . ." He runs a hand across his jaw while he searches for the correct word. "*Settled* now that you are here. Does that make sense? It was as if you were left on that beach for me to find, like the heavens sent you to help me recover. You have given me back my confidence. I know that you only ever want what's best for me."

I clear my throat. In that moment, I do not want what is best for Oliver. I want to slit his throat with a rusty blade, watch him fall to the deck and bleed out before me.

"Hello." Flora has returned. Up close, she is even prettier than I had thought. Perfect white teeth in a full-lipped smile, clear skin. "Apologies for taking so long, the queue for the loo was horrifying." Her speaking voice doesn't sound like mine, though; it is lower. More husky. *Sexy*, Rupert would say if he were here. She holds out a hand to shake mine. "I'm Flora," she says.

"Don't expect much in the way of conversation from Grace," Oliver says, elbowing me as if I am one of the boys. "She's more of the silent type."

"Grace?" Flora raises an eyebrow at me. "That's your name now, is it?"

"That's what we call her," Oliver says, adding sotto voce, "she's a mute, poor thing. My mother and I have taken her in at the estate." My hands curl into fists at my sides. As if I am a stray dog that they have rescued. An animal that can be easily cast aside again, when they grow bored of me.

"Well," Flora says, grazing her hand across my shoulder, an indistinct murmur of an electric current running between us. "It's very nice to see you, *Grace*."

"So," Oliver says, angling his body towards Flora, edging me out of the conversation. *That's rude, Oliver. Didn't your mother teach you any manners?* "You were saying before that—"

"That the uprising in the islands was essential? Yes, it clearly was."

"I disagree," Oliver says, as if that should be enough to shut down any counterarguments. I can imagine his parents reassuring Oliver that his opinions mattered when he was a child, sitting around the dinner table and asking their young son for his thoughts on the meal or his day at school. His voice would have been valued. I wonder if I would have been so quick to relinquish my own if I had experienced the same. "I don't think rioting is acceptable under any circumstances," he says. "Those people were just using the protest as an excuse to smash windows and loot whatever they could get their hands on."

"*Those people*? Are you serious?" Flora screws her face up at Oliver. "*Those people* owned the land long before you came, and *those people* have been treated abominably ever since. Do you expect them to wait politely while they're being shot down in the streets? I'm shocked they're not tearing the islands apart in fury; god knows they would have the right to."

I draw a breath in anticipation of how Oliver will respond to being challenged in such a public fashion, and by a woman at that. But he is quiet, his forehead creasing in concentration as Flora talks. "Yes," he says when she pauses. "I suppose you're right, Flora," and then: "That's a very good point, Flora, I never really thought about it that way."

The conversation moves from politics to music to literature to sports, Flora displaying an in-depth knowledge of each subject, as if she has spent years studying in preparation for this conversation. It's almost mystifying, her expertise. "You're so clever, Flora," Oliver says, eyes shining, and I want to scream. *What is it men actually want from us?* "How do you know all of this?" he asks. She cracks jokes that I do not understand, but which make Oliver throw his head back in laughter. People drift towards us, the group becoming larger and larger, but Flora remains the center of attention. No one can take their eyes off her. *She's so funny*, I hear people whispering. *And smart.* They stand in a circle around her, enthralled. And yet her eyes remain on me, as if this entire performance is for my benefit.

Who is this woman?

The evening plummets into night, the moon rowing across the ocean's skin. Voices spiking, people throwing words at each other but no one waiting for the replies. They are not having a conversation, these humans; they are merely delivering speeches, competing to see who can speak the loudest. The boat returns to the marina so a few guests can leave. Women with shoes in hands, makeup smeared down their faces as they stagger back towards the estate; some boys leaning over the side of the boat, vomiting. Two women wait to disembark, both petite and pretty, and they keep stealing kisses from each other. I can't help but stare at them, openmouthed.

"What are you looking at?" one of them asks me.

Nothing. I turn away hurriedly, and I think of Nia. Is this all that she has wanted? The freedom to hold another girl's hand? Why had my father deemed such a simple act to be so terrible?

"Come on, Captain, just another hour."

"No," says the man whose socks I am still wearing, ignoring their protestations. "Time to go."

And go they do, one by one, until at last, it is only Flora, Oliver, and me remaining.

"Good night, Captain," Oliver says as that man goes downstairs, the crew following him. The captain tips his hat at Oliver as he passes. "Good evening, sir," he says. "Or good morning, I should say. The sun is nearly up."

The sun is nearly up, I repeat to myself, feeling oddly resigned. The sun is nearly up and it brings my death with it. I will never see my sixteenth birthday.

Why must you always be so passive, Muirgen? Cosima's voice whispers in my head. If Cosima were here, she would march over there, run her fingers through Oliver's hair, and plant kisses on his mouth. Cosima would not be in the shadows, waiting for night to claim her for its own. But I am tired, so very tired. I don't want to have to fight anymore. My sisters might want me to rage against the sky tilting with light, beckoning a new day forward with fingers of streaking pink, but I don't have the energy. I feel weaker as the air gets brighter, wrapping itself around me, bending me transparent. I already feel as if I am dissolving.

Oliver leans closer to Flora. A question is asked. She nods. And a decision made. Her hand reaches out to his, leading him downstairs to where the bedrooms are. Just before she disappears around the corner, she turns. *Come*, she mouths at me, crooking her finger to beckon me forward. There is a glint in her eyes, something between mischief and malevolence, and I am shaken out of my lethargy. I stand up to follow—but I fall to the floor instantly, my feet buckling beneath me. And they are gone.

"What do we have here?" A harsh voice, slurring at the edges. "Gracie. All alone. That's not like you. Where has your master disappeared to? Doesn't he know that it isn't safe to leave his pets unattended?"

Rupert smells of anger and alcohol, his mouth streaked with the remnants of another woman's lipstick. If it were George, I would smile, hand him a handkerchief to clean his face. But I do not dare do so with Rupert. I have seen with my own father how dangerous certain men can become when they think you are laughing at them. They always want to punish you for it. "Grace? Are you listening to me?" he says, and I shrink away, pressing my body into the couch.

"What?" he says. "I'm not who you were hoping for? That happens a lot with me, I'm afraid. Everyone wants the dashing heir to the Carlisle fortune. My deepest apologies for disappointing you." He bends low, as if curtsying to me. "Or were you looking for George? No luck there either; George took Cordelia home. So chivalrous, is our friend George." He breaks off into a high-pitched voice and says, *"I won't allow you to take advantage of another girl, Rupert, it's not right."* Rupert laughs. "He did leave me in rather a bind. No other woman at this party was in as, ah, *acquiescent* a mood." He leans against the bow, watching me. *(Tell us the nymph-tale of the Big Bad Shark, Grandmother, that's my favorite, and the mermaid with the red ribbons in her hair. The shark and his sharp teeth. "All the better to eat you with, my maid.")*

"You look sad—sad that Oli's got a new playmate? She looks disconcertingly like Viola, I have to say. The perfect fucking couple," he seethes. "That's why I wasn't on the boat that day, little Gracie. I couldn't stand the idea of spending yet another afternoon with them, watching him slobbering all over her. Everyone pretending that they were so well suited when she was too good for Oli, she was *always* too good for him. She could have taken over the world if she had wanted to. She graduated first in her class, did you know that?"

I did not. Mermaids were not permitted to attend school in the kingdom. *A waste of time*, my father said. For what need would wives and mothers have of education? We would have our husbands to do our thinking for us.

"And Oli, he just . . ." Rupert's jaw tightens. "If he weren't a Carlisle, then Viola would never have even looked at him. Money and power, that's the only thing you whores seem to care about." He stares at me as if only just remembering that I'm still there. He crouches down. "Is that why you liked him too?" My heart feels as if it is pumping too much blood into my body; it is ferocious. "So odd," he says, grabbing my arms and dragging me to standing. "The way we found you on that beach, nearly a year to the day after Oliver washed up there. That's what happened to his father too. Isn't that a coincidence? Alexander's boat was wrecked, and when they found him, he was raving about a girl who saved him. *A girl who came from the sea*, Oli's old man said. He named this boat after her, the story goes. The *Muireann*." He pushes my hair back and my throat clenches at his touch. I don't want him anywhere near me. "Utterly mad, of course, and there was a lot of talk. You know how people like to gossip. Eleanor put him in that mental hospital to try and stop it, and Oliver never forgave her. Jesus, he wouldn't stop banging on and on about it, it got boring pretty quickly. What did he expect Eleanor to do? His father was a raving lunatic and she had to make sure Alexander wouldn't do any damage to himself." He snorts. "Or to the Carlisle name. She's canny, that Eleanor. But there was no keeping Alexander Carlisle locked up."

I can't move, my legs lifeless as a statue. I'm trapped here with Rupert, forced to listen. "Poor old Alexander Carlisle went back to the sea and he drowned himself." *Oliver's father took his own life?* Why did he not tell me that? "Giving Eleanor free rein to run the company and Oliver the perfect excuse to act like an asshole for the rest of his life."

There is a silence and he rubs his hand across his face. "Anyway," he says. "Enough of that. The past is in the past. It's just you and me now, isn't it? Whatever shall we do to pass the time?" His hand trails down my arm, then onto the skirt of my dress, inching it up a little. "Don't be so coy," he says. "I've seen the way you look at Oliver, like you're a bitch in heat. There's no need to pretend that you're some innocent virgin." He presses his lips against my ear, sticking the tip of his tongue into it, like Zale used to, and my stomach flips over, pushing vomit up my throat like a promise.

My mouth is open, searching for my voice—*please. Please help me.* But there is no help coming, and no sound save for Rupert's heavy breathing. He backs me into the wall, pressing his body against mine until my spine feels like it might crack. Undoing his belt, and a silent sob breaks from me at what is to come. He will finish what Zale started. "You'll like this," he says. A hand reaching down, pulling up my skirt, Rupert's fingers prodding that new place between my legs. *No. No.* But I cannot speak and worse, I cannot move. I am motionless, petrified, watching this man as he takes my body and does what he wants with it. My words are trapped tight in my throat, frozen, turning my limbs to stone.

Little mermaid.

Rupert is grunting, fumbling. He will take what he wants from me and he will destroy me as he does so.

Be brave, little mermaid.

Brave? I push Rupert off me, and he trips, trousers caught around his ankles. "You tease," he says. I turn left, right, the frenzy of dread making me clumsy and stupid, running to the end of the boat, but there is nowhere for me to escape to—unless I dive into the sea as cleanly as if I were diving into my nightmares.

There will be no protection there. The Sea Witch told me, she warned me. *There is no going back.*

Little mermaid, we are here.

Where are those voices coming from? Am I going mad, like Oliver's father? Is my sanity as lost to me as my voice is? Will they find me knee-deep in salt water, knuckle-white, mouthing words I will never be able to hear again?

"Where do you think you're going?" Rupert says, pulling his trousers up. He is walking towards me, oh so slowly. He is in no rush. He is standing in front of me now, his lips almost touching mine. He leans in to kiss the bare skin of my throat, ignoring my uncontrollable shaking. "Just relax, Grace."

Little mermaid. The hissing words are louder now, demanding my attention. They sound . . . *wet.* I look over Rupert's shoulder to find dozens of eyes staring at me from the dead of the water. They emerge, green hair slicked back, mouths open. *The Rusalkas.* The fallen women with arms outstretched, ready for their prey.

"Whoa," Rupert says as I push him against the side of the boat, kissing him forcefully. "Easy, tiger." His tongue invades my empty mouth. "So strange," he mutters. "There's just nothing there . . ." I allow my fingers to dip beneath the waistband of his trousers as I saw Flora do to Oliver earlier, and Rupert relaxes, his grip softening just enough for me to gather my strength. For I am Muirgen, daughter of Muireann of the Green Sea. I am Gaia, of the earth. And no one treats me in such a manner.

"Jesus!" His face gnarling in wide-eyed panic as he falls, his arms flailing for something to grab on to. The cry as he hits the water, hard, his body flinching. He resurfaces in a splashing fury. "You little—"

Then he sees the first Rusalka and his double take of shock is nearly comical. These are creatures that he has not given credence to since he was a small child on his mother's lap, listening as she spun stories to help him sleep. Monsters or mermaids? Maybe the Rusalkas are both. And maybe, in the end, they are neither.

Salka by Salka, they rise from the water, surrounding him in a circle, baring pointed teeth.

"Grace. Grace, help me. Get someone," Rupert begs. *"Anyone!"* he shouts when I stay where I am. The Rusalkas pull a tighter ring around Rupert, wrapping their arms around each other's shoulders, heads thrown to the skies, music slashing from their throats. A song of betrayal, of broken promises. Jilted brides, and babies torn from wombs, and imprisoned girls put to work in institutions, locked away by men who were supposed to be holy, men who told those same girls that they must atone for their sins of lust. (*Tell me about your impure actions, my child*, they whispered in dark corners, trying not to drool with anticipation. *Tell me in great detail about what you have done, and I shall grant you absolution.*)

Rupert is weeping as their song turns to a searing shriek, the windows in the yacht shattering and falling in shards of glass around my feet. Blood dribbles down Rupert's nose and his eyes start to cry tears of blood too. One of the Salkas breaks rank, Rupert's head between her clawed hands, licking his tears away, red tarred across her mouth. Then he screams no more.

I slump to the ground, shaking, my legs too weak to hold me any longer. What would I have done if the Salkas hadn't come to my rescue, if they hadn't smelled a bad man's rapacious appetite? I was so stupid to come here, to give up everything that I have ever known, ever loved, in an attempt to seduce a human man. A man I didn't know, a man that I had seen once and decided would be the answer to all of my problems.

Perhaps my father was right. I am just a stupid little mermaid.

My hands touch my throat. I will never hear my voice again. I stare at the sky. The light is turning and the moon slipping, calling her lover, the sun, to take her place. I use the rail at the side of the boat to drag myself to standing again and I begin to cry. I have no words in this world above the sea, but I will spell out the alphabet with my tears.

A head in the water (Have the Salkas come back?), then another. And another, another, another. No green manes this time, but clean skulls, hair plucked as finely as the kitchen maids pluck a chicken for yet another one of Eleanor's interminable parties. I strain to see, waiting until they swim closer and I can see features etched on those pale faces. Eyes so blue and lips so red. And then I realize who these maidens are.

"Muirgen," one of them says, and I squint at her to figure out that it's Talia. I had forgotten how homogeneous the mer-folk could appear. My father wants us all to look the same, act the same, think the same, and I just accepted that as natural. Why did I never understand how boring it was? And how stifling? Why did none of us realize that there could be strength in our differences as much as our similarities? "What have you done to yourself?" Talia asks when she sees me, her eyes wide in horror.

"You've caused so much trouble," Arianna says. "Father is furious. He and Zale have been planning—" She looks over her shoulder as if expecting our father to be there, like all of us do. "But he's right, of course," she says. "The Sea King is always right. For he is wise and good. We are fortunate to be living in the time of the Sea King."

My sisters are thinner, the bones pronounced in their faces. They're nervous, speaking quickly and yet choosing their words with a deliberation that is unusual. I look past them, searching for the other face that I want to see before I die. "Grandmother is not here," Sophia says, understanding instantly. "She would have felt obliged to tell Father, and there's no telling what he might do if he heard we went to the Sea Witch."

You went to the Sea Witch? I shake my head. I cannot believe my sisters would do such a thing.

"Our father would be right to be angry," Cosima says. "What would he think if he knew we had left the Shadowlands looking as we do? His daughters, *ugly*."

They're not ugly, exactly, but they do look rather strange. Huge eyes in pale faces, veins skimming blue over fine-boned skulls. *Why have you done this to yourselves?* I touch my own head, then point at theirs in question.

"Oh, Muirgen," Sophia says. "It's true what Ceto said. You have sacrificed your voice." Her own quakes as if she's holding back tears. "How could you do such a thing?"

"Forget her voice," Talia says, trying to peer over the side of the boat. "I want to see these human legs that you so desired." I wave her off, humiliated at the thought of my sisters seeing my ruined feet. "I cannot understand the fascination myself when our tails are beautiful."

"She was in love," Cosima says, her eyes downcast. She says it oh so quietly, as if she has come to a new understanding. That love is painful, love is someone harrowing out your chest and throwing your heart away as if it is of no value. *I know,* I want to tell her. *I know why you did it. I know that you sent me to Ceto because you wanted me out of the way.*

"Yes, she was," Sophia says. "Love can make you foolish."

"And what do you know of love, sister? You're not even betrothed," Talia says to Sophia. "Not like . . ." She looks at Cosima and she falters. "Not like Nia and Marlin," Talia rushes on. "They're perfect for each other."

Nia's weak smile, wobbling when Talia isn't looking. I remember those two girls on the boat, their obvious delight in each other. I wish I had my voice. *You are not unnatural*, I would tell her. Love is never unnatural, no matter whom you decide to give it to.

"Oh, Muirgen," Talia continues. "It has been such a mess these four weeks since you left us."

"A complete disaster," Arianna says.

"Yes," Talia says, frowning at Arianna. "There were many rumors at the beginning. Father was furious with Grandmother. He said that she had neglected her duties, he said . . ." She wavers, unable to repeat the words that the Sea King chose to berate our grandmother with. *Grandmother is in trouble because of me.* "He had the right to be angry, of course."

"Yes," my sisters chorus, and I cringe. Was I like this too when I lived in the kingdom? "Praise the Sea King."

"Father initially thought that you had been kidnapped by the Salkas," Talia tells me. "Zale left with a band of warriors, capturing the first greenhead they could find and strapping her to the dining table in the palace with rinds of seaweed." I can picture it, a group of men surrounding the struggling Salka.

"She was livid," Arianna says. "But she confessed in the end, told us that you had . . ."

"That you had gone to the Sea Witch *voluntarily*," Talia says, her forehead creasing, as if my reasons for doing so remained incomprehensible to her.

I remember the night I left, the utter despair driving me forward to the Shadowlands, any destiny preferable to the one awaiting me in the kingdom. Even death. Talia would never understand.

"And you asked her to give you two human stumps to walk upon the earth with." Talia takes an unsteady breath. "Father was so *angry*," she whispers.

"Sisters," Nia says, one hand over her eyes as she faces the horizon. "We do not have much time left. There is perhaps fifty minutes before the sun has fully risen."

"Muirgen," Sophia says, and tears prick my eyes at the sound of my own name. I did not think I would hear it again before I died. "The five of us went to the Sea Witch and we begged for her help. She has granted mercy on us." She gives a haunted smile and dread creeps over me. *What did the Sea Witch do to them?* "Granted mercy on you, I mean," Sophia finishes.

"We had to give her our hair, though," Cosima mutters.

"I don't know why you're the one complaining," Talia says. "It was your idea to go to the Sea Witch in the first place. You said that she was the only one who could help us, that no one else would know how to save Muirgen."

Cosima meets my gaze shamefacedly, and I feel as if she is trying to tell me something. An explanation of sorts. An apology. An image of the two of us as small children, hand in hand, flashes in my mind, sparkling with a beautiful intensity. I look away, allowing it to shatter. Too much has happened now. There is too much to forgive, and I am afraid I do not know where to begin.

"So, yes, we went to the Sea Witch," Talia continues. "What an expedition! I don't know how you went alone. It was very brave of you." She looks at me with something akin to admiration, an expression I am unused to seeing on my sisters' faces. "But Ceto wasn't as terrifying as we thought," she says, the rest of my sisters nodding in agreement. "It seemed like she wanted to help us, actually. We had to sacrifice our hair, of course. But she granted us this in return." She lifts her hand out of the water, her fingers grasped tightly around the hilt of a dagger, steel glittering in the growing morning light. It is the same weapon that I saw in the Sea Witch's cabin, the one she used to stir the magic potion with. "This is going to save you."

How?

"You must go to this man," Sophia tells me, as if reading my mind. "Immediately."

And what should I do when I find him?

I am so tired.

"Muirgen. Muirgen, listen to me. When you find him . . ." Sophia says, demanding my attention. "Gaia, you have to . . ."

"You must take the blade," Arianna says with relish. She is our father's daughter, that one; she's always enjoyed a story with gore. "And rip the human's chest apart with it, using the tip of the blade to spear his beating heart. The blood that spills must drip onto those human feet of yours, and your scales will reappear, and then your tail. Like magic."

"Like magic," Talia repeats.

I picture myself doing as they have suggested, Oliver's eyes opening when the blade pierces his flesh, screaming for mercy. I take a step back from them, a hand over my mouth in case I am sick.

"This is the only way, Muirgen," Talia says.

"She will not be able to do it," Cosima says as I stare down at them in shock.

"You must," Sophia says urgently. "Muirgen, you *must*. This isn't about you any longer. Zale is gathering the troops, placing spears in the hand of every mer-man, child and grandfather alike. You . . ." Something crosses her face that I cannot decipher, but which leaves me chilled. "You don't understand what things have been like for us since you left."

"Zale is only doing what he thinks is necessary," Cosima says, but her usual defiance has been markedly dampened. "We are bonded now, Zale and I," she says to me, a quiver in her voice. *What will Zale do to you when he sees your bald skull?* She is thin and pale, like the others, but there is a light sprinkling of bruises down her arms. Nothing too conspicuous. Nothing that would draw attention. But I see it. And I know. *Oh, Cosima.*

"Forty-five minutes . . ." Nia says, still counting the seconds in the sky.

Talia swims closer to the boat, her hand holding the blade out towards me. *I cannot do this. You cannot expect me to commit such a deed.*

"Muirgen," Sophia says again when I bend over, hands pushed into my stomach as if I'm trying to prevent my body from falling apart. "Muirgen. We cannot return without you. Father has, he has . . ."

"Father has been very angry," Cosima says. They stare up at me, their eyes flat. And I wonder what the Sea King has done to them. Cosima grabs the blade from Talia and reaches as high as she can. "You must do this, Gaia."

"Forty-four minutes," Nia says.

I take the blade. The handle is made of onyx, encrusted with ink-black jewels that resemble octopus eyes. It would be easy to tear someone apart with this, follow the route of their spine. The weight of it in my hands is shocking, somehow; the power it suggests. I like it, I am surprised to find. *I want more of it.*

"We are sisters," Sophia says. "We need each other, Muirgen. We always have."

Yes. I am ready to do what must be done.

Chapter
⪻ 19 ⪼

T HE STAIRS CREAK as I steal downstairs, a shrieking wail in the silence. I inhale sharply in the rushing fear that I have failed already, that my footsteps will rouse the crew from their slumber, that they will rush out to find me with this blade in my hands. But nobody stirs. I take the rest of the steps gingerly. Toes to heel, toes to heel, the bones peeling away from one another, bursting through the flesh. The pain is so agonizing that for the first time since I became human, or whatever it is that I am now, I am glad that I have lost my voice. I would not be able to stop myself from screaming.

There is a small kitchen to the left, two bathrooms straight ahead, and then four other doors. The door to one of the rooms is open, showing rows of empty bunk beds. Snoring is coming from another, so I presume this is where the crew reside. Two other rooms. I try one handle and it is locked. I silently curse. What will I do if Oliver has bolted his door shut to ensure privacy for him and Flora?

Praying to the gods, both of the air and of the sea, I test the other handle. It gives way, the door swinging open into a large room. Cream carpet, dark oak paneling, an enormous bed. And there they are, Oliver and Flora, foreheads pressed against one another as if waiting to kiss while they dream. They are both naked, the bedclothes crumpled around them. Her long, lean legs unblemished, untouched. Perfect in a way that I will never be again.

My grip on the dagger tightens as I stare at Oliver. I have sacrificed so much for this man; I have given up my family, my home, my identity. I have mutilated my body, carving it into something unrecognizable, just so he will find me beautiful. Not even beautiful, but *acceptable*. And I was silenced forever in the name of "true love." I wish Grandmother had never told me those stories, duped me into believing that a *happy ever after* was possible for women like me.

Oliver sleeps on, his chest rising and falling, his face serene. He thinks he has nothing to fear. He did not even lock his door to safeguard his chamber, so sure is he of his own immortality. I imagine myself stepping forward, bloody footsteps all over the snow-white carpet, leaving a mark on this human world that they'll never be rid of.

I have the sensation of splitting in two, as if my consciousness is peeling away from my body, floating to the ceiling, and watching the girl below me. The girl with the broken feet and the broken heart. The girl with no voice. What a fool she has been.

Yes, Gaia, yes, I whisper to her. Do what you have to do. You will stand at his bedside, his back towards you. You raise the blade to the sky (It is heavy, is it not, little one? So heavy.) and then you force the blade into his back, twisting it, feeling the flesh solid. And you twist deep again, carving circles in his skin, pulling out gristly chunks of him. You will search for his heart, the heart that he would not give to you of his own accord. Still beating, that heart, but not beating for you, never beating for you, Gaia. And you will hold it to your mouth and you will eat his heart whole, swallowing it, pushing it deep down inside your stomach. It will beat there, a second heart. Oliver will belong to you then. Finally.

I breathe in, a rasp in my throat as the air searches my mouth and finds it empty. I can sense that I am settling back inside my body, like loose sediment sinking to the seabed after a storm. I look at him again. Oliver. Oliver . . . *What is Oliver?* Spoiled. Weak. Heartbroken. Damaged, yes. But loved—he is greatly loved. I think of George, his steadfast loyalty to Oliver no matter how badly he has behaved. Daisy, who has become like a sister to me and who would never believe this of the Grace she knows. And Eleanor Carlisle, who has lost so much. I remember that night in the room of the paintings. Her hopelessness felt too raw to be ignored. The women of my family have caused her enough pain; will I be the reason for more?

My hands hang by my sides, yet I do not drop the dagger. I kneel beside the bed. I stood still while the Sea Witch sawed out my tongue, and I thought I could still make him love me. *I had my face*, as the Sea Witch told me. I had my face and my lovely form. *What else could a man want?* I reasoned. I have been told to stay quiet for so long, to listen to the mer-men, and to be attentive and respectful. To know my place. I did not imagine that a human man would want much more from me.

And yet he did. His delight in Flora's wit and her intelligence, her ability to challenge him, to make him laugh, is evidence enough. Why didn't I realize that such things would be important? I brush my fingers across Oliver's forehead. I thought he would save me.

Oliver stirs, as if to shake my hand off him. *My name is Gaia*, I tell him. *I want you to know my real name, since you have never known the real me.*

I should leave before he wakes up. I should leave before I change my mind, before I decide to claim his blood to turn my own back to salt.

I look at Flora, her lovely face, so peaceful in her sleep. She really is unbelievably similar to Viola. It's uncanny. It's . . .

Her eyes open. A snap rather than a flutter, as if she had been merely pretending to sleep. Like she knew that I would be there.

"I've been waiting for you, little mermaid," she says.

Chapter

20

ERROR IS SCRATCHING its fingernails across my heart, searching for blood. Flora climbs out of bed. She does so with a languid grace that suggests she is used to being nude and sees no shame in it. I stare at her naked body—those long legs and brown nipples—frowning.

"Very modest of you," she says. "You have become accustomed to the human ways." She opens the chest of drawers in the corner of the room, rifling through its contents. "His-and-hers bathrobes," she says, as she wraps a white gown around her. "I wasn't sure this man could become more of a cliché, and yet here we are."

She is being very loud, I think as a wooden clothes hanger drops to the floor. *She will wake Oliver.*

"I wouldn't worry about that," she says. She walks to the other side of the bed, a hand to his forehead. Unlike when I touched him, Oliver does not move. His breathing becomes slower, his body dropping into the mattress as if he's sinking. "They always fall asleep afterwards; it's pathetic how little stamina they have. You didn't miss much with this one, I can assure you."

Miss much? What is she talking about?

"He was adequate," Flora amends. "Concerned with his own pleasure, and annoyed I didn't seem to think it all a great honor. Male fragility can be exhausting at times, can it not?" She sits on the bed, grinning at me.

"It is okay to be confused," she says. "Understandable, in fact."

How can she—

"I can hear you. There's no need to look quite so terrified."

These shattered feet unsteady as I stumble away from her, reaching for the door handle. Grasping it between my fingers. Twisting and twisting.

This door is locked. Turning back to her, almost blind with fear. *Did she lock the door?*

"Yes," Flora says. "I didn't want you running away from me before I could explain."

But how did you do that? I can't seem to breathe out properly, my inhale coming more quickly with each passing second.

Who are you? Are you— Are you Viola?

"Viola?" she says. "You think Viola has returned from her watery grave to haunt you?" Viola, sinking past me, arms flailing. "Is someone feeling guilty?" Flora asks me. "You gave her up so quickly, did you not, to save him?" *I did.* I let Viola drown, and I did so without a second thought. Shame prickles my skin, breaking out like a rash.

Who are you?

"You haven't guessed yet?" Flora presses two fingers to her throat, and the voice that emerges this time is different and yet familiar.

"Hello, Muirgen," she says, but it is me talking, my lost words coming from Flora's mouth. I am too stunned to try to run away, so I close my eyes, listening to that which I thought I would never hear again.

"Don't cry," my voice says. "Don't cry, little mermaid." Flora's features soften, melding into one another before they begin to melt away. It's like water on a canvas, washing away the paint. And what is beneath? A beautiful face, a full body, but there is no tail this time. Fat, luscious legs, beautifully shaped. Pearls wound through her hair, gleaming. It is her.

The Sea Witch.

"I've told you before, my name is Ceto," she says. "Don't be rude. What a relief to be rid of that . . . insipid body. I don't know how people pretend to be something they're not; it takes so much effort. That was always my problem, ever since I was your age. I didn't care about what people thought of me. I only wanted to be true to myself." She laughs. "Your father didn't like that, I can tell you."

My father would kill you, Sea Witch, if he had his chance. I push my back into the door, fingers still grasping the handle in the hope it will open.

"You think I am afraid of your father?" she says, smirking at my attempts to flee. "You think I live in the Shadowlands because I fear his strength? No, little one. I live in the dark because I can be true there, and living true is the most important thing any woman can do." She tilts her head to the side. "But it takes courage, and we are not taught how to be brave, are we? Women are taught to obey the rules." One of her hair ornaments shimmers, catching my eye. So many pearls. *One, two, three . . .*

"Thirteen," she says. "There are thirteen of them. More than any maid you have ever known, am I right?

The Sea King used to say that thirteen was unlucky, but he was just annoyed that I was the firstborn. My brother always did want to win at everything."

Brother. I stop fumbling with the door.

"You're catching on at last!" She claps her hands with genuine satisfaction. "He was a nightmare when we were growing up," she says. "I had more natural powers than he did, that was obvious from the very beginning. He hated me because he was the boy, and boys were supposed to be more powerful. When Papa died, and my brother got his hands on that trident, I knew my days in the kingdom were numbered." She stares at the ground, her face somber suddenly. "I overheard him talking war tactics with his cronies, boasting about how he was going to be the one to finally wipe out the Salkas. I loved my father, I did, but I never agreed with his policy of exiling the Salkas to the Shadowlands. It was only breeding fear in the mer-folk, resentment in the Salkas. And resentment cannot be contained forever."

So the Sea King sent his men to the Shadowlands . . . I prompt her impatiently.

"Yes," she says, "But even that wasn't enough for my brother. He was obsessed with blood purity, with all of us being the same. He wanted to exterminate them for good. You have to understand, the Salkas didn't want war. They were just defending themselves against the kingdom's attacks, but he didn't care. He would kill them all, and then me in my turn, I presumed, even if I was salt-kin. Powerful women are often threatening to insecure men." Her eyes darken. "So I left, stealing away from the palace in the dead of night, and I went to the Salkas. And I told them I would help them. So I know what it's like to leave my family behind me, little mermaid. We are not unalike, you and I," she says, and I don't know if that is supposed to be a compliment. "Although you were much younger than me of course. I was at least forty-five when I left. And it was fine"—she clears her throat—"living in the Shadowlands. I have had my poor Salkas to take care of, and I have had freedom. That's more than most mermaids can hope for."

Why did you let me do it? Anger is building inside me, caustic and sour. *And why did you come tonight and distract him when you knew it was my last chance of survival?*

"Would you really want a man so easily distracted?" she asks. "I barely had to try tonight. He was ripe for the picking."

Why did you help me? I need to know, my whole body tense as it waits for her to respond.

Her smile fades suddenly. "I failed your mother. I couldn't fail you too."

My mother. Two steps, and I am in front of her. I catch her by the throat, cat-quick. Squeezing hard, for I am not afraid of her anymore. I will have the truth, at last. *Tell me. Tell me everything.*

She removes my fingers, her touch gentle. "I knew Muireann of the Green Sea. Not very well. She was just a baby when both my brother and I were into our fortieth decade, but her father was a favorite of the court so she was in the palace often as a child. She was like you, that same red hair, that same beautiful voice. A sensitive soul." *You're so like your mother, young Muirgen. So like her in every way.* "My brother was obsessed with her, ever since she came of age at twelve." Ceto shudders. "He kept badgering Muireann's father for permission, and he was told to wait, that a few years wouldn't hurt. Your grandfather wasn't afraid of the Sea King. Mac Lir was too well respected in the kingdom to be bullied into submission."

But my mother agreed to marry the Sea King. To end the war.

"She came to me first, arrived in the Shadowlands demented with grief over her brother, demanding to know which of the Salkas had slain him. As if it was the Salkas' fault!"

But it was their fault. They killed Uncle Manannán,

and they did it with glee. It was their fault that all of this happened.

"You still believe that to be true?" Ceto says. "I don't know what happened to your uncle, but my Salkas swore to me that they had no knowledge of his death. It did seem rather convenient, I always thought. Manannán disappears, the person Muireann loved most in the world. People do funny things when they're grieving, don't they? And the Sea King knew what Muireann was like, he knew that she didn't have a taste for war. I think he bet upon her doing anything to regain peace in the kingdom."

I try to connect the jagged edges of her jigsaw, assemble them in a way that makes sense. *Is she saying that—*

"I'm not saying anything." She cuts across me. "All I know is that the Salkas just wanted to be left alone in peace to live their lives, and yet their mere existence was enough to inflame my brother." The Sea Witch exhaled loudly. "I tried to explain to Muireann that this war was not of my doing, nor of my desire, and thus I could not end it, no matter how hard she begged me. I did not know the measures she would take next."

She married the Sea King. I try to imagine her, fifteen and wild with sorrow, betrothed to a man old enough to be her father. *The poor little mermaid.*

"She was reasonably content for a time," the Sea Witch says. "She had children, you and your sisters. Word reached me in the Shadowlands of how much she loved you."

But not enough. It was bad enough, as a child, knowing my mother had been reckless. But since learning of her relationship with Alexander, it has become clear that she was heartless too. *My father was right all along. She did abandon us. She did.* The melancholy that has been my shadow since the day my mother left me tugs at my hand like a small child demanding attention.

"That's not true," Ceto says fiercely. "She didn't mean to fall in love with a human; she meant to save his life. There was an accident, you see, and Muireann found this man in the wreckage."

It was Oliver's father, wasn't it? The paintings, my mother's face replicated over and over again. Hair so red and eyes so blue.

"Yes," the Sea Witch says, watching me closely. "The shipwreck occurred a few months after you were born. The man, Alexander, found himself rescued by a beautiful woman. They were attracted to each other, certainly, and like so many before them they mistook their lust for love. My Salkas said they saw her regularly sneaking away to the surface after that to go and meet this man, all the way up to your first birthday. They had decided to make things more permanent when . . ."

When what? Tell me more.

"What else is there to tell? He wasn't good enough for Muireann either, this Alexander." She gestures at Oliver, still asleep. "This bloodline does produce weak men, but I've found that weak men are often attracted to strong women. In the beginning, anyway. In time they come to resent that same strength they professed to love. They try to put you back in your place." *Just like Eleanor said, in that room of paintings.*

Was it you? The questions are tearing through me. *Was it you who gave my mother legs, so she could seduce Oliver's father? Did you take her tongue as payment too?* I picture my mother traveling to the Shadowlands, her fear pressing her forward as my own has done. My mother, on a beach with Oliver's father, dancing rings of blood around him.

"No," Ceto says. "Muireann of the Green Sea had no need of such help from me."

I don't understand. I bang one of my fists against the door behind me in frustration.

"Muireann could do it herself. Your mother was able to shed her tail like a snake when she reached the shore, and transform back into a mermaid the moment that her temporary legs tasted salt."

What? I sink to the floor, pulling my knees into my chest. *You mean—*

"Yes." Ceto remains still. "Your mother had powers. Impressive ones, at that."

But that's impossible. I shake my head. *Muireann of the Green Sea was only a mermaid.*

"All mermaids used to have powers, Muirgen." Ceto hands me a towel to wrap around my feet. I hadn't even noticed the wounds had reopened, spilling their guts onto the floor. I look at them in disgust. *What I would give to have my tail back.* "The powers would develop the day we came of age, when our bodies decided that we were women now. But we were told such powers weren't *mermaid-like.* We were told that no mer-man would want to be bonded with us if we were more powerful than they were. They warned us that our powers made us too loud. Too shrill. And so women became quiet because we were promised that we would be happier that way. And our powers were lost. And it happened so quickly too. That which we take for granted can so easily be taken away from us, if we do not remain vigilant."

I reach out for something to steady myself, shooting stars bursting bright in my chest. *But not yours, Ceto? Your powers remained.*

She laughs, showing perfect teeth. "No, not mine. I was too stubborn for that."

And my mother? I feel a growing sense of pride, something I have never associated with my mother. *My mother didn't give up either?*

"Muireann was stubborn too, but she was better at hiding it than I was. No one even knew about her powers, especially not the Sea King. He would never have married her if he had been aware. But she only had enough powers for herself; she couldn't ensure the safety of all you six girls as well. That's why she came to me, begging for help again. She wanted to flee from your father and take you with her, onto land. But I could not perform that spell without extracting a price, like I did with you," Ceto says. "The magic is too deep for that. Muireann would not allow my blade to touch your flesh, nor that of your sisters. And so, she let Alexander go. And she returned to the kingdom. She wanted to be home in time for her baby's birthday, she said."

But we were told that—

"I see your sisters brought you the blade," she interrupts my thoughts. The knife is still clasped in my right hand. I hadn't even noticed. "I knew you wouldn't be able to do what was needed of you. You are too soft."

If you thought I was soft, why did you perform the magic?

If you were so keen to appease my mother's memory, why did you do the one thing to me that she didn't want you to do?

"Your mother did not realize how desperate her youngest daughter would become." The Sea Witch bends her neck to one side, then the other, and I listen to the cracking joints. "I believe she would have approved of my decision, or understood it, at the very least. And I hoped that Oliver would fall for you, I really did, but I told myself that if he did not, I would come back for you. I would offer you another way."

Another way? I am too tired to do more than stare at her sullenly. *I will die when the sun rises. You have doomed me to my death.*

"No," she says. "You have a choice."

What choice? I am not used to choices.

"You can go to the deck," she says, brightening at my flicker of interest, however reluctant. "As the sun begins to rise—and it will rise very soon, little mermaid, do not be mistaken; my powers cannot stop the day from turning over—you can take the dagger and pierce your own heart with it."

No. I feel winded, as if she has sucked all the breath out of me and left me panting for air.

"Your body will fall into the sea," she says, "where my Salkas will be waiting for you. They will take you to the Shadowlands. I will make the necessary preparations there." She bends down to where I am sitting on the floor and puts a hand on my hair with such tenderness that something unspools inside me, softly. "I will confess that it seems a shame to see this red hair turned green."

I shove her away from me. *I could never be a Salka.*

"And why not?"

(*The Salkas are different to you and I,* my father said, *they are not of royal birth. Do not mistake them for anything less than pathetic and vicious creatures that must be controlled at all costs.* My sisters and I nodding in agreement.)

I look at her directly to emphasize my argument. *The Salkas are ugly and angry and—*

"And don't they have something to be angry about?" Ceto says, her lip curling in disgust. "You think your life has been difficult, Princess Muirgen. You don't know the meaning of the word."

I try to stand, my hand reached out to her. Begging for leniency. *But the Salkas—*

"The Salkas are the jilted, the victims, the orphans, and the abused." Ceto's eyes flash in irritation. "They deserve your sympathy. It is a hard thing to be a woman in this world, whether beneath the sea or if you break the surface. You had a taste of that tonight, did you not?" (Rupert's hand around my throat, the other pulling at my undergarments, seeking his pleasure without permission. I don't think he would have enjoyed it as much if I hadn't struggled.) "The Salkas have endured much worse than that," Ceto continues. "There was no one there to hear them scream *no*. Or maybe there was, but that *no* wasn't deemed worthy of being heard. Maybe they heard it and they didn't care. A woman's *no* can so easily be turned into a *yes* by men who do not want to listen."

I picture myself up on the deck, raising the knife, stabbing it deep, vomiting blood through my teeth. My sisters screaming. *I can't do that to my own body. I cannot inflict any more harm upon myself.*

"Gaia," she says, using my real name for the first time. "I am not sure a return to your father's kingdom is a good idea. I told Muireann the same when she came to me on your birthday. I warned her. *Go to Alexander*, I said, *and I will find a way of getting the children to you afterwards.* I promised her that I would find a way, and yet she went back to the kingdom's nursery anyway. She couldn't bear the thought of missing your birthday, I would wager. That was her mistake." Ceto takes a deep breath. "It was her last mistake. My brother made sure of that."

What do you—

Wait. Wait.

My father, his spear finding the nearest fish. Watching as it squirmed to death on a splinter-point. *Do you know what I do to little mermaids who fall in love with humans?*

"Yes," Ceto says, as I curl into the fetal position on the floor. I don't want this to be true, and yet somehow, deep within me, I think I had always known this was the case but I couldn't admit it. It was too dangerous to do so. "Your father is a proud man," Ceto says. "He would have rather seen her dead than in love with someone else."

Did my . . . did my grandmother know?

"Your grandmother is afraid," Ceto says gently. "She has always been afraid. She suspects that the Sea King might have played a hand in it, just as she suspects that Manannán's death might have been more complicated than was presented to her. But she doesn't ask too many questions or seek to know too much. It is safer for her that way."

Stop talking. I can't listen anymore. My hope breaks inside me, blistering, setting me aflame. I am bent double with the grief, my body heaving with silent sobs. My mother is dead and at the hands of my father. My mother, and everything she sacrificed for us. My mother, who only wanted to protect us. *She came back for my birthday. She came back for me.* And my father told us she didn't love us. He said that she was a bad mother, that she abandoned us. He let us believe that we were easy to abandon, because that kept us small. Scared. Easy to control. Something hardens inside me, and I allow it to happen. Nay, I welcome it. I will be hard. I will be made of ice. *He allowed us to believe that it was our fault.* I raise my head and meet the Sea Witch's gaze.

I am angry, Ceto. I have never felt so much anger. Are you happy now?

"Tick tock, little mermaid," she says. "Time is running out." She takes my hands in hers. "Like all women, you have the power within you, no matter what your father has led you to believe. Do you trust that power, Gaia?"

I have never had autonomy before. Besides going to the Sea Witch, I have always just done what I was told to do. It seemed easier that way. Safer. Maybe I was like my grandmother, looking away to remain comfortable.

"You will be safe with us," Ceto says, "Join us, I implore you. Join the true sisterhood in your mother's name. You can help us achieve peace, once and for all, by ridding the kingdom of your father and his army of rapacious mer-men. We can show the women how to reclaim their powers. They're still there, in every one of them, just buried so deep that they think they are lost forever. But we can teach them. That can be your legacy, Gaia."

If I join the Salkas, what does that mean? I am
Muirgen, daughter of the Sea King. I am Gaia, the mermaid who wanted so much and who looked up and who
fell in love with a boy. And I am Grace, the girl dancing
on shattered toes, smiling through the pain as if it were
nothing.

Who am I now?

"Who are you?" Ceto repeats my thoughts. "I would
wager the more important question is: Who *will* you be?
Who are you free to be now?" She sniffs the air, her
head snapping up. She smiles. "Right on time."

What? I look up too, as I have always done, but I don't
know what I am searching for now.

"A storm is brewing," she says. "Are you ready to sing,
little mermaid?"

Chapter

⤳ 21 ⤳

*T*HE BLAZING SKY bounces off the flat sea, rolling it purple. It is beautiful, this world. Why did I never fully acknowledge just how beautiful it was? I was so anxious to make Oliver fall in love with me so that my "real" life could begin, I forgot to stay still and appreciate what was around me. Just for a second, I breathe in the burning air, tasting the hint of coming sunshine on my tongue. I can hear my sisters talking amongst themselves.

"Where is she?"

"There is little time left."

"I told you that she wouldn't be able to do it."

"Do be quiet, Cosima."

"Don't tell me to be quiet, Talia."

"Sisters, *please*. This is not the time nor the place for these petty arguments."

I smile, despite myself. They never change, my sisters. Will they continue to fight in such a manner as the years pass? When Nia marries Marlin and the rest are sold off to the highest bidders? After their mer-babies are born, children I will never meet? Children I will never bear. Maybe becoming a mother would have made up for being motherless. Maybe it would have made me happy. But in the end, I can only wish that my sisters will be happy in my stead.

I wish for them only sons.

I close my eyes and I think of my mother. How she tried to save us, *she came back for us*, and was killed for her efforts. And I think of my father.

He waited for her by the rocks that are closest to the human world, slippy with sea moss and mussels, the Sea Witch told me. My mother had tried to conceal her fright when she saw him. *I was just going for a swim before Gaia's birthday*, she told him.

I know what you did, he replied, and he kept saying it until she admitted the truth.

But I can change, she said, *I've learned my lesson*. My mother would have started to beg then, for mercy. For her children. *It's too late*, the Sea King said as he took his trident. And he broke her spine with it.

I can hear screaming now, my sisters' voices reaming the air apart. The shrieking obscures any semblance of intelligible sentences; it is but a jumble of words, made up of *no* and *please* and *sorry* and *don't hurt us*. And *Father. Father. Father.*

The Sea King has come for us. That man does not deserve the name of Father, he who fastened strings into our hands, made us dance like marionettes. He murdered our mother and made us believe that she chose to leave us behind.

"What is the meaning of this insubordination?" the Sea King asks, and even now, the sound of his voice causes me to cast my eyes down, crouch my shoulders inwards, trying to show him that I am not a threat.

No more. I force myself to stand up straight. I will not cower before this man for a moment longer.

"We're sorry—"

"We didn't mean to—"

"But we just thought that maybe if—"

"Silence," the Sea King roars from the water. "What kind of maids are you, to disobey your father in such a way? Have you no loyalty? No gratitude for all that I have done for you?"

My sisters whimper in response. Someone is weeping hysterically, Cosima, I do believe, and I hear the sound of flesh meeting flesh, a savage clap, and a cry. *How dare he hurt another one of us?* "I told you to be quiet," he says. "Don't say that I didn't warn you."

I creep closer, making sure that I am still hidden from sight. I sit at the edge of the boat's hatch deck where the Captain brought me earlier, peeking around the wooden bow. My father is there, with my sisters, and he looks smaller than I remembered somehow, his tail submerged in the water, his hair more gray than I have ever seen it.

"What have you done to yourselves?" he says, rapping his knuckles against Talia's bald head. She recoils, then that learned blankness paints her face, stripping away any fear or hurt. Making her pretty again, the way our father prefers. "Where is your hair? Is this some sort of joke?"

"We wanted to save Gaia—"

"Do not call her by that name. It is cursed," he says. "That's what your mother wanted to call her. And look how she ended up."

I watch them, each face in turn, and I see reflected in them what I know to be true in myself. They try to hide it, but I can see it in their eyes. *If my mother didn't love me*, they wonder, *then is there something wrong with me? I am broken. My fault. My fault.*

We blamed ourselves. We hated our mother. And none of it was true.

"All I've ever asked from you is that you look pretty," my father says, "and you smile when asked to. Is that so hard? Is it? Why must you all be so useless?"

Leave them alone, I think, my hands curling into fists. I am spoiling for a fight.

"What was that?" the Sea King says, turning around to look at the boat. "Who said that?"

Leave. My. Sisters. Alone, I think again, and the words are seeping out of me, booming, reverberating in the wood of this yacht and soaring into the morning air. *It is my voice.*

"Muirgen," my father says, looking around to find me. "Muirgen, where are you?"

I do not move, my fingers at my throat. My voice has come back to me. My feet don't hurt anymore either, I realize. Has Ceto cast another spell, unbeknownst to me?

"Muirgen," the Sea King says, and his voice drops dangerously low. "If you don't show yourself immediately, I am going to scalp your sisters, one by one."

A low cry, swallowed back. My sisters are afraid, exactly as he wants them to be. He only feels like a true king when we are scared of him. "You wouldn't want that on your conscience, now would you, my sweet?" he says, the sound of the trident banging against the side of the boat, once, twice.

My father is getting impatient. He is so accustomed to us obeying him instantly; he does not know what it means to wait. "Which one is your favorite, Muirgen?" I peek again and see him grabbing Sophia by the neck, twisting her against him so he has the trident at her heart. She doesn't whimper, like my other sisters would have, but simply stares at the sky as if praying for divine intervention. "Beg her to come out, Sophia," the Sea King says. He is whispering into her ear, and yet somehow I can hear him perfectly, despite my distance from them and Cosima's relentless sobbing. "Tell your baby sister exactly how afraid you are right now."

Release her. I stride to the side of the boat, staring down at the Sea King and my sisters. I am not afraid, and my father can see that; it is as if he has a sixth instinct for our fear. This is not what he has been expecting. *Release her, I said.*

"Sister," Talia says, her eyes huge. "Sister, how are you talking without moving your lips?"

"Shut up, Talia," my father says, and Talia's face pinches. "No wonder no man has asked for your hand yet; you never do anything but yap."

Do not talk to my sisters like that. My voice is louder, and I find that I like the sound of it. *Did you hear me, old man?*

"Muirgen?" my father says, "Muirgen, how dare you tell me to—"

How dare I what? I thought I told you to shut up.

My sisters stare up at me, openmouthed. This is not how we have been trained to behave.

Cosima. She is still wailing, her hand covering her crushed face. *Cosima, it will be okay.*

"Stop that nonsense," my father turns and roars at her, ignoring me. "All you're good for is your pretty face—do you want to ruin that too?"

We're all worth more than that.

"Excuse me? You're worth more than what?" the Sea King asks, his face flushed with rage.

Worth more than our pretty faces. (I remember Eleanor's warning about beauty fading, and how she would have made her daughter strong, and I know my mother would have done the same, if she had been given the chance.) *You needed us to stay quiet, and scared, didn't you, Father? You pitted us against one another, forced us to compete with one another—and for what? Because you were afraid of what would happen if we worked together? Of how strong we could be?*

"Strong?" he spits. "You? Daughters are not meant to be strong."

Our mother wanted us to be more than your pawns, didn't she? We meant so much to her that she was willing to sacrifice her freedom to be with us. My whole life, all I have had is my hope that maybe my mother was still alive, that maybe she was waiting for me to find her and rescue her. That hope is gone, but truth is mushrooming in its place, spreading its hands out to feel the sides of my body. I could climb onto the side of the boat, balance on the railing with my hands to the sky. Take me, gods, I would shout, for I am no longer afraid. Take me and do what you will with me.

"How dare you?" my father says. His left eye is beginning to twitch; I'm making him nervous. "And do not mention that woman in my presence again. She was a slut. She deserved her fate."

Her fate? What fate would that be, Father?

"Oh," he says, sneering at me. A flash of anger spikes through me. He will regret that. He will regret all of this. "Have you forgotten about what the humans did to her? The humans you love so much, the humans that you have abandoned your sisters for." He brandishes his trident at them, and they grovel. "The humans took your mother. They destroyed her."

I laugh, a humming sound vibrating at the base of my throat until it explodes out of my mouth. It blasts against the water, charging waves like a tsunami against my father. He is left spluttering, wiping salt from his eyes, attempting to battle the water away from him with his trident. He should know at this stage that the sea always wins.

"How are you doing this?" he says. He is frightened. For the first time in my life, I have made my father frightened.

Looks like you're not the only one with powers.

"Gaia," Sophia asks, ashen. "Gaia, what's—"

Don't be afraid, sisters. I hold my hands up, so they will see that I am no threat to them. I want to protect them, to empower them. We are women. And women are warriors, after all.

"You should be afraid," the Sea King says, but he licks his lips nervously. "Your sister has gone mad. The time with the humans has rotted her brain." He picks up his trident. "We will retire to the kingdom and leave her here."

I can see Nia mouth, *Ten minutes, Gaia.*

Why don't we have a conversation about the humans, Father? Since you brought it up, after all. I lean forward against the railing, resting my chin on my closed fist, the very picture of nonchalance. *I'm sure my sisters would love to hear all about them. One in particular. Alexander Carlisle.*

"Girls." He grabs Sophia and Cosima by the back of the neck, snarling at the others to follow him.

Not so fast. I narrow my eyes, feeling a ring of fire raze my pupils. My father jerks his hands away, steam rising from the palms in smoke rings. He douses them in the water, screeching with pain, and I cackle wildly. I sound like a witch, I realize.

"Who are you?" he says, staring at his singed hands.

I am Gaia, daughter of Muireann of the Green Sea. My voice is strong, and so loud. The louder I speak, the more unnerved Father becomes. Was that what he feared, all this time? That his daughters would raise their voices and refuse to be silenced? *And I'm asking you to tell us what happened to our mother.*

"Your mother was infatuated with the human world," he recites the story that we all know so well. "She swam too close to the surface and she was caught. The humans took her and while I wanted to save her, I didn't want to endanger—"

No. I am howling, voice cracking and splintering, the sky dimming even though the sun is climbing. I am making the darkness rain. I have the power. *No. Tell us the truth.*

"Muirgen," he says. "Gaia, please."

She was beautiful, wasn't she? Muireann of the Green Sea. Beautiful but restless. Hungering for something more, something that she could not even name.

"She was unruly," he says. "You have to understand that. She wouldn't follow the rules. She was different from the rest of us."

And what is wrong with being unruly? I look directly at Nia as I say this. Her eyes shine with unshed tears, and I know she understands what I am trying to tell her. *What's wrong with being different?*

"I did it for her own good," my father says. "For your own good. You needed a better example from your mother, you needed a role model who was *pure*. I did this for you. I did this for all of you."

Shut up. I breathe out and a wind flares, blasting his beloved trident out of his hand. He tries to grasp at it, but I focus again, imagining a rope wrapping around his wrists. See how he likes being tied down. He cannot move. I will not allow him.

You killed our mother. The words split the sky apart, molding into black clouds. No one says anything; my sisters are silent. Their faces are gray as if, on some level, they too knew this was the truth all along.

"Mama," Talia says again and again, like a small child. "Mama."

Ceto told me the truth. My eyes boring into his, and I am not afraid. *You killed our mother.*

"I didn't—" the Sea King starts, but he can barely be heard over Talia's weeping. "I wanted to protect you." He looks at each of my sisters in turn, seeking support, before turning to Cosima. "My darling girl, you don't believe this, do you?" She is uncertain, her eyes darting between me and our father. She doesn't know what to believe.

You killed our mother, I say again.

And this time, my sisters swim away from the Sea King, leaving him alone. That was his greatest fear, of course. For who would the king be if he had no one to dominate? How could he stand tall if he did not have his daughters to look down on?

"No." He tries to go towards them. I will him to stay still, whispering incantations in my mind. I don't know how I know these spells; it is as if the words are carved within my soul. They have been there all along, waiting for me to find them.

The Sea King sinks, as if in quicksand. "Help me," he splutters, spitting out water, and yet none of my sisters move. I imagine his gills closing, taped shut. He will know what it feels like to have your last breath robbed from him, just as my mother did. "No," he says, gasping. "Muirgen. Muirgen, please don't do this."

Don't call me that. My. Name. Is. GAIA.

A forked tongue of lightning, a serpent licking the sky. *You will call me by my name, old man. You will do as I tell you to do, for once.* The light plunges dark, the sun painted over. *I will bend this world as I please, in ways you could only dream of.*

"Zale will come," the Sea King shouts, wrestling to keep his head above water. "No matter what you do to me, Zale will bring an army and fight this war. He will destroy you all."

I know Zale will come. My mouth waters at the thought of it, of what I will do to him. What I will do to them all. *And I will take care of him, Father; isn't that what you always told me to do? Don't you worry about Zale.*

"You cannot do this." He is crying now—my father, who told us that tears were a sign of weakness and should be avoided at all costs. "You are just *girls*."

We might be girls, I say, lifting my hand so that he can see the Sea Witch's blade. His head is bobbing up and down, his mouth forming the word *no* when he drops under the water, like a steel anchor has been tied around his tail. I swish the blade sideways and twist it, imagining a thick needle hovering above the Sea King's face, cutting into his flesh and sewing his lips shut with black thread. Perhaps it is time for my father to experience what it is like to be silenced.

But we "girls" don't have to do what you tell us anymore.

My father falls down, down, down. His body will sink to the kingdom, like all the human men before him, eyes still open as if searching for something. He will search for eternity.

Sisters, I say. They are huddled together, pale with shock. *I want you to remember always how powerful you are. Never allow anyone to take that away from you, or try and make you feel small. The kingdom needs you to be brave now.* I look at Nia again, and I think of what Ceto told me. *The kingdom needs you to be your true selves.* And my sister smiles at me. *Living true is the most important thing any woman can do.*

"Why are you talking like this?" Sophia asks. "There is still time for you to use the blade as the Sea Witch instructed. Why do you sound as if you are saying goodbye?"

Because I am.

I slice the blade through the air, lifting the blanket of night and calling the day in. The sun continues to rise. It is always there, the sun, even when we cannot see it.

"Gaia!" I hear my sisters screaming as I raise the knife, asking the sky to bless it, to sanctify it for this unholy task. "Gaia, no! Please don't do this."

(*Who are you?* Ceto's voice in my head. *And more importantly, who will you be?*)

I have a real choice, for the first time in my life. I can be whatever I want to be.

I will be a warrior, I decide, driving the knife through the air and aiming true at my heart, the searing pain muffling my sisters' cries. (*I love you, sisters. I love you all.*) I will grow my nails to claws and shave my teeth to blades. I will flay the skin from the bones of men like my father. I will tear them apart and I will eat them raw. Oh, I will set them on fire and devour their ashes whole.

I will be Rusalka. I will have my vengeance.

Mother. Mother, can you hear me?

Acknowledgments

I would like to thank Lauren Fortune for approaching me with the idea for *The Surface Breaks*, thus fulfilling a long-held dream of mine to reinterpret this story in a feminist capacity. Your enthusiasm, encouragement, and support made the entire process of writing and editing this novel such a joy. I've loved working with you.

I would also like to thank Genevieve Herr, David Levithan, Lorraine Keating, Róisín O'Shea, Eishar Brar, Andrew Biscomb, and everyone at Scholastic for working so hard on this book.

Thank you to my wonderful parents, as ever, and my sister, Michelle.

Thank you to my agent, Rachel Conway, and to Teresa Coyne for sending me incredibly helpful essays on merfolk mythology and fairy tales.

Thanks to my friends and extended family, whose patience with me while I wrote this novel was extraordinary. Special thanks to Grace O'Sullivan, whose lovely name I stole for my mermaid.

Bibliography

The Witch Must Die by Sheldon Cashdan

From the Beast to the Blonde by Marina Warner

Don't Bet on the Prince, edited by Jack Zipes

The Classic Fairy Tales, edited by Maria Tatar

Mermaids: The Myths, Legends, and Lore by Skye Alexander

Among the Mermaids: Facts, Myths, and Enchantments from the Sirens of the Sea by Varla Ventura

Mermaids 101 by Doreen Virtue

Author Bio

Louise O'Neill was born in West Cork in 1985. Louise has written two award-winning books, *Only Ever Yours* and her most recent, *Asking for It*, which won Book of the Year at the Irish Book Awards. She is currently working as a freelance journalist for a variety of Irish national newspapers and magazines, covering feminist issues, fashion, and pop culture.